WEB OF LIES

SALLY RIGBY

Storm
PUBLISHING

Ebook ISBN: 978-1-80508-617-8
Paperback ISBN: 978-1-80508-618-5

Previously published in 2021 by Top Drawer Press.

Cover design: Stuart Bache Design
Cover images: Shutterstock

Published by Storm Publishing.
For further information, visit:
www.stormpublishing.co

ALSO BY SALLY RIGBY

Hidden From Sight

Fear the Truth

ONE

11 April

'For goodness' sake,' Jenny Johnson said, turning to look in the back seat of the car where her two sons were squabbling, as usual, this time over a toy truck. 'The plan was for a nice day out, so stop arguing.' Her body tensed. Was it going to be like this for the entire day? If so, she'd sooner go back home and get on with the pile of ironing waiting for her.

It was late Sunday morning on a beautiful spring day, with the sky a soft pale blue and an array of yellows and oranges from the wild daffodils in bloom growing on the side of the lane as they drove through the countryside. She loved this time of year. It was perfect for a trip to Foxton Locks, their favourite place to visit. Though she suspected lots of other people would be there, too. Weather could be so hit-and-miss it was best to take advantage of it when you could.

'Are we there yet?' Lucas, the younger of her two boys, asked, fidgeting excitedly in his seat. 'I hope we see a boat coming through.'

'Yeah, that would be great, wouldn't it?' Tyler said.

At least it had stopped their latest argument.

She'd wanted the day to be special because it was the first time in ages since her husband, Kyle, had a day off. He'd been working seven days a week to get a big order shipped out. They were glad of the overtime, but it meant she'd had sole responsibility for the boys, who could be a handful, and that was putting it mildly.

'Boys, I've got a surprise for you,' Kyle said. 'But only if you're good.'

'We're good, aren't we, Tyler?' Lucas said. 'What is it, Dad?'

'Do you promise?'

'Yes,' Lucas said.

'Me, too,' Tyler agreed.

'Okay. I've booked us on a narrowboat for a trip down the canal after lunch. But if you keep fighting, I'm going to cancel it.'

'Yay. We're going on a boat. Thanks, Dad,' Tyler said. 'We'll be nice to each other. You can have the truck, Lucas,' he said handing it over to his younger brother.

Jenny smiled to herself and turned back to face the front of the car. 'Nice one,' she whispered to her husband.

He glanced at her and winked. Even though the boat trip had been her idea, she didn't resent him taking the credit if it gave her some peace and quiet. There were times when she could cheerfully take herself off and never come back. But those moments were few and far between. She loved her kids. And her life. It wasn't like every other family didn't have their share of problems. She saw the state of some of her friends' marriages and knew that she was luckier than most.

'There's the prison,' Tyler said, as they drove past it on the left. 'Do prisoners escape from there?'

'No. It's perfectly safe,' his mother said.

'If they do, I'll smash myself into them and knock 'em over. Then I'll kick and ...'

'Tyler, no one's going to escape from the prison.'

'But what if they did?' Lucas, who wasn't as fearless as his older brother, asked.

'They won't. Look out the window, boys. We're nearly there. There's the signpost for the Foxton Locks top car park,' Kyle said.

'Can't we get any closer? Let's try the lower car park, especially as we've got the picnic and blankets to carry,' Jenny said, not fancying the fifteen-minute walk with the boys in tow.

She'd been looking forward to having lunch at the picnic tables close to the lock and the gift shop, which she loved to look around.

'Okay, but at this time of day it's bound to be full. So don't blame me if we end up having to turn around and come back.' Kyle took a right turn and after driving for a few minutes, they came to the lower car park. It was full. People were milling around, heading straight to the canal staircase lock and the museum. And, of course, the pub.

'Sorry. Should have listened to you,' Jenny said, hoping it wouldn't set the boys off again, although judging by their shrieks of glee in the back they were so excited about the boat trip she suspected they wouldn't much care.

Kyle turned the car around and headed back along Gumley Road towards the top car park, joining a steady flow of traffic. 'Let's hope there's still somewhere in the overspill section.'

She sensed the frustration in his voice.

Luckily, there were still some spaces, although Kyle had to drive right to the far side where it backed onto some overgrown wasteland.

'Can we have lunch at the pub?' Tyler asked. 'I want some beer.'

Jenny laughed. 'First of all, no. We've brought a picnic. And second of all, you're only eleven and much too young for beer.'

'Henry's dad lets him have some.'

'Well, we're not Henry's parents and the answer's still no. It's a lovely day and we'll enjoy having our lunch outside watching the boats go by.'

'Can we get out now?' Lucas asked as the car came to a standstill.

'Yes, but stay close while we're sorting everything out.'

'Can I take the football?'

'Okay, but don't kick it close to the cars or you might do some damage. Go over there and stay where we can see you.' Jenny pointed at the piece of wasteland directly in front of them. 'And make sure to come back when I call, or there'll be no boat trip.'

For once it would be nice not to be the disciplinarian, but that seemed to be the role she'd adopted. Kyle was much more laid-back than she was. It made a good balance, though. It would be no good if they were both the same.

'Yes, Mum,' they both said in unison.

'Come on, Tyler, I'll race you,' Lucas said to his older brother, holding the ball and running off.

Jenny leant against the car and watched them. 'That's far enough,' she called. 'We're not going to be long, and I don't want to waste time waiting for you.'

The sun's rays beat down on her back and she breathed in the fresh country air. Market Harborough, where they lived, was a lovely small town, and they were happy there, but escaping to the country was still a perfect way to relax.

'You mollycoddle them too much,' Kyle said, cutting into her thoughts, as he came around the front of the car, stopping beside her. 'You know, they're ten and eleven and need to find their feet so they can manage on their own. You've got to stop being so protective. You're not going to be there for them all the time and it's not like they're going to run away or do anything stupid over there. Let them enjoy themselves. They're in no danger.'

She sighed. 'It's easy for you to say because you grew up in a rough and tumble house with three brothers. I was an only child, and only had to catch my breath and my parents would whisk me off to the doctor. But you're right. What harm can they come to over there?'

She headed to the back of the car, determined to relax a little, and pulled out the two cool bags which contained their lunch, and placed them on the ground. She then took hold of two blankets and closed the boot. She listened. There was silence. 'I can't hear anything. Where have they gone? I'm going to have a look.'

'I keep telling you, they'll be fine,' Kyle said. 'Leave them to play.'

Ignoring her husband, she headed to the spot where the boys had run in to the wasteland. The grass was overgrown, but not so much that they'd be hidden. 'Tyler. Lucas,' she called, scanning the area, willing them to appear. There was no reply.

'Kyle, they're not here and they're not answering,' she called out, swallowing back the panic.

Her husband strolled over. 'They're probably hiding in the bushes. Or one of them kicked the ball too far. They'll be back soon, you'll—'

'Daaaaaad.'

Jenny's heart pounded in her chest at the sound of the terrifying yell from Tyler. She ran in the direction of his voice and crashed into him. 'Are you okay? Where's Lucas? What's happened?' She wrapped her arms tightly around him.

'He-he's ...'

'Muuum,' Lucas came charging through the bushes over to where they were standing, his face ashen and his body shaking.

Kyle grabbed hold of him, picking him up and holding him close. 'It's okay, son. I've got you. Take some deep breaths and tell us what you saw. It was probably nothing.'

Jenny glanced at him. How did he know that? The pair of

them were clearly shaken. Sometimes Kyle's attitude was too laid-back.

'A b-body. Dead,' Tyler said, pulling out of Jenny's hold and trying to pull himself together.

'You saw a body?' Kyle asked, looking at Jenny and pulling a disbelieving face over the top of Lucas's head.

'A man lying on the ground. He's dead,' Tyler said.

'It's true,' Lucas said, as Kyle placed him on the ground so he could stand on his own.

'Are you sure he isn't asleep?' Jenny asked.

'No, Mum. He's dead. Half his head is missing,' Tyler said. 'The flies were ...' Tears rolled down his cheeks and Jenny pulled him back into her arms.

She'd never even seen a dead body herself, and now her two little boys had ... this could affect them forever.

'Kyle, go and see and I'll stay here with the boys.'

Lucas ran over to her, and she stayed hugging the pair of them, while Kyle headed in the direction the boys had come from. Lucas was shaking, and Tyler was ramrod straight, although she could feel his tears seeping through her T-shirt.

After a minute or two, Kyle came running back from through the trees, shaking his head. His face was devoid of colour.

'It's true. I've just seen the body.' He pulled out a phone from the back pocket of his jeans. 'Take the boys back to the car and I'll call 999. We'll have to wait for the police to arrive.'

TWO

4 May

Sebastian Clifford sat in his car and stared at the East Farndon church where the funeral of his cousin's husband was due to take place at eleven o'clock. The vibrant blues and reds of the wild flowers scattering the gravestones were at odds with the sombre occasion. He reached over to the passenger seat and picked up his black tie, flicked up the collar on his white shirt, and wrapped it around his neck. He pulled down the mirror and fiddled with the knot until it was acceptable. If his father had seen it, he'd have insisted on him retying it, using a full Windsor knot. But Seb wasn't there to make a statement.

It was thanks to his father that he was attending the funeral. He'd never spent a lot of time in the company of his cousin, Sarah, as she was nearly twenty years older than him, although he liked her. Because of the circumstances of her husband Donald's death, and the assumption that the media would be present, his father had decreed that Seb would represent the family. Being Viscount Worthington meant his father attended a number of royal occasions during the year, as did Seb's older brother, Hubert, who was in line to inherit the title, and it wasn't prudent to court the wrong sort of publicity.

Seb, on the other hand, had already stepped away from the family's confines by opting for a career in the police force, and so attending the funeral of a financier who had stolen millions of pounds from unsuspecting investors through his Ponzi scheme and then committed suicide, wasn't an issue.

What Seb had yet to discuss with his father was that he'd recently resigned from his position as a detective inspector in the City of London Police Fraud Squad. He'd actually been working at the Met Fraud Squad, where he'd been seconded, along with officers from other forces, to investigate a Singapore gambling syndicate that was responsible for match-fixing in sport. His particular focus had been on snooker, and he'd been closing in on them when the squad's whole operation had been compromised.

An undercover reporter had discovered that a detective sergeant in the special squad Seb belonged to had been feeding information to the syndicate. It had explained why they'd always been one step ahead of the squad's investigations. The team had been disbanded and he'd returned to the City of London force. But the only role on offer to him was in uniform. After fourteen years' service, the majority of which was as a CID officer, it wasn't something he was prepared to consider. So, he'd handed in his notice, and was now unemployed.

He'd booked into an Airbnb in Heygate Street, Market Harborough for a few days, and had left Elsa, his yellow Labrador, in the kitchen. He'd taken her for a quick walk before leaving, and she'd likely sleep for the rest of the afternoon. At nine years old, it was what she did most of the time.

He planned on using his time away from London to map out his future.

It had been many years since he'd visited Market Harborough, but it had still retained its quaint market town feel, very different from the hustle and bustle he was used to. He was looking forward to having a few days to explore and unwind.

A black hearse drew up outside the church, with a coffin in the back, followed by a black limo. The driver got out and opened the back door. Out stepped Sarah and her grown-up sons, the twins. Their faces set like stone. Sarah appeared much older than he'd remembered, her body slightly stooping and her face pinched. Although it was hardly surprising after what she'd been through.

He stepped out of his car and stretched his arms and legs. Despite it being considered roomy, it wasn't made for someone of his size. At six feet six inches tall, he struggled to find any vehicle comfortable. He headed over to where there were about twenty people waiting outside the 13th century church, well known for its historic spire. He nodded at those who glanced at him, not recognising anyone. Sarah and her sons walked into the church first, and the rest of them followed.

Were the boys not going to be pall-bearers? Surely they were old enough.

In his peripheral vision he noticed a man standing twenty yards away staring at the mourners. Was he from the media? He expected so, or why else would he be watching. No doubt the funeral would be reported on the local news later.

Once everyone was seated, the coffin was brought in and placed on the catafalque at the front of the church. The service was brief, comprising two hymns and a reading from the vicar. No one else spoke. After the coffin was taken from the church, Sarah and her two boys left, being the only immediate family present, followed by the rest of the mourners. It was a miserable day and had been raining on and off. They headed to the burial site and umbrellas were held up as the coffin was lowered into its hole in the ground.

Once it was all over, he was about to head back to his car

when he heard his name being called. He turned to see Sarah striding towards him.

'Hello, Seb. I see you drew the short straw.'

'It's not like that, Sarah,' he said, leaning down and kissing her on both cheeks. 'I'm very sorry for your loss.'

'I know exactly how it is. I'm part of the family, remember. Even my mother refused to attend. She said she wasn't well, but we all know the truth.'

Sarah's mother was Seb's father's sister. So, yes, he knew exactly what the truth was.

'You're right. Appearances have to be maintained. How are you coping?'

'Holding up. The boys have been a great help, although they're going back to university next week. Which will leave me rattling around in the house alone.'

Did that mean she'd had to get rid of the staff?

'It will get easier in time,' he said, more as a platitude than anything else, as he had no idea whether it would.

'What did you think to the service? It wasn't what I'd have wanted, but under the circumstances what else could we do?' she said, sighing.

'It was appropriate, I agree.'

'Will you be coming back to the house for lunch? We've put on a spread for everyone, though judging by the turnout we'll have enough food to last the rest of the week and into next.' She gave a wry smile.

He admired her stoicism. It couldn't have been easy for her or the twins, who he'd noticed were standing away from the other mourners, tight expressions on their faces.

Funerals in their family would normally attract hundreds of people to pay their respects. But no one wanted to be tainted by this one, especially if it meant appearing in the press.

'I'd be delighted to,' he said, lying. All he wanted to do was get back to Elsa to go out for a relaxing walk in the countryside, providing the rain eased.

'Are you going back to London today? You do still live there, don't you?'

'Yes, I do, but I'm staying here for a few days. I fancied a short break.'

'That's perfect. There's something I'd like to discuss with you when we're back at the house.'

He frowned. 'What is it?'

'I can't talk now as people might hear.' She glanced around conspiratorially.

What on earth did she want to speak to him about? They had nothing in common other than the family.

'Of course. I understand.'

She turned, and they walked together in silence to where the mourners were milling around by the cars.

'I'll see you back at the house. You know the way?' Sarah asked.

'Yes, I remember. It's on the edge of the village. The last time I was here was when your father ...' He paused, not wanting to mention the death of her father at a time like this.

'When Daddy died. It was a very different affair. No room in the church and a service which lasted several hours because of all the readings. A real celebration of his life. Not like ...' Her eyes filled with tears.

He leant in and gave her hug. 'It will be okay,' he said softly in her ear. 'I'll see you in a little while.'

'Thank you. I'm glad you're here, even if you were coerced into attending. You've always been my favourite cousin.' Her eyes, still glassy, shone as she gave a watery smile.

He waited until she'd moved on to speak to another person and then escaped back to his car.

'Excuse me?'

He looked up as a man holding a phone in his hand strode

up towards him. The same man who'd been watching them earlier.

'Yes?'

'I'm a freelance reporter sent by the *Harborough Mail*. Are you related to the deceased?'

He had two choices. He could either tell the guy where to go, or grit his teeth and answer his questions. What would be best for Sarah? Whatever he did it wouldn't stop there being something in the paper about the funeral.

'I'm related to his wife. Why are you here?'

'Donald Witherspoon defrauded hundreds of people, many of them from around here. People have lost their entire life savings thanks to him.'

'I understand and am very sorry for what has happened to them, but I'm here to support his wife during this difficult time.'

'Did she know about his activities?'

'I doubt it very much. Now if that's all, I'm leaving.'

He made a step towards his car and the journalist followed.

'Do you approve of what he did?' A phone was stuck under Seb's nose.

He drew in a breath and pushed the phone away. 'I know nothing about his investments. I'm here to be with my cousin. That is all. Surely, you don't believe the man should be denied his right to a proper funeral?'

'He *denied* his investors proper financial advice. As far as the public will be concerned, he should have been buried in a plywood box with no one present.'

'Well, the *public* don't belong to Donald's family. Whatever he did, that doesn't alter the fact that he had a wife and two children. For their sakes, I suggest you leave now. I'm sure you took plenty of photos of the mourners you can sell to the highest bidder. That should be enough for you. And I don't expect to read any of my comments in your article, as everything I have said is off the record.'

'Who are you?'

'It isn't important. You don't need to know my name because you won't be using anything I've said.' He took a step towards him, using his height to intimidate. It wasn't something he did often, but when he did, it was always effective.

'Okay, mate. I get your point.' The reporter took two enormous steps backwards away from Seb's potential grasp.

'Make sure you do. You can report that the funeral has taken place, and that's all. It's of no interest to anyone outside of the family. Got it?'

'Yes.'

'Right, off you go.'

Seb leant against his car, his arms folded tightly across his chest, until the reporter had returned to his car and driven off.

He'd had enough of the media after the special squad's demise. He had no desire to deal with them here as well.

THREE

4 May

Seb drove up the long drive towards Rendall Hall, which was situated on the edge of East Farndon village. It was the home his cousin had lived in for her entire married life and had been bought with money she'd inherited from her grandparents on her father's side. It dated back to the 17th century and he admired the distinguishing turrets which set it apart from many similar stone-built houses. It had been fully restored and was exceptionally beautiful. The ten acre grounds weren't huge, when compared with his family's estate, and manageable.

Would the property have to be sold? He hoped not, but he had no idea of Sarah's financial situation.

He parked the car on the gravel drive in front of the house and walked up the stone entrance steps, which were flanked by two pillars, to the large wooden double door that had been left open. He didn't imagine there would be many people attending lunch, if the number of people who'd been at the funeral was anything to go by. As he entered the main vestibule, a member of Sarah's staff, wearing a black skirt and white shirt, was there to greet him.

'Good afternoon, sir. We're serving drinks in the drawing room.'

'Thank you. I know the way.'

He headed to the room in question, which was to the left of the vestibule, and when he walked in, there was another staff member holding a tray of drinks.

'Sherry, sir?' he was asked.

Sebastian took one from the silver tray, although he could have done with a beer. Not that he'd expected there to be one on offer. He hoped lunch would be served soon as he really didn't want to stay too long. It wasn't fair on Elsa, especially as she was in unfamiliar surroundings. He wandered over to the rear window and stared out at the manicured lawns and immaculate flowerbeds, which were surrounded by fields and a small wooded area, also belonging to the hall. Elsa would have loved rummaging through there.

He glanced to the side and saw one of the twins standing alone, a pained expression on his face.

He headed over to him. 'Hello, Benedict, I'm Sebastian, your mother's cousin.'

'I know who you are. How do you know I'm not Caspian?'

He wasn't prepared to go into details about his *special gift*, as his mother had called it his entire life.

'We've met before, at your grandfather's funeral several years ago. I'm very sorry for your loss. It must have been very difficult for you and your brother, under the circumstances.'

'Yes, it is, and now we don't know what's going to happen. I can't believe that my father would do this to us. He left my mother with all these problems.' He turned his head, but not before Seb witnessed the tears fill his eyes and him blinking them away. 'I've got to go,' Benedict said, walking away without giving Seb time to answer.

More people arrived until Seb counted thirty. Not all of them had been at the church, so maybe they'd decided to pay their respects in a more private venue. Could he get away without staying for lunch? Sarah might not notice, except she had said she wished to speak to him. Could it wait? He'd no idea what it was about. Perhaps she wanted him to approach his father for help. Whether the viscount would was another matter. Maybe discreetly he could provide some support, after all he wouldn't want to see Sarah struggling at a time like this, considering she was a member of the family.

Where was she? If he attracted her attention now, they could have a quick chat. He scanned the room and saw her engrossed in conversation with an elderly couple. She happened to glance up and smile in his direction. It didn't look like she had time for him just yet so he turned and resumed staring out at the garden.

'Seb.' Sarah's voice startled him as he'd been miles away. 'Let's talk now, before lunch, as I might not have time otherwise. We'll go outside, where no one can hear us.' She opened one of the French doors which led into the garden and they walked out together.

'How can I help you, Sarah?'

'I read about what happened with your job, it can't have been easy. Were you in a lot of trouble?'

The media had reported on the incident and even listed the officers' names in the squad.

'I wasn't directly involved, so didn't get reprimanded, but my squad was disbanded.'

'I knew it couldn't be you. What's going to happen now?'

Should he tell her?

'Between you and me, I've resigned as there wasn't another position available that I was prepared to take. Please keep this to yourself, as I haven't yet told the family. They knew about the incident because it had been reported but as yet they don't know my decision to leave the force. Although I suspect they won't be too upset about me no longer being there. They were never happy about my career choice.'

If he'd have chosen to go into one of the armed forces, then that would have been acceptable, but the police force hadn't been viewed in the same way. After he'd finished university, he'd got accepted at the Metropolitan Police, in their fast track scheme, and had ended up in the fraud squad. From there he transferred to the special squad, and he'd enjoyed the role immensely.

'I wouldn't dream of mentioning it to them, but it does mean that what I'm going to ask you has come along at the right time.'

He frowned. 'I don't understand.' How could him leaving his job affect her?

'Donald's behaviour was inexcusable, and I was appalled that so many people lost their life savings thanks to him. I wish I could make amends on his behalf, but how can I? That aside, I don't believe he committed suicide. The reports were wrong.'

He hadn't been expecting that. 'What makes you say this?'

'I'm sure you know that he was found beside a car park at Foxton Locks having been shot in the head. The gun was close to him and he'd left a handwritten note addressed to me.'

'Yes, I had heard about the circumstances, and I'd have thought that to be conclusive evidence. Presumably, so did the coroner.'

It wasn't unusual for families to reject suicide verdicts and do what they could to overturn them. Sometimes for religious reasons, or simply because of any financial implications.

'Please hear me out. First of all, why did he choose to kill himself at Foxton Locks and not here?'

'Maybe he didn't want you to be the person to find his body. That often happens in suicide cases.'

'So instead, two young children found him and they'll most

likely be scarred for life. There's no way he'd have risked that happening.'

'If he hadn't been thinking straight then he might not have considered his body would have been found by children.'

'At a place like the locks where families go all the time? That's ridiculous. And even if what you're saying is true, where did he get the gun? He didn't own one like that. He has several shotguns for when he goes shooting on the land. But not a hand-gun, which is illegal, anyway. Why didn't he use one of his own guns? When I mentioned this discrepancy to the police, they said he could have easily accessed one.'

'I'm sorry, Sarah, but what you were told is plausible, and using a different gun, illegal or otherwise, is not, in itself, a cause for concern.'

She folded her arms tight across her chest and bit down on her bottom lip, staring at him. 'What about the note? It doesn't make sense, either,' she said after a few seconds.

Was she clutching at straws? It appeared so.

'It was in his own handwriting, and would have been nigh on impossible to forge it. What is it about the note that bothers you?'

Talking it through might help her come to accept the verdict.

'It said he couldn't go on because he felt responsible for all those people losing their money, and he hoped I'd forgive him. But he'd also lost all of our money, too. I'm left with nothing apart from the house, which is in my name and can't be touched. Donald had life insurance, which was invalidated by the suicide. He wouldn't want to leave me penniless. If he wanted to end his life and have it not classed as suicide, there are plenty of other means. Certainly not shooting himself. I've still got the boys to support while they're at university. That's not going to be easy. I'm going to need help and he'd have known that.'

'Suicide is covered under most life insurance policies now, isn't it?'

'We changed our provider eighteen months ago and there was a twenty-four-month exclusion period. He would have known that. He was meticulous about the details in contracts.'

'If he was depressed and not thinking rationally, he might have totally forgotten the exclusion. It's understandable now the full facts regarding his business have been disclosed. Were you aware of what was happening?'

'I had no idea whatsoever. Not that I'm believed. The media painted me as a willing participant, but it couldn't be further from the truth. Donald always kept details of his business away from me. It was how we'd always been from when we first got married. I'll admit that he'd been a little more distracted than usual, but business sometimes did that to him. I wasn't unduly concerned.'

'Why did you want to talk to me about this?'

It had to be more than to let off steam to a cousin she hadn't seen for a long time.

'I'd like you to take a look at the evidence and find out the truth. You'll be a fresh pair of eyes. I'll pay you, of course. I'm not expecting you to do it for free.'

'How can you afford to pay me, when you've already mentioned that things are pretty desperate?'

He couldn't take money from her, especially as so far he hadn't heard anything which changed his view on the verdict.

'I have a little put aside from a small inheritance from my godmother that I can use. It's not much, but it would be money well spent. Please, it's important to me. You're the only person I know with the sort of expertise that's required, and now you're not working, it's perfect timing.'

He couldn't simply dismiss her out of hand as she'd already been through enough.

'Before I make a decision, would you mind going through what happened on the day Donald died?'

'He wasn't himself and had been acting distant for a week or two. I'd asked him several times if there was anything wrong and he said he had a few business issues, but he'd sort them out. He wouldn't be drawn further, and I didn't push, because occasionally he was distracted, like I said before. I can't tell you how much I regret that.' Her eyes glazed over.

He touched her on the arm and she started. 'Are you okay?' he asked.

'Yes. Sorry. It's hard to put on a brave face all the time.' She sucked in a breath. 'On the Saturday of his death he told me he was meeting a prospective client in the afternoon and didn't know what time he'd be home. He didn't tell me where they were meeting and I didn't ask. I had plans with a girlfriend. We were going to visit some open gardens in the next village and I didn't mind him going out. When he didn't come home Saturday night I worried, but he'd stayed out before, especially if he'd had too much to drink. I left a message on his phone to call me. On the Sunday lunchtime the police came around and told me he'd been found dead at Foxton Locks. Then the financial nightmare started as what he'd done came out in the open. I don't believe it was suicide, and why go all the way out over there to do the deed? None of it makes sense.'

'If it's not suicide, do you think he was murdered?'

'I don't know. But I do think the police could have done a better job. It was as if they took the easiest route. They saw a note and a gun, and assumed straight away that he'd taken his own life. Especially as all the money issues came to light not long after his death.'

'Do you know how that happened?'

'One of his investors had contacted the Financial Conduct Authority, and they investigated. I let them have access to all of his records as I thought they would report me to the police if I didn't.'

'Did you explain your concerns about Donald's death to the police?'

'Yes, but they didn't listen. Even when I mentioned discrepancies with the actual note, they just dismissed it.'

'Could you be more specific?'

'I'm not denying it was his handwriting, but there were issues with the wording that made it not ring true. For a start, he didn't put an 'h' on the end of my name, he wrote *Sara*. He's hardly going to forget how to spell my name.'

'He could have missed that off by accident, in his hurry to write to you. It's easily done.'

'He also referred to the boys as *the twins*.'

Seb frowned. 'But they are twins.'

What was he missing?

'But he never called them that. He was obsessive about wanting to differentiate between the two of them and not act as if they were one person, like so many people do with twins. If he wasn't using their names, he only ever called them *the boys* or *the children*. Never the twins. Surely that's got to mean something.'

That piqued his interest. Could Sarah be right about this? One questionable thing in respect of the note could be explained. But two? Had there been something suspicious about Donald's death?

'You have to understand, I can't interfere in a police investigation especially as I'm no longer a serving officer.'

'I'm not asking you to do it as a police officer, but as a civilian.'

'Investigations like this are delicate and complicated, Sarah. I haven't worked suspicious death cases, and I'm not a private investigator.'

Nor did he have any desire to be one.

'Surely you've got contacts you could use. I just want to know whether he committed suicide. Please, Sebastian. I need somebody to listen to me. You're family, and I thought out of everybody you'd understand.'

Her pleading eyes locked with his and tugged at his heart. He wasn't normally swayed by emotion, but after everything she'd been through, how could he let her down? And there certainly were some unanswered questions.

'Okay, I'll take a look. I'll need to check all of Donald's files. Do you have them here?'

'Everything's in his study, including his laptop which the FCA also returned.'

'Is it password-protected?'

'Yes, but I know his passwords. He kept them in a notebook in his office. Hardly secure, I know, but he said he didn't have the capacity to remember them. Not everyone can have your memory.'

'It's overrated,' he said, shrugging. 'You get back to your guests and I'll return first thing in the morning. I don't want you to get your hopes up because I might find nothing to indicate that the police and coroner were wrong.'

FOUR

5 May

Detective Constable Lucinda Bird tore into the police station car park in her old Mini and came to a screeching halt in one of the empty bays. She was half an hour late for work, which meant the morning briefing would have already started and she'd be getting her arse kicked. Again.

She grabbed her bag and jacket from the passenger seat and charged into the station, a 1960s three-storey building in Fairfield Road, in a mainly residential area which, in her opinion, was way past its sell-by date. Why couldn't they have a brand new, swanky building close to the town centre and all of her favourite cafés?

'Late again, Birdie,' the desk sergeant called out as she passed him.

'Oh, shut up,' she muttered, making sure he didn't hear as he was her superior officer, and wasn't averse to calling her out on her behaviour.

She ran along the corridor until she reached the CID office. The door was open, and she tiptoed in hoping no one would notice. She could pretend she'd been at the back of the room the whole time, if anyone asked. Although as there were only five of them in the team, not counting Sarge, she doubted she'd be able to get away with it.

'You decided to grace us with your presence today, then,' Sergeant Jack Weston said, arching an eyebrow.

Crap. Now she was for it.

'I'm sorry, Sarge. The traffic was ridiculous this morning,' she lied pitifully, knowing that he'd see through her excuse. This was Market Harborough. There was no such thing as a rush hour, just a *rush five minutes*.

'Sit down. I'm giving out today's duties.'

She hurried over to her desk and pulled out a chair next to another DC, Neil Branch, aka Twiggy, and dropped down on it, dragging in some much needed breaths. She glanced around at everyone else in the room. Tiny, Rambo and Sparkle. All their eyes were on her, too. They'd no doubt have something to say once he'd finished. Being the youngest on the team meant they didn't hold back on the teasing. Not that it bothered her. She'd been a member of the team for two years now and was well able to give as good as she got.

She was silent while Sarge continued until, finally, he stared in her direction.

'Birdie, you're on desk duty.'

He'd got to be kidding. How long did he intend to make her suffer for one *tiny* mistake?

'Come on, Sarge. You can't be serious. Not still.'

'I had been thinking of sending you out today, but you were late. *Again.* It's desk duty for you for the foreseeable future. You need to pull your socks up. And I don't want to hear any complaints, or I'll make sure you're stuck in here until the end of the year, at the very least.'

Ten days ago, she'd had an accident in the police car she was driving. It was totally her fault, she hadn't been paying attention. She'd got so many things on her mind that she'd run into a skip on the side of the road, beside a construction site. It had totally wrecked the car and landed her in a load of trouble.

It wasn't like she hadn't told the truth, though. She could've said she was swerving to miss a car or cyclist. But no, she'd told Sarge exactly what had happened and was now being punished for it. If only she'd lied, she wouldn't have found herself in this crap situation. It wasn't fair if Sarge added being late today as a reason for keeping her chained to her desk.

'I'm fed up having to answer the phone and do all the filing. Why can't I go out with Twiggy today?'

'Because I said not. If you want to get back to proper duties, then start acting responsibly. And that means arriving at work on time and not looking like you had a skinful last night and are nursing a hangover.'

How did he know? She'd piled on the make-up this morning, being particularly heavy with the under-eye concealer.

'Sorry, Sarge. I promise to be on time tomorrow.' She made a cross sign over her heart, to emphasise she'd meant it. Not that he'd take any notice. Her timekeeping had always been poor, despite her best intentions.

He'd been right about her having a hangover, though. She had a massive one. But in her defence, she'd a genuine reason for going out last night and getting totally wasted.

'You'd better be. Right, the rest of you continue with your duties and keep in touch.' He turned and walked out of the room in the direction of his office.

'What's the matter with you?' Twiggy said, turning to her, shaking his head.

They'd been friends ever since she'd joined CID after her apprenticeship as a police constable in Oadby, near Leicester. He was in his late forties and had been there forever. He'd taken her under his wing and showed her the ropes. He was a good mate.

'Nothing. I just think it's unfair being left here on my own for another day. You could've stuck up for me and suggested I went out with you.'

'Why would I do that? Look at the state of you. Do you think Sarge is the only one to notice? Why were you out drinking on a Tuesday night when you'd got work the next day? What the hell was going on that head of yours?' He folded his arms over his well-rounded belly.

'It's complicated.'

'It's always *complicated* with you.' He gave an exasperated sigh.

'Look, I'm good at my job and I help solve crimes, don't I?'

'Yes. But you also crash police cars and get up the sarge's nose. You've got a lot to learn if you want to make something of yourself in CID. Having a natural instinct will only get you so far.'

'It's not like I turn up with a hangover on a regular basis. It was a one-off, that's all. That's the trouble with you being old and married. You've forgotten what it's like to go out and have fun.'

Except that wasn't the reason why she'd been drinking. Last night, she'd spoken to her parents about searching for her birth mother. It had been on her mind for a long time, but she was worried over how to broach the subject. Rightly so because when she mentioned it to her mum and dad, they took it the wrong way. It wasn't what they said, but the hurt in their eyes was evidence enough of how upset they were.

She'd hated herself for hurting them, so instead of staying in and talking it through, she'd gone out for a drink. A group of her friends were in the pub, and one drink led to another. It wasn't helped by seeing her ex-girlfriend, Shelley, out with her latest who was tall, blonde, elegant, and nothing like Birdie.

Maybe she'd talk to her parents this evening and explain that searching for her birth mother was nothing to do with them. She'd never told them, but growing up she'd always felt like there was something missing. There was a burning need inside her to find out where she'd come from. It wasn't going to change how she felt about her mum and dad. She'd always love them. They were the best parents in the world and had always supported her.

Finding her birth mother was just something she had to do. She hadn't told anyone else. Not Twiggy, or her friends. She was going to do it alone, but not behind her parents' backs. She'd already started making enquiries about how she should go about it.

Her parents had adopted her at six months, after being told they were unable to have children. Except then her mum became pregnant. Twice. Birdie now had two younger brothers. They'd never treated her any differently from the boys. They were one big happy family. Until you looked at them. She was the only one who was short with a mass of red curls, green eyes, and pale freckled skin which turned pink as soon as the sun even dared to show its face. The rest of the family were tall, had dark hair, dark eyes and skin which tanned easily.

'You can't do both,' Twiggy said, interrupting her thoughts. 'I'm not that ancient. I do remember what being single is like. If I was you, I'd get on with my work and show more commitment by being here on time, or even early, and staying late. Then the sarge might let you out with the rest of us.'

'Has he said anything to you?'

'Not in so many words. But if you carry on like this, you'll be stuck on desk duty forever, even if you are a great detective.'

'We could do with a juicy murder to work on. Sarge would let me out then.'

'I'd rather not, thanks, as it would play havoc with my home life. When we get big cases regular hours go out the window.'

'Think of all the overtime you could earn though, enough to pay for your next holiday abroad.'

'True. But if you're looking for more action then apply to a larger force. What about Lenchester? It's like the murder capital of the world over there. Certainly enough to keep you occupied.'

'How can I move somewhere else? It's cricket season and we're going to win the league this year. There aren't many of us left-handed bowlers around and it makes a big difference, believe me.'

Plus her attention was now focused on finding her birth mother.

'I'm sure Lenchester has a team.'

'I couldn't leave you, you'd miss me too much.'

'You think about it. In the meantime, have fun answering the phones and dealing with irate members of the public who've had their washing pinched off the line, or distraught grannies whose cats are stuck up a tree.' He grinned, grabbed his jacket from the back of the chair and headed to the door.

'Piss off and leave me alone.' She threw a pen which hit him on the back of his head as he left the room. 'Come on,' she said, glancing upwards. 'Bring me something big so I can show Sarge what I'm made of.'

FIVE

5 May

Following a leisurely walk through the town, stopping at a café on High Street for a late breakfast of bacon and eggs, Seb collected Elsa, and they drove out to East Farndon to see Sarah.

After he'd left Sarah's the day before, he'd spent time googling Donald and his Ponzi scheme. There were thousands of results. He started at the top of the first page. It was an interview with some of the hundreds of people who had lost all their money after investing in Donald's schemes.

Those interviewed talked about him as being charming, friendly and, so they believed, trustworthy. That was the Donald Seb remembered, too. He'd been well liked, and the family had approved of him. He'd never asked Seb to invest, probably because he thought being a police officer, he wouldn't have money to spare. He was right.

He'd read several more articles, and they were more of the same, saying that Donald had operated one of the worst Ponzi schemes in UK history and how he'd destroyed the lives of so many. Sarah had been right about the scheme coming to light after one of Donald's clients had alerted the FCA, the independent regulator in the field, that they were owed several interest payments.

Many people were calling for the family to make some sort of recompense, but he knew they couldn't do that. People automatically assumed that because Sarah and the boys lived in a big house, and were related to a viscount, that they were wealthy. The articles did make mention of Sarah, pointing out her connection to Viscount Worthington. But other than that, there wasn't much about her and the twins. A small blessing.

Sarah's house was only ten minutes away and, when he arrived, he turned up the long drive and parked in front of the house. He knocked on the door, expecting it to be opened by one of her staff but, instead, it was Sarah.

'Morning,' he said, staring at his cousin, pleased to see the tight lines were a little less accentuated around her eyes. He hoped she was feeling less stressed than the previous day.

'I was wondering what time you were going to arrive. I didn't want to go anywhere in case I missed you.'

'I thought you wouldn't appreciate me arriving too early in case you wanted a lie-in this morning, after the difficult day you had yesterday.'

Elsa poked her nose around Seb and rubbed against Sarah.

'Oh, you've brought your dog. Hello.' She leaned down and patted her on the head. 'Let's go for a walk in the grounds and she can have a good run. Then I'll show you Donald's study.' Sarah held open the door for them to head into the house.

'How are you doing after yesterday?' Despite there being less tension on her face, there were dark circles under her eyes. He suspected she'd hardly slept.

'It was a long and strenuous day and I was glad when it was over. The boys are still here, but they're in bed. I'm not going to disturb them as they need their rest. It's been so hard for all of us.'

'Yes, I could see how on edge they both were, yesterday. Understandably.'

'Like me, finding out what their father had done shocked them to the core. They'd always got on well with him and held him in high esteem. Now, everybody in the country, probably the world, knows what he did to all those people, and that the boys are his sons. It's hard when you love someone to find out what a monster they'd been. But it's not like there's a switch inside of you to turn off the love you had for them. It's just ...'

Her face crumbled, and he drew her into a reassuring hug.

'It's only natural for you to have these feelings,' he said softly. 'You have to give it time. It will get better, I promise.'

She pulled out of his arms and stood up straight, giving a sniff. 'I know. Less of me going silly, it's not going to help anyone.'

He followed her into the kitchen and out of the back door, unhooking Elsa's lead as they went. She charged off into the garden. Unlike the day of the funeral, it was warm, and the sun was shining through the few fluffy clouds. 'Do you mind Elsa running here or should we go into the woods?'

'She's fine. It's nice to have a dog around. I'd been saying to Donald about getting another dog after we lost Mitzi, but he didn't want a puppy because they're hard to train at our age. He didn't want a rescue dog either because he said he didn't know where they came from. Some of them can turn nasty. So, we were left dogless. Now I'm on my own ...' She shrugged, letting out a long sigh.

'You should get one, they're splendid company,' he encouraged, convinced it might help her get over her loss, and give her something to focus on other than questioning Donald's death.

'Tell me more about Donald's business. Are you familiar with what he did?'

'More so now than when he was alive. I'd always believed that he gave people financial advice and helped with their investments. That's all he ever told me. I know more now, having read the papers and seen on TV what he'd done to his investors.'

'So, you understand that for many years he operated a Ponzi scheme. He persuaded people to invest their money through him, only instead of investing it into a particular scheme which gave a return, he kept the money for himself and used money others had invested with him to make their interest payments.'

'A bit like using Peter to pay Paul,' Sarah said.

'In a simplified way, yes. This went on for more than ten years. Think back to then, can you remember whether something specific happened around that time which made him change from being a legitimate financial adviser to doing this?'

'He didn't ever say anything to me. I'd always thought his business was doing well, and he was making a success of it, even during the recession.'

'He took people's money for himself. What did he spend it on?'

'Us. The house. In recent years, the house has started eating money. We've had to replace the roof. The boiler – which was as old as the hills – stopped working. The grounds take a lot to maintain. We also had school fees to pay and now we're supporting the boys at university.'

'Did you go on holidays? Did he buy expensive clothes and gifts?'

'Donald always had a good car and his suits were made at Savile Row, because he said people wouldn't invest in someone if they thought they didn't have a lot of money themselves. We did go on delightful holidays, several times a year.' She blushed.

'Sarah, I'm not blaming you for any of this, you weren't to know the situation.'

'You might not blame me, but I do. Why didn't I notice

anything? You must think me so stupid, but Donald never involved me. And foolishly I didn't ask. I'll regret that for the rest of my life.'

He rested his hand on her arm. 'You must stop being so hard on yourself. He duped you in the same way as he did to everyone else. It isn't your fault.'

'I suppose you're right,' she said, sighing. 'Why don't you spend some time going through his files now and then we'll have lunch. Unless you have somewhere else to go?'

'Lunch would be lovely, thank you.'

He followed Sarah back into the kitchen and down a corridor to the east wing of the house, stopping at the last room. Elsa was running close behind them.

'Here's Donald's study,' Sarah said, opening the door.

It was a large rectangular room with a floor to ceiling book-case running along the far wall, a gigantic ornate wrought-iron fireplace on the other and in the centre, standing proud, was a magnificent mahogany antique desk with a dark green leather inlay. The desk was bare other than a laptop in the middle and, next to a brass photo frame, an antique silver dual-footed inkstand with glass inserts to one side of it. Behind the desk stood a Victorian style captain's chair, with a burgundy leather seat. It was stunning. The large window and French doors over-looked the garden, and the sun's rays made a beautiful dappled effect on the desk.

'This is a lovely space,' he commented.

'Yes, we recently had it refurbished.' Her voice fell away, as if she was embarrassed at spending the money.

He glanced around the room at the large paintings on the walls and the cream sofa with cushions that matched the deep red and cream striped curtains, pulled back with curtain ties. No expense had been spared.

'Did Donald spend a lot of time in here?'

'Too much. He'd be in here for hours, unless he was out

visiting clients. Occasionally he'd even sleep on the sofa if he was too tired to make it upstairs. I'd moan sometimes, but it fell on deaf ears. I didn't like to complain too much, though, because it was his hard work that gave us the lifestyle we enjoyed. Now we know the truth it's made a mockery of our whole existence.'

'Did he have regular contact with his clients?'

'Yes, most weeks he'd be out with them, as far as I know. I couldn't tell you who they were, but you'll find details of meetings in his diary. He'd often travel to London as many of his clients were there, and he'd stay overnight if he was taking them out for dinner.'

'Whereabouts did he stay in London?'

'A small hotel in Knightsbridge. He talked about buying a small flat for when he was there, and for us to use when we went to the city, but he never got around to it. Thank goodness.'

She walked behind the desk, opened the middle drawer and took out a small black leather notebook which she handed to him.

'This contains all of his passwords.'

'Do you mind if I look through his files?' Seb asked, pointing to the four-drawer dark wood cabinet situated in the corner of the room.

'Not at all. Look at whatever you want. Nothing's off limits. I don't know what you'll find, though, as I couldn't bring myself to touch any of his work-related belongings.' She stepped away from the desk and he sat down and opened the lid to the laptop.

'I'll be fine on my own, no need for you to hang around. You don't mind Elsa being in here with me, do you?'

'Of course not. I'll pop back with a bowl of water for her. You can open the doors if she wants to go out in the garden. I'll let you know when lunch is ready.'

The laptop password was written on the first page of the notebook, along with passwords for his bank accounts, his accounting software, and all sorts of other organisations. Sarah really should look into making password changes to any which related to her as well, as this lack of security made her far too vulnerable. But that was a discussion for another time. He didn't want to overload her with too much to think about.

He opened the laptop and was impressed at how organised the documents were. Every folder and file within it were labelled using an easy-to-understand system, which made the task of going through everything a lot easier.

First of all, he opened the folder containing a list of clients, recorded in alphabetical order. Each client had their own file, which included a signed copy of their agreement, followed by a list of investments they'd made and when they were paid dividends. Some clients received theirs monthly, some quarterly, some every six months and some once a year. The agreements appeared watertight, requiring the client to invest their money for a minimum period. These investment periods mainly fell between five and ten years, with most of them falling into the latter. There was the provision for clients to withdraw their funds early, however, this incurred a hefty penalty of fifteen per cent of the initial investment. As some clients had invested up to two hundred thousand pounds, that was indeed severe.

At the time of Donald's death, he had forty-nine active clients in the Ponzi scheme. Each client's individual file had a note stating how often dividends were paid.

Seb was able to ascertain those clients whose money had been invested legitimately and those whose funds weren't. The turning point was 2010. From that date onwards, Donald falsified documents to his clients when they received their interest using information he received for his legitimate clients to create them. That way, anyone who tracked their investment independently would be getting accurate information. How did he account for this on his tax returns, though? A question for another time.

Seb moved from the client files into Donald's main business

bank account where all new investors' monies were placed. There were no outgoing payments made to any external investments, contrary to what the agreements stated. All interest payments to his clients were made via direct payment. The only withdrawals were made into Donald's personal bank account and from there he paid for the family housekeeping and living expenses. A large monthly amount went into Sarah's own account, more than his salary as a detective inspector with the Met.

It was quite a juggling act and, for many years, had worked very well. Donald had managed the money expertly. From what Sebastian could see, however, towards the end of the previous year, Donald's outgoings began to exceed the amount of money he had coming in, as he was taking on fewer new clients. He missed dividend payments, but he did it in such a way as to not alert people. When a payment was missed, Donald emailed the client and explained there were issues with the bank due to the hacking of accounts and they would be paid as soon as possible, at the latest by the time the next payment was due. He made sure not to miss more than one dividend per client until it got to the time when he died. By that time, very few people were receiving their money.

He leant back in the chair and stretched out his arms. The chair wasn't comfortable for someone of his size. He glanced at the bank account again, ensuring he'd checked every item. At the start of this year, there was a large investment of two hundred thousand pounds from Donald's brother Edgar. Sebastian had met him, but he wasn't at the funeral yesterday. This wasn't the first time Edgar had invested. His initial investment had been eleven years prior, and he'd signed a ten-year agreement. Yet he put in more money.

Had he done it to help him out?

Was he aware of the fraud Donald was engaging in? And if he was, how deep did his involvement go?

SIX

5 May

Sarah glanced up at the kitchen clock from where she was standing at the island chopping lettuce. Seb had been in the study for two hours. He was her last hope. She'd thought about employing a proper private detective, but changed her mind. She didn't want someone she didn't know or trust going through everything.

It had to be Seb or no one.

Footsteps echoed down the hall, and the door opened.

'Sorry, Sarah, I don't know where the time went.'

'I was about to come and fetch you for lunch. I thought we'd have a salad with the leftovers from yesterday. There's cold chicken and cold beef, if you're okay with that?'

'Sounds wonderful, I'm starving. What can I do to help?'

'Nothing, it's almost ready. We'll eat in here as the boys haven't surfaced yet and it's only the two of us. There's no need to stand on ceremony.'

He washed his hands and headed over to the Welsh dresser. 'Are these okay?' He held out two white china plates.

'Yes, they're fine.' She stared at him. His eyes gave nothing away. 'Have you found anything yet?'

He took the plates over to the island, before turning to face her.

'I have some questions regarding the business which need answering.'

She placed the knife on the work surface and stepped towards him, enveloping him in a huge hug.

'I'm so relieved that you agreed to investigate Donald's death. Thank you.'

Whatever he found she'd be prepared to accept because then, at least, she'd know Donald's death had been properly investigated.

He stepped away from her, leaning against the worktop. 'Sarah, you must remember, it's highly unlikely that my investigation is going to make any difference to the official outcome. The suicide verdict will most likely stand, unless we have hard evidence to persuade the police and the coroner to change their decisions.'

She nodded. 'I understand. If I'm wrong, then so be it. I just want somebody to look into it and to actually listen to me. You're the first person who has and I can't begin to tell you how good it feels to be heard. You'll have to advise me how much to pay you, as I've never done anything like this before. What's the going rate for private investigators these days?'

She'd looked on the internet but couldn't find anything. Then again, she wasn't sure if she'd looked in the right places. Donald used to call her a technophobe, and he was right ... up to a point. She'd never been interested. She used her phone and would read on her tablet, but other than that she hardly went online.

'First of all, I'm not a PI, nor have I any intention of becoming one. Second, I'm not prepared to take any money from you. I have some free time since leaving the force and this will keep me occupied.'

'Are you sure? I do have some money set aside, as I mentioned to you. It's not much but—'

'And you need it to take care of yourself and the boys. I want no more said about it. This is non-negotiable.' He wagged his finger in her direction.

Her lips turned up into a relieved smile. 'In that case you should come and stay here with me at the house. There's plenty of space and it would be no trouble. It's the least I can do after you're being so generous with your time.'

It would be nice to have someone around, especially as the boys were going back to uni tomorrow. It would force her into preparing meals and keeping the house looking nice. At the moment, those things were an effort, and often she didn't bother.

'Thanks for the kind offer, but I like being in walking distance to the town centre. I've already paid until Thursday morning and I'll check with the owner of the property to see if I can stay a while longer.'

'The offer's there if you change your mind, or if the property owner can't fit you in.'

'Much appreciated, thank you. I'll let you know what she says. My plan is to continue in Donald's office after lunch, as I haven't yet looked in his filing cabinet and then tomorrow start to investigate in earnest. I can't stress enough, though, please don't get your hopes up.'

'I understand, and promise not to. Will you be giving me regular updates on how the investigation is going or do I have to wait until you've completed it?' She bit down on her bottom lip.

'I'll keep you informed of my progress as I go.' His stomach rumbled. 'Excuse me.'

'Come on, let's eat.'

She took the plates of meat and bowl of salad over to the table and brought out some warm crusty rolls from the oven.

After they'd eaten, he placed his napkin on the table. 'I'll go back to the office now. Do you mind if I take Donald's laptop away with me, and anything I find in the filing cabinet which might be of use?'

'Help yourself to whatever you'd like to take. I know it's in safe hands.'

What would Donald have thought, if he'd known that everything he'd done while in business was being put under scrutiny? Her husband had been well liked, prior to it all imploding, and it was something he'd worked hard at. He would've known that once his fraud had been found out everyone would turn their back on him. It would have destroyed him.

But was that enough for him to take his own life?

* * *

Seb returned to the study and opened the French doors, letting Elsa out into the garden. 'Go and have a run, you've been a very good girl.' His dog didn't need telling more than once and she charged outside, into the garden, sniffing everything she came across. He left the door open, letting in the warmth of the sun.

It was kind of Sarah to offer he stayed at the house, but that wasn't going to happen. He couldn't investigate with her knowing his every move all the time, however much she tried to keep out of his way. He needed to keep some distance between them, especially if he was led down a path that put Donald in an even worse light. If that was possible.

Thanks to his *super memory* as his mother referred to it, he already knew every electronic bank statement and client record belonging to Donald. His next job was the filing cabinet. He began his search in the top drawer. It contained personal documents relating to the family and the house. After a quick flick through, he left them alone. It was Donald's business he was concerned with initially.

The second and third drawers contained hard copies of the signed agreements Donald had in place with his investors. That was either very brave or stupid. A paper trail showing all the dealings he'd made over the years would have been ample evidence if he'd ever been found out. Seb assumed he'd done it in case his laptop broke, or was compromised, and he hadn't trusted the cloud.

Elsa came bounding in, holding a chewed tennis ball in her mouth. She wagged her tail proudly, dropping it at his feet.

'You do know this isn't yours, don't you? What's Sarah going to say when she discovers you've ruined her ball?'

Elsa continued wagging her tail, totally oblivious to his fake reprimand.

'Come on, I've seen enough. Time to go.' He picked up the laptop and left the study.

Sarah was sitting at the kitchen table when he walked into the room, her hands wrapped around a mug, staring into space.

'Are you okay?' he said.

She started. 'Sorry, I didn't hear you come in. My mind was on other things, in particular whether I should look for a job. The problem is I'm not qualified for anything. After Donald and I got married I stayed at home and took care of the children and house. Not the modern way, I know. But it was different in my day.'

'You could go back to working in an art gallery, like you did before you settled down,' Seb suggested.

'You remembered that,' she said, jerking her head back. 'Of course you did,' she added before he had time to answer. 'I forgot about your memory. There aren't many galleries around here, but it's something to consider. Have you finished in Donald's study already?'

'Yes, I've seen as much as I need to for the moment. Can you remember the name of the person at the FCA who you dealt with?'

'FCA?' she frowned.

'The Financial Conduct Authority,' he reminded her.

'Oh, sorry. I didn't recognise the acronym. Yes, it was a nice woman called Linda Stallion. I've got her card somewhere.' Sarah went over to one of the kitchen drawers and rummaged through. 'Here it is.' She passed it to him and he placed it in his pocket.

'Thanks. One last question. Do you, by any chance, have Donald's phone? I'd like to check it his text messages and any apps he used.'

'His phone?' She bit down on her bottom lip. 'He had it on the day when he … he … It might be in the bag of things the police gave to me after the post-mortem. I put it in his bedroom, because I couldn't bring myself to open it. I haven't been in there since he died. The cleaner dusts every week, but other than that it's as it was when he left home that day. Do you want to check? His room's up the stairs and off to the left. It's the second door on the right.'

Seb went upstairs and found the room. He pushed open the door. Anyone who didn't know would believe that someone still slept in there. On top of the large antique chest of drawers was a black plastic bag. He opened it and the smell of dried blood and dirt wafted out. He felt inside, but it wasn't there.

He returned to the kitchen, where Sarah was still seated. 'I couldn't find it. Let me know if it turns up. You need to dispose of the bag and its contents as it didn't smell good. But not until I've completed my investigation in case, we need it for evidence if something untoward did happen to Donald.'

'You mean … murder.' She looked at him. 'Of course you do. If it isn't suicide, then what else could it be.'

'Let's take it one step at a time. There's no point in second-guessing what I'm going to discover.'

'You're right. I'll see you out.'

She went with him to his car, and he gave her a kiss on the cheek before leaving.

First thing in the morning, he'd contact the police and ask to see their report. He'd also like to view the coroner's report if they could access it for him.

How would they take him wanting to investigate a case they'd already closed?

They could complain, but that wouldn't stop him. He had questions and he wouldn't rest until they were answered.

SEVEN

6 May

Seb glanced up at the kitchen clock on the far wall. It was eight-thirty and time to contact the police. They had every right to refuse his request, although they might acquiesce and let him see it on the QT with him being an ex-officer. Unfortunately, he had no connections with the Market Harborough force and didn't know the size of their CID. It was bound to be small, but that shouldn't make a difference to their ability to assist him.

He googled the number and called it.

'Good morning, Market Harborough police, how may I help you?' a male voice answered. He had to be careful how he worded his response as the front desk acted as a gatekeeper. He wanted to keep quiet that he was investigating the case. In a small town like this, if it did turn out that the death was suspicious, he didn't want to alert anyone unnecessarily.

'I'd like to speak to someone in CID, please.'

'May I ask what it's about?'

'An existing police matter. My name's Sebastian Clifford.'

He doubted very much that they'd know him from working at the Met.

'One moment, please, and I'll put you through.'

'DC Bird,' the female officer answered. She sounded young. And bored.

'Good morning, my name is Sebastian Clifford. I'd like to speak to you about the Donald Witherspoon case.'

'There is no case,' she answered, her tone flat and dismissive. 'It was recorded as a suicide by the coroner.'

'I'd like to view the police report, if I may.'

'Why?'

'I'm related to his wife, and she's asked me to look into it.'

'Why?' the officer repeated.

This was going to be more difficult than he'd assumed. He'd have to tell the officer more than he'd originally intended.

'Mrs Witherspoon believes that her husband's death wasn't suicide.'

'Both the police and coroner's reports would disagree, so what makes Mrs Witherspoon think she knows better?' she responded sarcastically.

He could sense the rolling of her eyes. Didn't they provide interpersonal skills training in Market Harborough? If she'd been one of his officers, she'd have been reprimanded for her manner.

'Nevertheless, I would still like to read the police report,' he cajoled, already having the measure of the officer. One word out of place and she'd most likely end the call.

'So you can tell us how we got it all wrong?'

Clifford stifled a laugh at the continuing belligerence in DC Bird's voice.

'I also wondered if you could contact the coroner's office for a copy of their report as you won't have it on file as there was no prosecution involved?' He chose not to respond to her comment.

'You seem to know a lot, are you a lawyer?'

'No, I'm a former officer.'

'That explains it.' Her tone softened a tad. 'Where did you serve and what rank were you?'

'I was a detective inspector at the Met in London.'

Silence hung in the air.

How was she going to deal with his reveal? Provincial forces often had a stereotypical view of officers from the Met, believing them to be full of their own self-importance. Some officers, maybe. But in the main it was untrue.

'What? So now you're here with your *big city experience* to tell us we messed it all up and us country bumpkins don't know what we're doing?'

'Not at all. My cousin has asked me to look into the case while I'm here. I'd like to see the police report if there's any chance that you could do that for me, please?'

'What evidence does your cousin have for believing his death might not be suicide, bearing in mind both CID and the coroner's office have investigated?'

Should he tell her? If it meant she'd let him see the police report, then he had no choice. He could threaten to speak to her DS, but he got the impression that it would have no impact. If anything, it might work against him.

'If you could please keep this to yourself. My cousin doesn't believe he would commit suicide and leave her and their children in such a dire financial situation.'

'Despite what he did to all those people? That's rich.' He winced at her facetious tone.

'There's also the fact that he didn't own a gun like the one he supposedly shot himself with.'

He waited for her next comment …

'He left a note.'

She was only answering in the same way he had when Sarah had first approached him.

'Which also had some anomalies.'

Was she going to ask what they were? He didn't want to play all his cards at once, in case he did have to go higher.

'It seems to me that your cousin is clutching at straws because she's finding it hard to deal with such a tragic situation. Tragic on so many levels.'

She wasn't wrong. Even if his death turned out to be suspicious, it didn't change the fact that he'd ruined so many lives in pursuit of a good life for himself.

'Maybe she is,' he admitted, allowing his uncertainty to show. 'But, nevertheless, I promised to look into it for her. Will you help me or not?'

'Give me your number and I'll get back to you.'

'When? I'm not staying long.' What he didn't want was for her to put his request to the bottom of the pile. He needed the information straight away ... if not sooner.

'Don't push it just because you used to be inspector, and I'm a lowly DC.'

He coughed to hide the laugh which had erupted from his throat.

'I have no rank to pull. And even if I did, it's not the way I operate.'

'I'll check out a few things and phone you later this morning. Take it or leave it.'

'Thank you,' he said, giving her his number and ended the call.

He detected interest in her voice and that could only be a positive thing.

Whether she'd let him have the report, however, remained to be seen.

* * *

Birdie replaced the phone after her conversation with ex-Detective Inspector Clifford and stared at it. Was he really from the Met? He could be anyone. She wasn't going to consider helping until she knew more about him.

She googled his name and her jaw dropped. Bloody hell. He was royalty. There were photos of his dad, *a viscount*, standing next to the Queen. There was also an article about his family which mentioned Sebastian being in the force. What the hell was the son of a viscount doing being a police officer, or even an ex-police officer?

She opened more of the results on the screen. This was interesting. He was part of a special squad, tasked with investigating fraud overseas, that had been disbanded after being compromised by one of its members. Was it him?

Was he fired, or did he resign?

Could he be trusted?

She was in enough trouble as it was, without adding to it.

Her gut told her that he was genuine. And it rarely let her down.

Should she show him the file? She was bored to death at the moment. The phone had hardly rung and the filing was up to date. She went over to the cabinet and pulled out a buff-coloured folder which contained everything there was on Donald Witherspoon's suicide. She hadn't been involved in the case as the body had been found on her day off. Except it could hardly be called a case, considering how little work it entailed.

The file was thin. A few scribbled notes. Copies of interviews with the wife, the family who found the body, and the suicide note. No witnesses? That would be most unusual at Foxton Locks.

Surely it wouldn't hurt to let Clifford look at it. Then again, she didn't want to get herself in trouble with Sarge, which she would if he found out. But why would he?

With Clifford's experience, he wouldn't take up the case unless he was convinced there was something not right.

Birdie pursed her lips as an idea popped into her head.

Could she get away with it? Yeah, of course she could.

She'd help Clifford with his investigation. That way, if it did turn out to be murder and she was involved in solving it, she could say goodbye to desk duty. If it did turn out to be nothing, then no one need know that she'd helped him. She had nothing to lose. It was a win-win situation.

She copied the contents of the file and then phoned him. First making sure that no one was around to hear.

'Clifford,' he answered almost immediately.

'It's DC Bird. I've decided to help you.'

There was a long pause. Had he hung up?

'I don't recall requesting your help, I asked for a file,' he finally said.

She hadn't expected this reaction. He should've jumped at the chance to have some assistance. Well he'd got it whether he wanted it or not.

'The file and I come as a job lot. Take it or leave it.'

'What about your work?' he responded almost immediately.

'I'll fit it in around my shifts.'

Would that be possible? Sleep was overrated, anyway.

'Can you get hold of the coroner's report for me?'

'I have a contact there who might be able to assist.'

To refer to him as a *contact* was a bit of a stretch. She'd had a drunken fumble in the pub car park where they'd held the police Christmas party last year, with a guy who worked there. She'd persuade him to let her see it.

'Excellent. When can I have the documents?'

'Meet me at seven tonight at the Red Lion pub in Little Bowden. The food's good and you can shout me dinner.'

Did he just laugh? It would be a small price to pay for her help.

'As you wish, DC Bird. I will meet you at the pub and dinner will be on me. What's your first name? I can't call you DC Bird all the time.'

'Lucinda.' She cringed at the sound of her name which she despised. 'My name's Lucinda. But use it even once and you'll regret it forever.'

'Noted. So what do I call you?'

'Birdie's just fine.'

'In that case, *Birdie,* I look forward to meeting you this evening. And you may call me Seb.'

'Yes, m'lord.' Ooops. Did she just say that out loud?

'Excuse me?'

'Nothing. I'll see you later. You'll recognise me by the hair. It's red and wild.'

She ended the call before insulting him further.

The day might have started off badly, but now things were looking up.

EIGHT

6 May

Seb drove out to Little Bowden, which was on the outskirts of Market Harborough. He'd intended on bringing Elsa, thinking they could eat outside, but at around five o'clock, it clouded over and the heavens opened. The worst of it was over, but as he was about to leave it had begun spitting, so he fed her and left her at the house. She'd probably sleep for most of the time he wasn't there, which he thought would only be a couple of hours.

When he reached the pub, he parked in the street opposite and stared at the building, which was painted cream, and had a delightful thatched roof. Hopefully, the food would match the quality of the exterior. As for the company, he had to admit that he was eagerly anticipating meeting with Birdie, and not just because she was bringing the documents he required. He'd found her refreshingly amusing, although whether they would manage to work together remained to be seen.

He glanced at his watch. It was six fifty-five, so only five minutes before they were due to meet. He crossed the road and pushed open the dark wooden door, ducking his head as usual when he entered buildings like this. The room was empty apart from a couple seated at a table in the corner and two men standing beside the bar, with pints in front of them.

'Can I help you?' the bartender asked as he approached.

'A pint of stout, please. I'm meeting someone here and would like somewhere quiet to talk and eat. Where do you suggest?' Seb asked while his drink was being poured.

'The dining room's your best bet. Most people eat in here or outside during the week. There's a table at the far end where you shouldn't be disturbed. It's through there.' He pointed towards the back and to the left. 'Here's the menu. You'll need to come back here to order.'

'Thanks,' Seb said, taking the menu, picking up his drink and heading off.

The dining area had a homely feel and was light and airy. The table in the corner was next to the fireplace. It was the perfect spot for him to meet with Birdie as it was unlikely their discussions would be overheard.

He strummed his fingers on the table and glanced at the time on his phone. She was ten minutes late. Surely she wasn't standing him up. That would be ironic, considering he hadn't intended working with anyone, let alone someone he'd never even met, as he much preferred to be alone. It meant that if anything went wrong, he only had himself to blame. But as she had the information he wanted he wasn't left with a choice. Once she'd handed it over, he might consider phasing her out of the enquiry. He'd make that decision in due course.

'Here you are.' He looked up, and standing in front of him, a smile on her face, holding a half-pint in her hand was Birdie. It couldn't be anyone else. She wasn't wrong about the wild red hair.

He stood, towering over her, and held out his hand. 'How did you know it was me?'

'I asked at the bar if they've seen anyone strange.' She shook his hand. A firm grip for someone of her size.

He frowned. 'Strange?'

'As in, not from around here. This is a *locals'* pub, and they know most of the customers. The guy behind the bar told me you were tall. But bloody hell, I hadn't realised you were that big. You'd make a great goalie. Do you play football?'

'Rugby's my game.'

'League or Union.'

'Union. I'm not fast enough for League.'

'Fair enough,' she said nodding. 'Cricket's my sport.'

They sat, and she placed a paper carrier bag on the far end of the table.

'Is that the report?'

'In here is everything you asked for, including the coroner's report,' she replied, patting the bag. 'You owe me big time for that as I had to reacquaint myself with someone who, after a Christmas party, I'd hoped never to see again.' She pulled a face.

He laughed. 'Despite having only just become acquainted, I imagine you manged to deal with the situation in a satisfactory manner.'

'That's beside the point. So, if you're thinking of dropping me now you have what you want, think again.' She leant forward slightly and locked eyes with him.

Was she a mind reader in her spare time?

'I won't insult your intelligence by saying the thought hadn't crossed my mind, but knowing how you've already gone over and above what I would expect then you have my word that you won't be excluded from the investigation.'

'As you're a *viscount*, of course I believe you.' She smirked.

Already? He should get a sign printed and then he could hold it up when he was asked the inevitable question.

'I'm not a viscount. My father is. And, before you ask, I

don't inherit the title, my older brother does.' He paused. 'I don't spend my days playing polo, either. Nor am I related to the Queen and we definitely don't hang out together. I think that just about covers everything.'

'Touched a nerve, have I?' she asked, tilting her head to one side, her green eyes twinkling.

'You follow a long line of officers who have something to say about my background.'

Her face fell. 'Oh. Sorry.'

'Don't worry, I've learnt to deal with it.' He shrugged. It annoyed him, but he'd grown used to it. It came with the territory.

'It's not that. I always thought I was unique, especially in the force, and now you're telling me I behave just like the rest of them. Crap.' She bowed her head, and glanced up at him from under her lashes, grinning.

Working with her was going to be most entertaining. Not that he envisaged them being together for long. It wouldn't take them long to look into the case. He expected to be back in London by this time next week at the very latest.

'From the little I know of you, I doubt that very much.'

'Come on, let's order some food, I'm starving. All I've eaten today is a bag of crisps.'

'Here's a menu,' he said, handing it to her.

'I already know what I'm having. A medium rare rib-eye steak with a large portion of fries, please. No salad. You have to order at the bar.'

'I'm on my way,' he said, as he stood and made his way into the other room.

After ordering their food, Seb returned to the table and sat opposite her.

'Did they say how long it would be?'

'I didn't ask, but as there are very few people in here I

suspect not long. While we wait, tell me about yourself. How long have you been in the force?'

'What's this, an interview?'

'I'm curious.'

'I joined at twenty-one after a string of boring jobs, the longest lasting six months at a local kennels.'

'You're a dog lover?'

'Yeah. But the owner was a bastard and didn't treat them well. I told him what I thought, and he fired me.'

He approved. Not of her being fired, but the fact she chose to stand up for the ill-treated animals.

'I have a yellow lab. I've left her at the place I'm renting.'

'Why didn't you bring her with you?'

'The weather.' He took a sip of his stout. 'You've stayed in the force, so you must enjoy it?'

'If I say it's *my vocation,* it makes me sound like a do-gooder. But I love it. The five years since I joined have flown by.'

'It's a good career.'

'It would be if I could learn to play by the rules but, you know, sometimes rules are there to be broken.'

'And sometimes they're there for a reason.'

'Yes, Dad.'

'How old do you think I am?'

'No idea. A lot older than me from the way you talk.'

'I'm thirty-eight.'

'Old then.' She shrugged. 'Your turn to tell me why you joined up. It's gotta be more interesting than my story.'

'I went to a police recruitment event at uni and liked the sound of it.'

'I bet that went down well with the family.'

He gave a dry laugh. 'You could say.'

'What did they think about the scandal you were part of?' She paused. 'I googled you.'

'The whole team was disbanded. We weren't all guilty.'

'That must have been tough. Were you fired?'

'No. But the only job they offered was one I didn't want to take.'

They were interrupted by the waiter bringing their food and he breathed a sigh of relief. He didn't fancy rehashing everything when they had more important matters to discuss.

After they'd eaten, Birdie took out the folder from the carrier bag. 'Shall we go through this now?'

'Yes, let's. Is there a copy of the suicide note?'

She opened the folder and pulled it out, handing it to him. 'Here.'

He cast an eye over it and then read it aloud:

Sara,

Please forgive me. I can no longer live a lie. You'll find out soon enough what I've done. Take care of the twins. I love you.

Donald

'Short and to the point,' he said.

'Why is his wife concerned? Does she think it was written by someone else?'

'No, it's definitely his handwriting. But she believed he was forced to write it and was leaving her clues. First of all, he misspelt her name, the 'h' at the end is missing. Second, he referred to the children as *the twins.*'

'They are twins.' She frowned.

'That was exactly my reaction. But it transpires he had a thing about wanting them to have their own identity. If he referred to them collectively, it would be *the children*, or *the boys*, but *never* the twins.'

'Is that it?'

'He left the family with nothing. Something he wouldn't have done to them.'

'He had no money, so there was no choice.'

'Not entirely, there was an insurance policy but Sarah's unable to claim because of the suicide verdict. There was a two-year exclusion period and he only took out the policy eighteen months ago. Surely if he took his own life he would've waited until the time he knew she'd definitely be paid out.'

'Hmmm. Could he have thought it was one year and not two?' she suggested.

'That had crossed my mind, especially if he was depressed and not thinking straight.'

'Did Mrs Witherspoon mention her thoughts to the police?'

'She did, but they were brushed aside. Let's take a look at the police report.'

Birdie took it out of the bag and passed it over to him. 'It's thin because there was nothing to report, other than where the body was located and the circumstances. Also, copies of interviews with the family who found him, and his wife.'

He flicked through it, his insides churning when he read about the two young boys who had found Donald with his head blown off.

He glanced up at her. 'What about the coroner's findings?'

'They confirmed it was suicide. Witherspoon died between seven and nine on the Saturday night, the day before his body was discovered. The gun was found close to his right hand. He was right-handed. The note was influential in the final verdict, as were his financial problems, which came to light immediately after his death.'

'Were there any witnesses?'

'None noted in the file. Although, you'd think there might be someone there. Foxton Locks is a busy place. Unless ...'

'The officers didn't look for any,' he said, completing her sentence.

She shrugged. 'Or the weather was bad ...'

'I'll go through the reports in detail later when I'm home. I like to be armed with all the facts and while I'm not saying I think the death isn't suicide, there are definitely some questions that need answering.'

'I wasn't part of the investigation, otherwise my instinct might have told me otherwise and we'd have looked a bit closer. What have you done so far?'

'I've gone through Donald's laptop and identified how he operated the Ponzi scheme. He used money from new investors to pay dividends to the existing ones. He was very organised, and all transactions were methodically recorded, both electronically and as hard copies. He would leave twenty thousand pounds in his current bank account and regularly topped it up with new investments. At the beginning of the year there was a substantial investment made, by an existing investor who happens to be Donald's brother. Interviewing him is a good starting point, and from there I'm going to contact the FCA to find out who alerted them to the fraud.'

'Surely a visit to Foxton Locks, the crime scene, is a better place to start.'

She was right.

'Good point. I'll go in the morning.'

'Wait until my shift ends and I'll come with you. Pick me up at five-fifteen tomorrow afternoon, outside the station. I'm on the eight-five shift.'

NINE

7 May

Birdie stared at her birth certificate which she'd taken out of the drawer where the family's important documents were kept. She'd been born in Leicester on 7 November. A Scorpio baby. That made sense. Nonconformist. Passionate. Determined. How many times had those traits been levelled at her?

Father: Unnamed

Mother: Kim Bakirtzis

She called up the Adoption Contact Register website on her screen and read through all the details. It wasn't a tracing system as such, but a register for people affected by adoption to record they wished to be in contact with their birth relatives. She opened the application form. Her heart raced as she keyed in the information regarding her birth and adoption details and, after paying a fee of fifteen pounds, she submitted her request to be added.

That was it. She'd done it. There was no turning back. She just had to wait to see if her mother was also on the register and then, potentially, they could be in contact with one another.

She'd no idea how long it would take to get a response, but hopefully ... she caught sight of the time on her phone.

Crap. She was meant to have met Clifford fifteen minutes ago.

She grabbed her jacket and raced out of the station, shoving her arms into it on the way. She came to an immediate halt. What car did he drive? By the time they'd left the pub last night, it was dark, and they'd headed in opposite directions, so she didn't see.

She scanned the small car park. Close to the entrance was a large, black BMW four-wheel drive that she didn't recognise. Was that him? She jogged over and saw him sitting in the front seat. She waved, and he responded.

'You're late,' Clifford said as she opened the passenger door and hitched herself up into the seat.

'Sorry, things got away with me. You know what it's like, having been in the job. Um ... One thing you better know about me is my timekeeping's not brilliant.'

She might as well tell him now rather than have him discover it down the track. That way he couldn't moan at her. She hoped he wasn't one of those obsessive, gotta to be punctual or the world will come to an end, freaks.

'It's good to be forewarned,' he said, giving a warm smile. 'Put on your seat belt and we'll go.'

'Have you been to Foxton Locks before? she asked, pulling the belt over her and clicking it in place.

'No. Have you?'

'Oh, yeah, loads of times. We used to go when I was a kid. Everyone goes. It's a great place. Obviously not because we're going to see where the victim was found. But it's lovely and it doesn't get dark until nine, so we've got plenty of time.'

She'd thrown in that last comment so he realised that being a little bit late didn't matter. It wasn't like she didn't try to be on time, but more often than not she failed. She didn't want to tell him the real reason for her tardiness that evening. That she'd been engrossed in adding herself to the Adoption Contact Register to try to find her birth mother. That was her secret.

'I've put it in the satnav,' he said as they drove off.

She sat back and enjoyed the smoothness of the ride. His car was far nicer than hers, which is why she'd asked him to pick her up. The old Mini she owned had belonged to an old woman who'd lived down their street. When she'd died, Birdie had bought the car off the estate for three hundred pounds. It was reliable and got her from A to B. But it was what it was, and nothing like the luxury she was experiencing now. She'd love to buy a new car, but she was saving up for a deposit to put down on a place of her own. She'd also got her student loan to pay off, which was a hefty amount even though she had dropped out after two years.

She glanced across at Clifford, whose eyes were focused on the road. For an older guy he looked good, although maybe a bit too perfect, with his chiselled jaw, dark eyes, and that quality that made a person want to keep looking at him. His height and build added to that. He wasn't her type. She didn't do perfect. She imagined he wouldn't be short of offers, though.

He turned his head, catching her staring at him.

'How was your day?' she quickly asked, acting like that was her whole purpose in looking in his direction.

'Quiet. Apart from when I went out for a walk with Elsa, I spent most of the time going through Donald's records. What about yours? Any interesting cases come in?'

'Yeah, but not for me,' she said, letting out a long sigh.

'Why not?'

Crap. She'd forgotten she hadn't mentioned it last night. Would he still want her working with him if he found out?

'If you must know, I got into a bit of trouble and have been put on desk duty for the foreseeable future.'

He glanced at her and frowned. 'Isn't that part of your job anyway?'

'Yes, but usually we take it in turns. At the moment it's only me.'

'What did you do?'

'Let's just say I had an argument with a skip and the police car I was driving came off worse.'

'Were you hurt?'

'Thanks for asking, because not many people did. My boss was more concerned about the car. I was fine. A couple of bruises, that's all. The problem was, it was all my fault. My mind was on other things and before I knew it, the skip and the side of the car had collided. The car was a write-off.'

'Why are you being disciplined if it was an accident?'

'It's unofficial. My sarge is doing it to teach me a lesson. It doesn't help that I keep being late for work.'

'You said you were a poor timekeeper, but I thought you meant outside of work. Why don't you set your alarm clock?'

'I already have a mother, I don't need another, thanks.'

Really? Was that a Freudian slip?

'And I'm not ready to be one,' he said, tossing a glance in her direction and grinning.

'Sometimes ... well, often ... I sleep through my alarm,' she said, totally disarmed by his response. 'Sorry, you'll get used to me and my big mouth. Lucky for you we're not going to be working together for long.'

'Why do you want to be part of this investigation, if you believe my cousin's mistaken in her view of her husband's suicide?'

'Isn't it obvious? There's no end in sight to my desk duty and I hoped helping you would be a chance for me to get out and do something worthwhile. The whole point in me joining the force was to make a difference. I don't want to be a glorified receptionist for my entire life.' She clenched her fists and banged them on her legs.

'I thought you'd only been on desk duty for a short while.'

'Well, whatever,' she said, waving her hand dismissively. 'Turn right here, it's a shortcut.' He drove them down a windy country road. 'Now take a left into Gumley Road. The body was found in the top car park. We'll go there first and then call in at the pub beside the lock to have a word with the landlord to find out what he knows. According to the file, he wasn't questioned before and you know what these places are like. You can get to know a lot through informal gossip in these close-knit locations. I don't suppose you hung out with locals when you were at the Met and in a big city.' She paused. 'Here's the car park.'

He drove in. 'Where exactly was Donald's body discovered?'

'On the wasteland over there.' She pointed to the far side of the gravelled area.

He parked beside it and she walked on ahead, with him following.

'You wouldn't even know a body had been found here,' Clifford muttered as they got further in.

'It's been a month already, which is long enough for everything to get back to normal. Follow me,' she said, heading deeper into the grassed area. 'According to the report, the boys who found Witherspoon's body were playing within eyesight of their parents' car. They disappeared over there.' She led them towards a clump of trees.

'I thought you hadn't been to the scene.'

'I spoke to Twiggy about it earlier today. Don't worry, I didn't tell him about you and me working together on the case. It's not going to get out.'

'Didn't he wonder why you were asking?'

'I told him I'd come across the case when I was filing and

wanted to know more. I ask a lot of questions anyway so it didn't alert him to anything being odd.'

'In the report you gave me, it mentioned that Donald's car was found in Foxton village, near the pub. Why not leave it here?'

'It's pay and display and no overnight parking. Perhaps he didn't want to be found immediately. Or ...'

'If it wasn't suicide, the killer didn't want him found,' Seb said, finishing off her sentence. 'So someone else could have driven his car there.'

'Or he left it there himself and then walked here to commit suicide,' Birdie said.

'Did Twiggy give you any other useful information?'

'Nothing that wasn't already in the report. He did mention the young boys who found the body, and how traumatising it must have been for them.'

'Do you know whether they were offered counselling?'

'There's nothing about it in the file, but I'd have thought social services would have arranged it for them. Do you want to interview them?' She hoped not. Surely there wouldn't be anything to gain from it.

'No, we don't need to. I don't expect they'll be able to tell us anything other than what we've already got from their original interviews. It would have been hard enough for them to deal with without us dredging it up again.'

Not to mention, it would be difficult to set up an interview without alerting any of the services.

They came to a clearing where the grass was flattened.

'This must be where he was found,' Birdie said, scanning the area. 'There are still some blood splatters around the place.' She pointed to a tree dotted with specks of blood. 'You'd have thought the rain would have washed them away.'

'The leaves are acting as shelter.' Seb picked up a long stick and pushed away at the surrounding grass. 'If the gun went off between seven and nine in the evening, what are the chances of someone hearing it?'

'This car park gets busy during the summer, which this wasn't, or when the weather's good. If there was anyone around up here they'd have heard. They wouldn't in the lower car park or by the lock, as they're too far away.'

'So, if no one reported hearing a gunshot, then most likely the weather wasn't good.'

'I'll check to make sure but, yes, that's right.'

She continued scanning the area, but there was nothing out of the ordinary that captured her attention.

'Do you have an evidence bag with you?' Clifford asked.

'Always,' she said, pulling one out of her jacket pocket and handed it to him. 'What have you found?'

'An old cigarette butt. It was buried under the leaves. It may or may not be important, but worth taking anyway. I'm fairly certain Donald didn't smoke.'

'You know I can't send it to forensics for testing?'

'I know' he said dropping it into the bag. 'Are there any CCTV cameras around?'

She glanced around. 'It doesn't look like it but I'll find out. The land is owned by the council, so if there are any we can take a look at the footage.'

'Assuming it's kept for this long.'

'I expect there isn't any or Twiggy would have requisitioned it to see the time Witherspoon arrived and what his movements were.'

'Are you sure he'd have done that when it was assumed to be suicide?'

Would he? She'd like to think so, but she couldn't be sure. If it had been a busy weekend he might not have.

'I think so. There doesn't appear to be anything else here, so let's go to the pub,' she said, anxious to move the conversation on.

TEN

7 May

'Is the pub within walking distance?' Seb asked, as they left the scene of Donald's death and headed back to the car.

'It depends on how fit you're feeling. We should drive, it's beside the Foxton Locks staircase. FYI, it's one of the largest in England and has ten locks.'

'Impressive.'

'Never let it be said that my education was wasted.' She grinned in his direction.

'I was referring to the locks, not your knowledge of them.' He paused a moment. 'I didn't mean that—'

'I know,' she said interrupting. 'I was joking.' She pointed to the left. 'If we drive back down Gumley Road that will take us to the pub and the lower car park.'

'Is the pub likely to busy at this time?'

'I've no idea. In the summer, when the weather's good, it is. People sit outside watching the boats go by.'

'Let's hope it isn't, or the staff might be too busy to talk to us.

Where exactly were the parents parked when the body was found?' he asked, scanning the deserted car park.

'It would have been close to where we are, if they could see their sons playing over there. I'm not sure exactly. Does it matter?'

'Most likely not. It helps to get a complete picture in my mind of everything that occurred. Especially if it turns out that the time at which Donald died there were other people around. Although, one would assume that if there had been, someone would have reported hearing shots. But at the moment we don't know because there's nothing recorded in the file about that.'

'Look, the investigation deemed Donald's death to be suicide from the start. If there was anything suggesting other- wise it would have been investigated. Twiggy did his job the best he could.'

Had he touched a nerve?

'He's your partner, and you're bound to feel protective of him. All I'm doing is getting an overview, I'm not here to appor- tion blame.'

'That's all right then,' she muttered, scuffing her shoes on the gravel.

He drove them to the lower car park, and they walked to the pub, an attractive building overlooking the water. As they entered, he glanced around; it was much larger than it appeared from the outside, and not as quaint as he'd imagined. There was a group of men in suits standing beside the bar, and several couples sitting at tables.

'Would you like a drink?' he asked.

'I'm starving. I haven't eaten for hours.' She stared longingly at the bags of crisps hanging behind the bar.

'Is this going to be a theme of us working together? Every- where we go you need feeding?' He arched an eyebrow.

'I did come straight from work, remember, and it's way past

six,' she said, an incredulous expression on her face. 'What do you expect me to live on? Thin air?'

'Fine. Food it is.' He laughed to himself as they headed to the bar.

'Can I help you?' the man serving said as they approached.

'I'm Sebastian Clifford, and this is DC Bird from the Market Harborough police. We'd like to speak to the landlord, please.'

He hadn't intended pulling the *police card*, but decided it might help speed things along.

'We have a manager. Will he do?'

'Yes, he would, thank you.'

'I'll fetch him. I won't be long.'

They stood to the side and waited. After a couple of minutes, a tall, overweight man, who looked to be in his fifties came over to them. He wore a red Foxton Locks polo shirt which pulled tightly across his stomach.

'I'm Freddie Evans, the manager,' he said in a broad Welsh accent.

'Sebastian Clifford and this is DC Bird. We'd like to speak to you about this man.' He held a photo out of Donald. 'Do you recognise him?'

'Yeah, course I do. He's Donald Witherspoon, who screwed everybody out of their money and then decided to commit suicide on our doorstep. How could I forget him?'

'Did he ever come in the pub?'

'He was a regular over the years. To be honest, I'd always thought he seemed a like decent bloke. Friendly, chatty. Never rude to the staff. But what the hell do I know? He had us all fooled. I've been managing the place for twenty years, and we've never had a suicide here before. It played havoc with our business. Plenty of press around, but the locals kept well away. Why are you investigating now, after everything has settled and things are going back to normal?'

'This isn't a police investigation.'

'You said you're police.' His brow furrowed as he glared at Birdie.

'We're looking into his death on behalf of his wife,' Seb said.

'I have nothing else to tell you. I'm busy with admin and only came out because I thought you were police. I don't like being lied to.'

'I am an officer, Mr Evans,' Birdie said, holding out her warrant card. 'Off duty.'

'What does that mean? That I don't have to answer your questions?'

'It wasn't my intention to mislead, but would you have spoken to us otherwise?' Seb said.

'I suppose not.'

'So you understand our dilemma. We didn't lie to you, but maybe we were a little economical with the truth.'

'You can say that again. I'm going back upstairs to my work.'

He'd risk asking some more questions, as he suspected he wouldn't get another chance.

'Before you go, when Mr Witherspoon visited who was he usually with?'

'Clients, I believe.'

'How do you know that?'

'Because he'd ask for somewhere quiet in the restaurant, and often there were documents spread out on the table.' He pointed to the large dining area over the far side of the pub.

'Did he ever come in with his wife?'

'I don't know. I didn't keep track of the man. I wasn't his keeper.'

'When was the last time he was here?'

'The day before his body was found, he was here for lunch with a man who I assumed was another client.'

'Did the police question you about this?'

'No. We didn't have a visit from your lot.' He nodded at

Birdie. 'But why would they if it was suicide? The top car park isn't exactly on the doorstep.'

'Would you recognise the other man again?'

'Possibly. He was tall, stocky build, shaved head. Looked a bit rough. I'd probably put him in his late thirties, or early forties.'

'What sort of mood was Mr Witherspoon in that day? Did he seem different?'

'Come to think of it, I remember serving him and he didn't seem his usual self. He wasn't rude, he was never rude, but he did seem a bit not with it, if you know what I mean. I didn't read anything into it. Sometimes people are friendlier than others.'

'Are there any members of staff or customers who could give us a bit more information about him?'

'I doubt it. He didn't mix with people when he was here.' He held his hands up. 'You've had more than enough from me. I'm going.'

'Thank you for your help.'

'Do you have a menu?' Birdie asked.

The manager picked one up and handed it to her. 'They'll take your order at the bar,' he said and walked away.

'What do you think?' Birdie asked.

'We need to find out who Donald was with on the Saturday.'

ELEVEN

8 *May*

Seb had met Donald's brother, Edgar, on several occasions at family gatherings, usually weddings and funerals, and the brothers had always appeared close. Should he phone or email to ask if Edgar would speak to him? Seb had no idea what reception he'd get. He'd phone. It was more immediate. Fortunately, he had his number stored in his mobile.

'Witherspoon,' the soft voice echoed in his ear.

As comfortable as Donald had been in the company of others, Edgar was the opposite. A pleasant enough chap when talking on a one-to-one basis but put him in a group and he would hardly ever contribute.

Edgar had always seemed to live in his outgoing older brother's shadow. It reminded Seb of his older brother, Hubert, who was the more outgoing of the two of them.

'Hello, Edgar. It's Sebastian Clifford, Sarah's cousin.'

'I know who you are. How are you?'

'Well, thank you. I came down for Donald's funeral the other day but didn't see you there.'

He didn't reply for a while, and if it wasn't for his breathing Seb would have thought he'd ended the call. 'I thought it was best to stay away, under the circumstances,' he eventually said. 'How did it go?'

'Not many people turned up. It was a simple service. Adequate.'

He'd be lying if he said it was anything other.

'I'm not surprised people kept away after what my brother had done. He was certainly *persona non grata* in every circle I know of.'

'I'd like to speak to you and wondered if you were around sometime today so we could get together.'

'What about?'

'Sarah has asked me to look into the circumstances of Donald's death, and I thought that as you'd invested with him, and were also family, I'd approach you first. Not only do you have first-hand experience of his business practice, but you knew Donald better than most.'

'You're not the first person to ask me for an interview for that very reason. The press has been hounding me ever since he died. As soon as I think it's dying down, something else crops up and they're at my door again. The funeral being a point in question.'

'I'm very sorry, it must be hard.'

'That's an understatement. But, in case you wondered, I don't hold any malice against Sarah. I'm pretty sure she knew nothing about his activities. Donald told me that he rarely shared business matters with her. He often joked that the less she knew the better, so she couldn't incriminate him. I've got a lot on today, but have an hour free at one. Let's meet for a drink at the pub in Guilsborough.'

Seb sighed with relief, as he'd been bracing himself for a no.

'Thank you. It's much appreciated. I'll see you later.'

He ended the call, surprised that Edgar had agreed so

readily to see him. It was only eleven-thirty, and he had an hour before he needed to leave for the meeting so after he'd done some research on Edgar, as he had no knowledge of what business he was involved in, he called Linda Stallion from the FCA to see if he could ascertain who it was that had reported Donald's financial irregularities.

'It's Sebastian Clifford, Ms Stallion,' he said when she answered the phone. 'Sorry to bother you on a Saturday but I was given your card by Sarah Witherspoon as you dealt with her regarding the investigation into her husband Donald's company.'

'How may I help?' Linda Stallion replied, sounding puzzled.

'Sarah's my cousin and she's asked me to look into the nature of Donald's death. I've gone through his business records and wondered if you could tell me which one of his clients contacted you and reported him? I'm assuming it was a client who hadn't been paid their dividends.'

'That is correct, but I'm not at liberty to give you an actual name. All I can tell you is they were long-time investors and lost their life savings.'

'Was it the Blacks?' he asked remembering some media coverage which had featured them.

'What makes you ask that?' The pitch of Linda Stallion's voice increased. Was he correct?

'They were prominent in the press and from my research, I discovered they'd invested with him before he began the fraudulent scheme.'

'You didn't hear it from me,' Linda said.

* * *

He left Market Harborough at twelve-thirty, not wanting to be late, and headed for the pub. He'd been there fifteen years ago, when he was in town for a party Sarah had given to celebrate her parents' fiftieth wedding anniversary. When he arrived, he was surprised that the 16th century pub was exactly as he remembered it and hadn't been updated.

He walked in and, even though he hadn't seen him for many years, he straight away recognised Edgar, sitting in the corner with a drink on the table in front of him. There was a definite family resemblance between him and his older brother. They both had a full head of thick grey hair, were stockily built, and around five feet nine inches in height.

He stopped at the bar, got himself a pint, and then headed over.

'Good to see you,' Edgar said, standing.

'You too, despite the circumstances.' Seb shook his hand and sat opposite.

'How's Sarah coping?'

'Haven't you been in touch with her?'

'To be honest, no. We kept away.' He couldn't meet Seb's eyes.

Feeling guilty? He should be.

'She could do with some support, Edgar. Especially from family who are likely to be more understanding of the situation, and you've already told me she knew nothing about what Donald had done.'

'I'll mention it to my wife, Celia, and see what she says. She might agree, but I wouldn't bank on it. We're still reeling over what has happened to us. He's left us virtually penniless.'

'Do you mind if I record our interview?' He could remember it all verbatim, but Birdie might like to listen to what Edgar had to say.

'For what purpose?' he asked, frowning.

'It's for my partner. I wanted to speak to you alone as we know each other. I can assure you it won't be used for anything else. I'll delete it once she's listened.'

'Okay, you have my permission.'

Seb took out his phone, clicked on *record* and placed it in the middle of the table.

'You invested a lot of money with Donald. How did you first get involved?'

'He was doing really well at a time when the bank interest rate was heading towards zero. After discussing this with Donald, he suggested I invest with him as he could get me a good return on my investment. I trusted him, so I did. Each quarter I received a healthy dividend.'

'According to his records, you invested another large amount with him at the beginning of this year.'

Edgar picked up his glass took a long drink. 'That's correct. He asked me to invest some more … because he had this big deal coming up and he wanted to include me as family.'

What wasn't he telling him?

'And you agreed to do it?'

'I'd have been foolish not to and at the time I was still getting my quarterly returns.'

'What happened?'

'A couple of months in, the dividend from my existing investment didn't appear and there was nothing coming from the new one, so I asked for my money back. He said no, because it was all tied up. What I didn't know until after his death was that he'd lost all my money.'

'How much did you invest with Donald in total?' Although he knew from the records, he wanted to double-check everything had been recorded.

'Three hundred and fifty thousand. One hundred thousand initially and then a further two hundred and fifty. The dividends from the original investment have always gone towards the children's school fees, and I thought the additional dividends would help, as their fees increase annually.' He bowed his head. 'The children have to leave their school at the end of this academic year. I could just about manage to scrape enough money to pay for the last term, but not now. We're in dire straits.'

'What about your house?'

'I have a large mortgage on it which I'm struggling to service. I took out a second mortgage to cover some renovations a couple of years ago. We've always lived well. We'd go skiing twice a year and take a holiday in the Caribbean. Without my investments, I don't earn enough to cover our expenses. Celia is barely talking to me at the moment.'

'Why? It wasn't your fault. You can't be held responsible for Donald's actions.'

'She ... she ... didn't know about the latest investment.'

Ah ha ... that's why he was acting strangely.

'Why didn't you discuss it with her?'

'Donald wanted a decision immediately, and she was away with some friends on a no-contact spa week. He was most insistent.'

'May I ask where you got the money from to invest? Two hundred and fifty thousand is a lot of money to get your hands on at short notice.'

'A variety of places. I had money in savings accounts, and I sold most of my share portfolio.'

'You work as an accountant in Leicester, I believe.'

How could someone with such financial acumen find themselves in a situation like this?

'Ironic, isn't it? No one understands how I managed to get caught out.'

'Did you have any idea at all that Donald was operating a Ponzi scheme?'

Edgar frowned. 'You think I'd have given him all of my money if I had? That's ridiculous.' He waved his hand in the air.

'He didn't start the scheme until after your first investment.'

'I'll take your word for that. He didn't share business decisions with me. We used to be close, but not so much recently.'

'Why's that?' Seb asked, honing in on the hostile tone in his voice.

'No reason. We just seemed to drift apart.'

That was a cop-out answer, but he wasn't going to pursue it now, as he didn't want the man to totally clam up.

'Where were you on the day Donald died?' he asked, deciding to move on or they'd end up going around in circles.

'I was at home with Celia when they found him. I remember getting the call from Sarah.'

'He died the day before on the Saturday. Can you remember your movements then?'

'Not without my diary. Most weekends, if we don't have any functions, we spend relaxing.'

Seb wasn't going to push him. This wasn't a police investigation, after all.

'How did you feel when he died?'

'What a stupid question. He was my brother, of course I was devastated.'

'Even though you'd drifted apart?'

'That didn't change the fact that he was my brother and he was dead.'

'When his financial mismanagement came out in the open, how did you feel then?'

Edgar glanced either side of him, as if checking that no one could hear. 'I hated him for what he'd done to my family.'

'Didn't you suspect anything was wrong before it all came out in the media?'

'At the back of my mind there were some niggles after I'd asked for my money back. But Donald was a great salesman. When he said the money was tied up and it would be there by the next dividend payment, I believed him. I *had to* believe him. Then he died, and the truth came out. Celia can't bear me to even mention his name, but he was still my brother, despite him screwing us over and losing everything we have. That's what makes everything so hard to deal with.'

'What are you going to do now?'

'Like I said, the kids will be leaving their current school and we may have to sell the house, but we'll try to avoid that if at all possible, as by the time the mortgages are paid off it won't leave us with much. Celia's looking for a job in the interim, which will help with day-to-day expenses. I shouldn't be saying this, but we'll be sitting pretty once her parents kick the bucket because she's in for a hefty inheritance.'

'Why don't you ask them for help?' It seemed the most logical thing to do under the circumstances.

'And admit what I've done? What do you take me for? I do have some pride.' He shook his head.

'No one could blame you if you did go to them.'

'You don't know her folks. They've always thought she could do better for herself. They were probably right.' He picked up his drink and finished it. 'I've got to go. Things to do.'

'I appreciate you sparing the time to see me.'

'I'm not sure what good it's going to do.'

'If he didn't commit suicide and his death was suspicious, then there will be an investigation.'

'And I'll have to find an alibi because I'll be a suspect, no doubt. Not that it matters because I'm sure he did commit suicide. You know what he was like, he wanted everyone to like him. This would've destroyed him. I hope you don't discover that it's murder. Enough damage has been done from this.'

'Sarah needs to know the truth, so she can get on with her life.'

'But it's not going to make any difference, is it?'

'It will to her. What she really needs right now is some support. It's hard being ostracised for something she didn't do.'

'I hear what you're saying, and I'll think about it.'

They left the pub together, and Seb had just got into his car when his phone rang.

'Clifford.'

'It's me, Birdie. Where are you?'

'I've just had a drink with Donald's brother, Edgar. He was one of the investors.'

'Why didn't you tell me? I could have come with you.'

'Because I know him, and he wouldn't have opened up with you there. He's much better on a one-to-one basis.'

'Did he tell you anything useful?'

'He's angry and blames his brother for what's happened to him. He thinks Donald committed suicide because he didn't want to face the fallout that would have happened when his financial losses and the Ponzi scheme came to light.'

'Good point. While I remember, there's no CCTV by the top car park at Foxton Locks, so we can't check who was there on the day Donald died.'

'Okay, thanks.'

'Where are you going next?'

'There's a retired couple, Bert and Pearl Black, who were Donald's clients from a long time ago and were the ones who reported him to the FCA, who then uncovered the Ponzi scheme. They live in Marston Trussell, a village on the outskirts of Market Harborough.'

'I know where it is.'

'I was going to phone and see if they'll see me this afternoon.'

'Let me come with you. Give me an hour to get ready as I've just got up.'

'It's nearly two o'clock, how come you've only just arisen?'

'I went to bed late.'

'I'll call them now and get back to you.'

He phoned and Mr Black answered. Seb explained why he

wanted to visit the couple and the man was amenable, so after making the arrangements he got back to Birdie.

'They've said we can see them at four, so I'll pick you up at three-thirty. Where do you live?'

'Gardiner Street. You'll see my car parked outside the house, behind a Citroen which belongs to my mum.'

'You still live with your parents?'

'Yeah. So what?'

'No reason, you just seem to be the sort of person who would've flown the nest a long time ago.'

'I have lived away from home, but … you know … circumstances. Anyway, this isn't about my living arrangements. When you get here, you're to stay in the car and not knock at the door. I don't want anyone thinking we're going out on a date. I don't date older men.' She paused. 'Or women, for that matter.'

'I'll wait outside your house. Shall I put a hood over my head?'

'Don't be stupid.'

TWELVE

8 May

Seb checked his watch for the tenth time. If Birdie didn't hurry up, he'd go to the door and knock, despite her insistence that he didn't. He was parked outside the front of the detached Victorian house where she lived, which wasn't far from the house he was renting. It was half-brick and half-rendered and had ivy growing around the front door.

He placed his hand on the door handle, ready to get out of the car when her front door opened, and she came tearing out of the house. She ran around the front of the car and opened the passenger door.

'Don't say anything. I know I'm late. We'll be there on time.' She jumped into the car, pulled down the seat belt and clicked it in place.

'My lips are sealed,' he said, before starting the engine and driving away.

'Is there any chance we can stop off somewhere to pick me up something to eat? A burger from the drive-through would do the trick.'

'We're expected at the Blacks' house at four.'

'It's only a slight detour and won't take long. I can eat it on the way. Please.'

'Okay.'

He drove them through the town centre and stopped at the first fast-food restaurant they came to. Luckily there wasn't a queue.

He ordered her a burger, which she wolfed down in a couple of bites, and a coffee.

'Thanks, I needed that after the night I had.' She rested her head on the window.

'What happened?'

'I was out with friends clubbing, that's what young people do on a Friday night.'

'But we were together last night.'

She looked at him from under her lashes and laughed. 'You crack me up. I didn't go out until eleven. I know in your day people would go out early, but they don't do that now.'

'What do you mean *my day*? I'm not a geriatric.' He couldn't remember the last time he'd been dancing at a club, but he wasn't going to admit that. He much preferred concerts or the theatre.

They arrived in Marston Trussell with time to spare, and stopped outside a semi-detached, cream pebble-dashed house with a white door and a gravel drive.

At exactly four, they walked up the short drive to the front door and, after knocking, an elderly man in his seventies appeared. He was wearing a shirt and tie, with a pair of suit trousers. The only concession to him being at home and not in an office was his tartan slippers.

Had he dressed up to meet them?

'Mr Black? I'm Sebastian Clifford, I phoned you earlier. This is my colleague DC Bird.'

'I'm always happy to help the police.' He smiled at Birdie.

'I'm not actually on duty today, sir. I've come with Sebastian to talk to you.'

'Oh. Never mind. Come on in, my wife's in the lounge.'

They walked into the nicely decorated house and followed him to a small living room with a brick-built fire in the centre of the wall facing them. His wife stood up from the sofa and smiled. She too was dressed nicely in a floral print dress which buttoned up the front.

'Hello, Mrs Black. It was very kind of you and Mr Black to agree to speak to us,' Seb said.

'Please, call us Bert and Pearl.'

'Are these all your family?' Birdie said, gesturing to the walls which were covered in mounted photos.

'Yes they are. We have four children, twelve grandchildren and three great-grandchildren. They're scattered all over the world, as far away as New Zealand. We had planned to travel overseas to see them all, but ...' Her voice fell away.

'We can still speak to them on the computer. It's amazing what you can do nowadays. You can actually see them, and the picture is so good you feel like you can almost touch them,' Mr Black said, putting his arm around her shoulders.

'Except we can't.' She gave a sigh.

'Please sit down,' Mr Black gestured to the two rust-coloured easy chairs which were either side of the sofa. 'You want to talk about Mr Witherspoon?'

'Yes, if you don't mind. Please could you tell us how you first got involved with him,' Seb said.

'We invested all our money with him after seeing his advert in the paper. We wanted to make sure we had enough money once we'd retired to do all those things we'd planned. Like travel. We'd sold our house when we downsized after the last of the children left home and had a large amount of money. The bank rates were appalling, so I contacted Donald to find out more.'

'Did you know him before this?' Seb asked

'He was a member of the Rotary club I belonged to. We were acquaintances. He came around to see us and talked about investing and what we could do with our money, to give us the best return. He suggested we reinvested our dividends, to build up our capital sum, and said that we could change that at any time and also take out the lump sum we'd put in once the initial investment period was over.'

'How much did you invest?'

'A hundred thousand pounds. It was the money we had left after selling our house and buying this one. At first, we reinvested the dividends and when we retired we changed and received an income every month which we used to top up our state pensions.'

'He seemed so nice,' Mrs Black said. 'He took us out to a fancy restaurant to celebrate when we signed all the papers. The Elm Tree, in Husbands Bosworth. I don't know if it's still there because we haven't been since. He was charming, and we trusted him.'

'Did you take any other financial advice?' Birdie asked.

Mr Black hung his head. 'I wish we had. But he was reputable, we knew him, and for years there were no issues at all, until ...' He paused.

'What happened?' Seb asked.

'Six months before he died the payments stopped. He said there was a financial crisis in the Middle East and that we shouldn't worry. He was working hard to sort out the situation.'

Seb shook his head. 'And you believed him.'

'Yes, we did. We then left it for a couple of months and after there were still no payments, I contacted him again and left a message on his voicemail. He didn't call back. I tried several times with no joy, so in the end I sent an email saying that we want all of our money back. After that, he called. He apologised profusely and promised our money within two weeks. It didn't happen. So, I contacted the FCA and told them what had happened. They said they would investigate and let me know what they'd found. They reported back that there were some *anomalies* ... that was the word they used, and they would be taking matters further. But then he died.'

'And we lost our money,' Mrs Black said, a single tear rolling down her cheek. 'All we have is our pension to live on, which barely covers the bills. God help us if something big needs replacing like the boiler. We don't want to bother our children because they have their own families to care for. We'll probably have to sell the house and move into a small flat, or a care home. All thanks to that man.'

'I'm sorry to hear that,' Seb said. 'You should consider telling your family, though. They might want to help you.'

'We got ourselves into this mess, and we're not going to ask our children to help us out. Nobody, apart from you, knows exactly how much we've lost, and that's how it's going to stay,' Mr Black said, banging a fist on the arm of the sofa. 'All they think is that we'd invested a small amount with Witherspoon. We had to tell them that because our names are out there on a debtors' list. Although we didn't expect anyone to notice, we wanted to cover ourselves just in case.'

'Why are you investigating him now, isn't it all over?' Mrs Black asked.

'Mr Witherspoon's wife doesn't believe he took his own life, and she wants us to look into it,' Seb said, hoping it wasn't going to drag up too many awful memories for them.

'Do you think he was murdered?' Mrs Black asked, her eyes wide.

'We haven't got that far. I'm just taking an extra look to make sure nothing was missed during the investigation.'

'I believe he committed suicide because he didn't want to be seen as a failure. He always came across as being so proud of his success. He should have stayed and faced up to what he'd done to all of us.'

'I expect you're right, but we want to make sure.' Seb stood. 'Thank you for taking the time to talk to us. We really appreciate it.'

Seb and Birdie left the house and returned to the car.

'This makes me so sick,' Birdie said. 'Witherspoon goes in there all smarmy and smiles and wanting them to trust him and then he takes the money, not caring what would happen to them. It's a fucking disgrace. What's gonna happen to those poor people? They've got nothing and are too proud to ask for help. It's disgusting.' She thumped the dashboard.

'Remember that when they first invested with him, his business was above board. He didn't start the Ponzi scheme until years later.'

'I don't care. He's still a bastard.'

'I knew Donald and there was nothing about him which made me think he would resort to this kind of behaviour. He always came across as being above board and genuine.'

'Nothing? I find that very hard to believe. No one can be that perfect.'

'Perfect he wasn't, and I suppose he did smile a lot and maybe liked to ingratiate himself with people. But I never witnessed anything which gave me cause to believe that he was operating fraudulently.'

'Did he ever ask you to invest in one of his schemes?' Birdie asked.

'Not once. I was a police officer, and he thought I had no money, as well as thinking I'd lost the plot by joining the force.' He sighed as the familiar conversations he'd had with his family regarding his choice of career forced their way to the front of his mind.

'What's wrong with being a police officer?'

'Nothing, as far as I'm concerned, but it's different for my family. They'd rather I'd done something else, and now they've had their wish granted.' He turned his head and stared out of the front window. He wasn't prepared to discuss it further with her. With anybody, in fact, until he was clear about it himself.

'What happened, do you think, for Donald to embark on this fraud, because surely something must have? And then what went wrong for it all to go to tits up?' Birdie asked.

'If I was to hazard a guess, I'd say he had a cash flow problem ten years ago and found himself short of money. At that same time, he signed up an investor, and instead of actually putting the money into the scheme it was earmarked for, he borrowed it, believing it would be like a short-term loan. It then snowballed from there, and he was continually borrowing money from new investors to pay the old. It worked well, for a long time, but Ponzi schemes can only flourish as long as there's a steady flow of new investors. Problems arise when the money runs out and there isn't any new money coming in. The house he lived in required upkeep and he took Sarah and the boys on expensive holidays. He wore bespoke suits and drove top of the range cars. It was a delicate balancing act, one which he obviously failed to keep going.'

'If he was murdered, then there are a number of people with motives.'

'We don't know that he was, yet. Remember it was only reported to the FCA shortly before he'd died, and they didn't get access to the records until after his death and following that it was announced.'

'But if people like the Blacks wanted their money back, and he refused then they could've murdered him.' Her brow furrowed. 'Except that would make it even worse because they'd never get their money back. Why didn't he sell his house if times had got desperate?'

'It's in Sarah's name and he couldn't touch it. He'd have had to go to her and explain what was going on. He always kept Sarah well away from the business, and I imagine he was too proud to admit he'd failed.'

'Maybe he did tell her, and she killed him. She wouldn't be the first wife to murder her husband.'

'Then why ask me to investigate his death after it had been classified as suicide? That doesn't seem at all feasible.'

'True. Is there any way people like the Blacks can get their money back?'

'They could make a claim on the estate, except there's nothing left. He was bankrupt.'

'I wish we could do something to help that poor couple get their money back. Would they have a claim against Sarah and the house?'

'I'm not a lawyer and can't answer that. But Sarah shouldn't be blamed, and I'm not debating with you if that's right or wrong. Our job is to investigate Donald's death, not worry about Sarah's input or otherwise. Did the Blacks have reason to kill him? Yes. Except they didn't know about the Ponzi scheme until after the FCA had investigated.'

'Do you believe them?'

'As much as I'd believe anyone in that sort of situation.'

'You mean yes. And so do I. What are we going to do now?'

'Continue interviewing investors, but first I want some more background on Donald and not just from his brother. I'm going to speak to Sarah tomorrow and get a list of his friends. I'd like you to take a look at his active investors. Another pair of eyes might spot something odd and worth investigating further. Check up on anyone who you think appears suspicious in any way. I'll email the list to you later.'

'Thanks. You might as well take me back home. I've got to get ready to go out.'

'Again?'

'Yes. Do you expect me to stay in on a Saturday night?

Don't answer that. A gang of us are going rollerblading at the leisure centre. You're welcome to come.' He turned to see the smirk on her face.

'Thank you, but no. I'll let you know how I get on after speaking to Sarah.'

THIRTEEN

9 May

The moment Seb turned into the long drive leading to Sarah's house, Elsa started getting excited, wagging her tail and pushing her nose up against the car window. She clearly recognised where they were and remembered the fun she'd had playing in the grounds. He parked outside the front of the house. There was only one other car there, which belonged to Sarah.

He rang the bell several times, and after a few minutes Sarah came around the side of the house, mud smeared on her face, wearing gardening gloves and old clothes.

'I thought I heard the bell. I've been working in the garden. It's extremely therapeutic, and I get so engrossed that it makes me forget about everything else. I hadn't realised the time.'

He leant down and kissed her on both cheeks. When he'd called earlier to ask about Donald's friends, she'd invited him over.

'I thought you had a gardener?'

'We used to, but I've had to let him go. There's a man in the village who comes in once a fortnight to mow the lawns as it's such a big job. The rest I can manage myself. I've had to let most of the staff go as I can't afford to keep them. All I have now is Dee, a local woman, who does the cleaning and helps with other jobs when I need her. Really, she's a luxury, so I don't know how long I'll be able to keep her. Come on around the back.'

He let Elsa off the lead, and she went charging ahead of them. 'She had such fun the last time. I expect she'll make for the woods.'

'Will she be okay on her own?'

'She never goes far. She'll find us soon enough once she's had enough of running around.'

'I'm parched. Let's go inside for a cup of tea.' They walked around the back and into the kitchen and she filled the kettle. 'I've got Earl Grey, English Breakfast, or peppermint and ginger herbal tea.'

'The latter would be lovely.'

'I'll join you,' she said, taking out two mugs and pouring boiling water over the tea bags. She took two small plates from the dresser and a tin from the pantry. 'Cake?'

'I haven't long since had lunch, but what the heck,' he said, the smell of the chocolate invading his senses as she opened the tin and wafted it under his nose.

'Home-made. All I've been doing recently is baking to keep me occupied.'

'Have the boys gone back?'

'They left this morning to give themselves time to get settled before their lectures.'

'Do they share a flat?'

'They're both in the same halls of residence and they see each other often, although they do have their own sets of friends. They don't tell me much, but you know what kids of that age are like.'

'How were they after the funeral?' If Donald's death did

turn out to be suspicious, then the police would want to question them.

'Okay, as far as I can tell, which is hard because they don't confide in me. They think it's manly not to share their feelings. They're both very like Donald in that respect.' They sat at the big oak kitchen table in the centre of the room. 'So how's it all going?' she asked just as he'd taken a bite of cake. He held up his hand to signal that he'd speak once he'd finished.

'I'm working with a DC from the local police force.'

'The police are getting involved in the investigation? How on earth did you manage that? At the time of Donald's death, they took very little notice of anything I said. Is it because you used to be in the police?' she asked, her eyes bright.

'No, this is someone I phoned regarding accessing the police report, and the only way I could get it from her, together with the coroner's report, was if I let her work with me on the QT.'

'That sounds a bit odd. Who is she?'

'DC Lucinda Bird. Known as Birdie. She's very different from most officers I've come across of her age. But certainly entertaining. She's helping me during her time off and so far, has been very useful. I wanted to ask you about Donald's friends. I thought I'd speak to one or two of them to get a better picture of how he was in recent times.'

'Donald didn't really have any friends. Plenty of acquaintances and he was always being invited to various events, or charity golf tournaments, but no one really close. In fact, the only friend of his he's had for many years is Tony Yates. You might have met him at our silver wedding party.'

'I didn't meet anyone of that name, but considering there were around two hundred people there, that's hardly surprising.'

'Tony was Donald's best friend from university. We used to go out occasionally as couples, his wife is Pauline. To be honest

he was more Donald's friend, and although Pauline was pleasant, we didn't hit it off enough to meet up outside of any
couple's activity we did together. In fact, I can't even remember
the last time I saw them.'

Tony Yates. Seb's mind was filtering information he'd seen.
'Is his proper name Anthony?'

'Yes, I believe it is. Why?'

'He was one of Donald's investors. I will definitely contact
him.'

'Would you like his number?'

'I already know it, from the records. Are you sure you can't
think of any other friend I could talk to?'

'No, sorry,' she said, shaking her head.

'Did Donald ever mention Bert and Pearl Black, they were
clients of his for many years?'

'I haven't heard their names before. Should I have?'

'Bert knew Donald from the Rotary club.'

'Donald was a member for many years, and I went to their
charity events with him, but I don't recall ever meeting them.'

'No problem. I spoke to Edgar yesterday, and he's still bitter
about what happened. He'd actually made two large investments with Donald and neglected to tell Celia about the latest
one, which was the reason behind them losing everything as
he'd cashed in all his other investments to fund it.'

'Goodness ... he kept it from Celia. That's a surprise. Edgar
has kept well away from me since Donald's death. I don't blame
him, I suppose, but he has to know it was nothing to do with me.
Does he hate me?'

'No, he doesn't. He realises that you wouldn't have known
anything about Donald's scheme. To be honest, the issue is
more with Celia.'

'That doesn't surprise me. Has he been forbidden to
see me?'

'Give them time and I'm sure they'll come around. Birdie and I went to Foxton Locks to the location Donald was found, and then we went into the pub close by. The manager knew Donald as he often used the place for meetings with prospective clients. Did you ever go there with him?'

'Yes, occasionally I did. Maybe a couple of times a year. It's a lovely location, and the food is good.'

'Donald was there with someone on the day he died.'

'I told you he went out to meet a client, but he didn't give me their name and it wasn't in his diary, nor did he tell me exactly where they were meeting.'

'Did the police ask you about it?'

'No because I think they thought he'd made it up, to give him an excuse for going out that day. It didn't help that I couldn't give a name or provide any record of the meeting.'

'It's an understandable conclusion to make. According to the report, Donald's car was left in Foxton village itself and not in the car park where his body was found.'

'Yes, that's right.'

'Did the police explain why they thought it was left there?'

'I didn't think to ask and no one mentioned it to me. The first I knew of it was when the tow truck brought his car back.' She sighed. 'That makes me sound so stupid, but at the time I wasn't thinking straight.'

'You're not stupid. It's hard to think rationally when you're grief-stricken. Could I take a look at the car?'

'I no longer have it. I sold it a few weeks ago. The man who does the lawns took it to the car auctions in Northampton as I couldn't face doing it myself. I'm sorry.'

Damn. It would have been cleaned by now so nothing for him to look at.

'It's not important, don't worry about it.'

'After what you've done so far, do you think I'm justified in my beliefs about the death?'

'It's too early to say. Yes, there are some anomalies, but none so far which have caused me to question the police and coroner's verdict. But that doesn't mean I'll stop investigating.'

FOURTEEN

10 May

Seb parked in Newarke Street car park and headed down York Road until reaching Oxford Street. He pressed the button on the crossing and waited for the green man to show so he could cross the busy Leicester road. He'd arranged an appointment for two o'clock with Donald's friend Tony Yates who had a large quantity surveying practice in the city. Birdie had moaned that he was going without her, but she was working and he wasn't prepared to sit twiddling his thumbs waiting for when she was available. He'd never visited the city, although he'd recently read that it was in the top ten places for people to live in terms of quality of life, ahead of London, Nottingham, and Derby. From what little he'd seen of it, so far, he liked the vibe.

Yates and Co was in a large office block, and after studying the board listing the companies housed there, he took the lift to the seventh floor. The reception was chrome and glass, and behind the desk sat a twenty-something man wearing a suit and tie.

'Good afternoon. The name's Clifford and I'm here to see Tony Yates. I have an appointment at two.'

'If you'd like to take a seat over there, I'll let him know you've arrived.' The receptionist pointed him to a waiting area where there was a black leather sofa and matching chairs.

Seb headed over and sat down. He picked up a book on iconic buildings around the world from the glass-topped coffee table in front of him, and flicked through the pages. Buildings had always fascinated him.

'Mr Clifford?' He glanced up at the woman standing a short way from him, smiling. 'I'm Dawn, Mr Yates's executive assistant, if you'd like to come with me, I'll take you to his office.'

He followed her down the corridor until they reached an open door with *Tony Yates Managing Director* on the brass nameplate. Inside were two desks, one empty and the other with a young woman speaking on the phone. An internal door was situated to the right of the two workstations, and Dawn gently knocked and opened it.

'Mr Clifford to see you, Tony.'

'Come on in,' Yates said, walking around his desk to where Seb stood and shaking his hand. He was slim with salt-and-pepper short hair and stood six inches shorter than Seb. He was dressed conservatively in a pair of dark navy suit trousers, the jacket hanging on a coat stand beside the door, a white shirt and paisley tie.

'Would you like anything else?' Dawn asked.

Was he going to be offered a coffee? That would be most welcome.

'No, we're fine, thank you. Please take a seat.' Yates gestured to the large table by the floor-to-ceiling corner window.

'What a magnificent view,' Seb said, admiring the one-hundred-and-eighty-degree skyline, a mix of old and new buildings, all blending effortlessly.

'There have to be some perks of being the owner of the

company, and having the best office is one of them,' Yates said, standing by the window and giving a contented sigh, before returning his attention to Seb. 'You informed my assistant that you wished to speak to me about Donald Witherspoon, on Sarah's instruction.'

'Yes, that's right. Thank you for seeing me, I wasn't sure you would under the circumstances.'

'Initially I was going to refuse, then curiosity got the better of me. Why did Sarah want you to speak to me?'

'She isn't convinced by the suicide verdict and I'm investigating for her.'

'Clutching at straws, I suspect,' Yates said, shaking his head. 'How's she doing?'

'As well as can be expected. It's been tough for her and the boys. Have you been in touch with her? I noticed you weren't at the funeral.'

He already knew the answer to that question but hoped to trigger a response to help him gauge the depth of his feelings about the situation.

'I should have gone, but how could I after what had happened? I realise it wasn't Sarah's fault, but ...' He shrugged.

'Unfortunately, many people felt the same as you and she's been left on her own to deal with her loss and the fallout from the discovery of his financial mismanagement.'

'Do you agree with Sarah about the suicide verdict?'

'My investigation is ongoing and as yet I don't have a definitive answer.'

'Are you a private investigator?' he asked, frowning.

'No, I'm not.'

'What skills do you have, in that case? I hope you're not taking advantage of Sarah in her vulnerable position.'

The irony of the comment, coming from someone who hadn't even bothered to contact her, didn't escape Seb.

'Aside from being Sarah's cousin, I'm a former police officer, and my colleague on this case is a serving officer.'

Perhaps he shouldn't have mentioned that, not that it would get Birdie in trouble as he hadn't mentioned her name.

'Fair enough. Fire away. What do you want to know?'

'I'd like a little background on the two of you. I know that you and Donald went back a long way, and that you were his only real friend. Can you give me a potted history of your relationship?'

'We were in the same halls of residence at Leicester University and met during freshers' week. We hit it off straight away and were friends ever since. I admit we didn't see each other as much as we'd have liked in later years, but we would meet up every now and again, at charity events or social functions. And then sometimes, when our diaries allowed, we'd go out for drinks to catch up. Occasionally, we'd make up a foursome with him and Sarah, but my wife Pauline wasn't keen on doing that. She liked Sarah well enough, but she disliked Donald and thought his friendly outgoing nature was all a facade. She saw what the rest of us didn't, as it turned out.'

Was that enough for her to take matters into her own hands after discovering the fraud? Which would mean she'd have had to have known about losing their money before the death and it had become general knowledge.

'From what I've discovered from his records, you invested a substantial amount of money with him at the beginning of this year.'

'Yes, that's right, I did. Two hundred thousand.'

'Can you confirm that you'd never invested with him before?'

'That's correct, because I like to keep business and pleasure separate.'

Except he didn't this time.

'Why did you change your mind and invest in January?'

Yates leant forward slightly, and lowered his voice, as if wanting to make sure that no one else could hear. 'He contacted me because he was desperate. He was having a difficult time financially and asked me if I could help.'

'Had he ever asked you to help him out before?'

'No, that was the one and only time.'

'And you were happy to invest two hundred thousand pounds. That's a lot of money to find.'

'I have a thriving business and he was in trouble. He'd have helped me if the situation was reversed.'

'How were you able to lay your hands on such a large amount?'

'It has nothing to do with you.' His body stiffened.

Seb immediately went on alert.

'I'm trying to get a picture of how desperate he was and how deep your friendship went. Judging by your comments, I'm guessing you had to either liquidate some stocks or borrow from the bank.'

'What else could I do? He was my friend. I borrowed from the bank.'

'Did he discuss how he was going to pay you back?'

'It was an investment, and I was going to get a return on my money, in the same way as the rest of his clients. I agreed to a five-year term.'

Nothing was sitting right.

'So you tied up two hundred thousand pounds for five years. How did you receive your dividends?'

'I was due quarterly payments and, before you ask, no I didn't receive any. After the first due date had been and gone, I contacted him and he said there was a problem and he promised that next quarter it would be fine. There wasn't a next quarter because he was dead before the time came around.'

'And now you've lost that money and you're left having to pay back a loan for which you having nothing to show.'

He nodded. 'Yes.'

'When was the last time you saw Donald?'

'We met up in early January, when he came to see me about borrowing the money.'

'After you'd agreed to invest, did you meet up again?'

'No, because we were both too busy. We conducted our business electronically.'

'What were you doing on Saturday, 10 April? We know he'd gone to Foxton Locks pub with a client, and I wondered if that was you?'

Yates didn't match the vague description the pub manager had given, but Seb sensed something going on and he wanted to check.

'I told you only moments ago that I hadn't seen him since January. What are you implying?'

'I'm not implying anything. Just trying to get an idea of Donald's life recently. I thought you could help.'

'I have nothing further to say and have work to do.'

He was being dismissed.

'Thank you for speaking to me. Do you mind if I get in touch again if I have further questions?'

'If you must.'

FIFTEEN

11 May

'It's me,' Birdie said, when Seb answered the phone.

He'd just finished his lunch and was intending to give Sarah a call to update her on his meeting with Tony Yates. He didn't have much to tell her, but he wanted to keep in touch to check on how she was doing. Someone had to.

'What have you got?'

'I've been at it for hours.' She paused. 'In between my proper work, obviously. You'll be so impressed. I even arrived early this morning to get cracking. Sarge nearly had heart failure when he turned up for the morning briefing and found me sitting at my desk, head down. Don't worry, he didn't see what I was doing. I just told him I was planning a new filing system. Maybe he'll let me out of the office soon.'

'You never know your luck.'

'I haven't been through the whole list of his investors, but this is what I've got so far. One of them is Andrea Wood.'

'She invested one hundred and fifty thousand with Donald, what's so special about her?'

'She's *Andrea Wood* the TV star.'

'You'll have to enlighten me.'

'She presents the morning breakfast show, Monday to Friday, and has a home locally that she mainly uses at the weekend.'

'How do you know that?'

'One of the girls I play cricket with told me. Her mum cleans for Andrea.'

'Does she come back here every weekend?'

'I've no idea. I've seen her wandering round the Harborough antique shops in the past on a Saturday. Her name was Ann Smith until she changed it. Why wouldn't you, it's hardly a celeb's name is it? Anyway, I did a bit of research on her and found nothing on her at all for either name. Not even a speeding fine. Can you really get to almost thirty-nine without doing anything? She's way too perfect if you ask me.'

'Not everyone's committed a misdemeanour, even an inconsequential one.'

'That aside, I think she's a person worth interviewing. I also checked out Witherspoon's friend, Tony Yates. He had a drink-driving charge from when he was a student. Other than that, there's nothing to report ...' She paused.

'I'm sensing a *but* coming.'

'This might be nothing, but one of the investors was very interesting. He's Grant Truss, who also goes by Grant Dixon, a fellow financier who was involved in some dodgy dealings fifteen years ago. What I want to know is, why would he be investing with Donald when he's a financier himself? He was the director of Victory Finance, a company which went into administration causing many people to lose their savings. It wasn't a Ponzi scheme like Donald's but the FCA got involved because the company had misled clients into thinking they were buying into a safe scheme as well as promising them a ten per cent return on their investment.'

'That's an excellent find. See if you can find out where he is so we can interview him.'

'Already done. I'll text you his details.'

'I remember his name and know he invested forty thousand pounds on 6 February 2004, and he also invested a further twenty thousand on 30 May the following year. With the initial amount he reinvested the dividends, and the second he opted to be paid annually.'

'You've got that all written down in front of you, have you? How could you find him so quickly?'

'No, it's not in front of me. I remember.'

There was a few seconds' silence. He knew exactly what she was going to say next.

'You've got a photographic memory?'

And now he had to explain it.

'No, that's a misconception. I have a very rare condition known as Highly Superior Autobiographical Memory, or HSAM for short. It means I can recall past events in detail, and the exact day and time they happened. Ask me what I had for dinner three years ago yesterday and I'll tell you.'

'Whoa. That's amazing.'

'That's what everyone thinks. But it's not all it's cracked up to be. It's like having a search engine in your head the whole time, only unlike Google or whatever, it can't be switched off. It can get extremely tiring at times.'

'It must have helped during exams.'

'In a way it did. I remembered the facts I'd read, but they still had to be applied. Studying wasn't plain sailing for me. I wasn't a straight A student.'

'Got it. But I still think it's awesome.'

That's what most people thought. They should only walk a mile in his shoes and then see if they had the same opinion.

'I'll contact Grant Truss and arrange to see him.'

'Do you think Truss investing with Witherspoon was something to do with his company going to the wall?'

'That's what we need to find out. Whether it's related to Donald's death, however, is a different matter. When did Truss's company go into administration?'

'After he began investing with Witherspoon. Maybe Truss knew his company was on dodgy ground and wanted somewhere to stash some cash without anybody knowing.'

'I'll find out more when I see him. Keep digging and see what else you can find out. What happened when the regulator got involved in his company?'

'They weren't prosecuted, but their assets were frozen and they went into administration. I'll keep looking and update you with what exactly happened. I don't have a day off until Saturday, so you'll have to interview Truss without me. Can you manage that?'

'I'll try my hardest.'

'Keep in touch ... crap. Someone's coming. I'll text you Truss's details, let me know how it goes.'

Within a few seconds his phone pinged, and he'd received a text with the details. Truss worked in London. He called the number.

'Fast Finance,' a woman answered.

'I'd like to make an appointment to see Mr Truss.'

'What's it regarding?'

'Finance,' he lied. 'Does he have any appointments tomorrow?'

'He's available at eleven. Shall I book you in?'

'Yes, please. The name's Clifford. Thank you for your help.'

He ended the call before she had time to ask for his first name, in case they googled him.

Things were progressing well. He hoped to have an answer for Sarah soon, one way or the other.

SIXTEEN

12 May

Seb caught the nine-thirty train to London and took the Piccadilly line on the Tube to Southgate where Truss was based. His office was above an estate agent in Chase Side, close to the art deco station. Seb pushed open the green door which was in definite need of a coat of paint and headed up the narrow staircase covered in well-worn patterned lino which looked like it dated from the sixties. At the top of the stairs was another door, and in faded gold lettering on the glass was written *Fast Finance*. According to Seb's research, the company offered payday loans, mainly operating online.

He walked in and behind a large cheap looking desk, filling most of the room, sat a woman in her fifties with blonde hair framing her oval face. Her fingers, with long pink nails decorated with gemstones, were frozen in mid-air as she stopped tapping on the keyboard and glanced up, craning her neck until they made eye contact.

'May I help you?'

'I'm here to see Mr Truss. The name's Clifford, I called yesterday.'

She rested her hands on the desk and nodded. 'You were lucky to catch him in today as on Friday he goes to the Bahamas for a month, and he's been busy getting everything sorted.'

'Will someone be carrying on with his clients in his absence?'

'There's no need to worry, he can still sort out everything for you. It's possible to work anywhere nowadays thanks to the internet and having a laptop. We don't have many face-to-face customers, didn't you want to apply online? It's so much easier. Though I never thought I'd hear myself say that. When I first started here, we did everything in person and I was useless on the computer. Mr Truss was very patient while I learnt how to use the software and ... I can even help my grandson with his homework.'

'I'm impressed,' Seb said, flashing a smile in her direction.

She sat upright, her shoulders back, a self-satisfied expression on her face, and picked up the phone on her desk, pressing one of the buttons. 'Mr Clifford's here to see you,' her voice boomed out. After replacing the handset, she looked up at him. 'If you'd like to go through that door, that's his office' She pointed to the door to the right of her desk.

As he walked in, Truss stood up and held out his hand. He was a small man, maybe five feet six, with a rather large protruding belly, short grey hair cut around his ears, and a well-trimmed beard.

'Mr Clifford, good to meet you. Please take a seat.'

Seb shook his outstretched hand and sat on the chair in front of the desk.

'Thank you for seeing me at such short notice.'

'Can I get you something to drink?'

'Coffee would be lovely.'

Truss picked up the phone. 'Violet. Two cups of coffee and

don't forget the biscuits.' He replaced the phone and then patted his stomach. 'I can't miss my mid-morning snack or I won't be able to concentrate.' He laughed, and his double chin wobbled. 'How may I help you? What sort of loan are you looking for?'

'I'm actually here for a chat.'

Truss frowned. 'Didn't you tell my assistant you were here about organising some finance?'

'That's correct and I'm sorry to have misled her, but I wanted to speak to you about Donald Witherspoon and I wasn't sure that you'd agree to see me if you knew the real reason for my visit.'

Colour drained from Truss's face. 'Are you the press?'

'Most definitely not. His wife has asked me to investigate her husband's death as she's not convinced it was suicide.'

'What am I to do with that?' His voice was stiff and stilted.

'Going through Donald's records, I can see that you invested with him on a couple of occasions.'

'And let me guess, because of my background, you thought I was something to do with this Ponzi scheme he was operating. Well, let me tell you, I had nothing to do with it. I lost everything I'd invested with him, along with everyone else.'

'Why were you investing with him at all, if you had your own finance company and the knowledge to make investments?'

'When I was a director of Victory Finance, I decided to keep some of my investments private so I invested it in a variety of different places, including with Donald.'

'What made you go with Donald out of all the investment companies around? Did you know him before you invested?'

'We went back a long way from when we both worked for the same loan company back in the nineties. We both left the company to work for ourselves. I bought into a finance company that gave loans, and he decided to go it alone. We kept in touch over the years. Not regularly, but maybe every six months or so.'

'What other places did you invest in on the quiet?'

'That's nothing to do with you and not relevant to this.'

'Did you keep some of your investments separate for tax purposes?'

He didn't expect the man to tell him, but he asked, anyway. If he was operating a tax dodge and Donald was in on it, that could be an angle to investigate.

'I don't discuss my personal taxes with other people.'

'Did you take dividend payments from the investments with Donald, or reinvest them?'

He knew the answer, but wanted to check that Donald's records were accurate, or that Truss was telling the truth.

'The initial investment I took out was one hundred per cent reinvested. The later one I took an annual dividend as it helped with my cash flow.'

That matched with what he'd read.

'Did you know or suspect that he was operating a Ponzi scheme?'

'No. And he certainly wasn't doing it originally, I'd stake my life on it.'

Seb scrutinised Truss for any telltale signs of deceit, but there were none. His breathing, eye contact, blinking, and overall body language didn't give him cause for alarm.

'How can you say that so categorically?'

'I knew him well, and it wasn't how he operated. When we first started working together, he was shit-hot on following the rules and regulations of the industry. I'm sure, initially, his investments would have been legitimate.'

'In which case, what happened to make him switch to doing something illegal?'

'I can only guess, but it could have been because the bottom fell out of the financial market. Interest rates plummeted, and investing was a nightmare. It was impossible. He had a certain lifestyle which he needed to maintain, and that was the only way he could do it. I don't know for sure, but he might have initially done it just once and one thing led to another until he used the money from every new client to pay the existing ones.'

He had repeated Seb's thoughts exactly.

'Were you struggling at the time, too?'

'No, if anything my business increased. I offer payday loans and the market for those tends to increase during times of recession when people find it hard to go from week to week.'

'When it came out about the Ponzi scheme did you come forward and speak to the FCA and register your claim against the company?'

'It would have been pointless as there were no funds available to pay creditors and I had no desire to be on the FCA's radar again.'

'When was the last time you spoke to Donald?'

'Several months ago when I asked him for my money back. I ...' His voice fell away. Had he not meant to disclose that information?

'You hadn't mentioned that.'

'I have now,' he muttered. 'Donald explained that he couldn't get it straight away and asked if I would mind hanging on for a while longer. I had to agree, I had no choice in the matter.'

'Were you worried?'

'A little. I needed the money to pay off my mounting debts, thanks to having a young wife who doesn't know the meaning of the word restraint. She thinks because I'm a financier I have a bundle of cash burning a hole in my pocket.'

'When your old company went under, you left a lot of small-time investors with nothing. Like Donald has done with his company. What I don't understand is why you put your trust in Donald and didn't realise there were issues.'

'My company was different from Donald's. We weren't

operating a Ponzi scheme, so I didn't see any signs when dealing with him.

'Regarding the debts you mentioned, surely it can't be that bad if you're planning a month in the Bahamas.'

'I make investments in my wife's name, so we always have some backup funds. But I'm telling you now, we're not rolling in it.'

'Where were you on Saturday, 10 April, during the day and into the evening?'

'I don't know offhand, let me look in my diary.' He opened his phone. 'At home.'

'Can anyone vouch for you?'

'My wife was there. The dogs, too.'

'We'll be ...' He was about to say checking, but of course he couldn't. He was no longer in the force. 'Thank you for your time.'

On the train on the way back, he gave Birdie a call.

'How did it go with Truss?'

'There was definitely something underhand going on there, but I don't know that it's related to Donald's death. As far as their relationship is concerned, they've known each other for years, since working together at a finance company. Truss now does payday loans out of a run-down office in Southgate. He claims to have a mountain of debts, but he's off to the Bahamas for a month. It's a shame we don't have access to his financial statements.'

'I could try, but I'd have to be careful in case I get spotted.'

'I don't want you to put yourself at risk. There was nothing that alarmed me about his relationship with Donald, and he has an alibi for the day of the death, so let's leave it.'

'What about the friend, Yates? We got sidetracked yesterday and you didn't tell me how the meeting went.'

'Again, another person who'd known Donald for a long

time, since university in fact. They saw each other rarely these days, yet according to Yates they had a deep friendship.'

'Deep enough to invest two hundred thousand pounds at a time when Witherspoon was on hard times. He must be loaded if he could afford that.'

'He didn't have the money to invest. He took out a bank loan.'

'Whoa. That's a whole different story. Who on earth goes into hock for that much money, even if Witherspoon was his friend? Unless ... Do you think Donald could've been black-mailing him? Donald might have known something so bad the only way Yates could keep him quiet was to give him the money. Then again, he could've murdered Donald and saved the money. So that doesn't work.'

'That thought had crossed my mind but, like you, I couldn't see any sense to it. You don't loan a huge amount of money then kill the person before you get a penny back.'

'Maybe they really were good friends, and Donald had helped him out in the past and so he was returning the favour. He could have done it out of duty.'

'It's possible. I'll see if there's anything in Donald's files showing a payment made to Yates in the past.'

'Can you go back to him and ask?'

'I could, although, he didn't appear pleased to learn that we were investigating the death. I asked why he didn't go to the funeral and he said he couldn't bring himself to. He also mentioned that his wife didn't like Donald.'

'We should interview her. She might have had something to do with it.'

'Yes, I agree. But we'll have to tread carefully as we have no reason, and she could easily report us to the police.'

'You mean she could report me to myself.' Birdie chuckled. 'Did he have an alibi?'

'He avoided the question, but it wasn't something I could push as I'm no longer in the force.'

'Where to now? It seems to me that we're going around in circles. Have we moved forward at all?'

'Not forward but we have gone deeper. We have his brother and best friend lending him money in the guise of an investment. He'd approached people he knew who could help him out. We know he's very persuasive and a good salesperson, so did he borrow from anyone else?'

'What about Andrea Wood? We should interview her and see if she knew him personally. Not only is she a celebrity, she also invested a big chunk of money. If we can talk to her, that is. She might refuse.'

'Rob, my friend at the Met, might be able to help. I expect I'll have to travel to London for the interview as I don't want to wait until the weekend in the hope she might be visiting her home here. I'll let you know once I've spoken to him and we'll go from there.'

SEVENTEEN

13 May

The next morning Seb got up at six and grabbed the lead from the side.

'Come on, Elsa, let's go for a walk before I have to work.'

He drove to the Welland River where she had a good run around. It was surprisingly busy for so early in the day, but it was still enjoyable walking down by the river. It helped clear his head, and he was able to plan his next steps. Later, he'd give Rob a call to see if he could arrange an interview with Andrea Wood. It was Seb's best chance of getting to see her without alerting her agent or management team, which he didn't want to do at the moment as this was meant to be an unofficial enquiry. Also, as a TV personality, she wouldn't want her dirty linen aired in public, if there was any.

Sarah had invited him around for tea later so he could give her an update on the investigation. She'd sounded very keen to see him when they'd spoken on the phone which didn't surprise him. Now the hard work of arranging the funeral was over and the boys had left, she had a lot of time on her hands. She needed to start planning her future, whatever that was going to be. He hoped that eventually the family would come around and see that what had happened wasn't her fault and give her the support she deserved. But he imagined they would want the dust to settle in case the press was still hanging around, especially as the funeral had reignited media interest.

That was the trouble with their family being so high profile. They were overly concerned with what the outside world might think and how it could damage their reputation. It wasn't all selfish. Members of the family were patrons of various charities, and bad publicity could have an adverse effect on them.

'Elsa,' he called, spotting her playing near two dogs who were in the water. It wasn't warm enough for her to go for a swim as it would make her arthritis worse. The dog glanced up at him. 'Come on, girl. You know you can't go in there.'

She reluctantly ran back to him. Many people anthropomorphised their pets and he was one of them. But how could he not when Elsa clearly understood everything he was saying? And she made her feelings known to him.

They'd arrived back at the house by seven-thirty and, after breakfast, he opened the computer and started researching into Andrea Wood. She was aged thirty-nine. Used to be a journalist and then worked in the newsroom for a local BBC station. From there she secured a position at an independent TV station, eventually ending up hosting their breakfast show. She was an attractive woman with short blonde hair, tucked behind her ears, and large green eyes. She appeared much younger than her age. Unless the photo had been Photoshopped. She'd been to York University to study English and was married, now separated, to a radio producer. Currently, she was dating a celebrity chef. Provided Wikipedia was to be believed, of course. He didn't recognise her from the image, but that was hardly surprising, as he seldom watched TV, and never in the morning. Nothing in what he'd read set off any alarm bells.

At ten-thirty he picked up his phone and called his friend and ex-colleague Rob Lawson, hoping he'd be able to assist.

'Sebastian Clifford. Hello, stranger,' Rob said, answering almost immediately. 'How are you?'

'Very well, thank you. I'm staying in Market Harborough at the moment.'

'What are you doing in that dump?' Rob had an aversion to any place outside of London, unless it was New York or Paris.

'You're such a snob,' Seb said, laughing.

'Anyway, to what do I owe this pleasure? It's not like you've called regularly since leaving. Come to think of it, you haven't called at all. I was beginning to feel I'd done something wrong.'

When Seb had left the force, he'd decided to cut all ties. It was more of a defence mechanism against missing the career he'd forged for himself. He had missed Rob, though, as he'd been the closest friend he'd had at work. Had he made a mistake?

'It's complicated. I'm actually after a favour.'

'Fire away.'

That was what he liked about Rob. They hadn't spoken for ages, but he clearly didn't hold that against Seb.

'Does your wife still work at the TV station?'

'Yes, why?'

'I want an interview with Andrea Wood who presents the breakfast show.'

'What do you mean *interview*? Don't tell me you've joined the press. I know your views on the media.' He laughed. 'Or do you want to ask her out?'

'I'm working on a case and her name has cropped up. I don't want to make a big deal of it, just speak to her quietly.'

'How can you be working on a case when you've left the force?'

'Between you and me, this is something I'm doing on the side for my cousin, Sarah. Her husband was Donald Witherspoon, and he died about a month ago. You may have heard of him.'

He could trust Rob to keep it to himself.

'I have indeed. He was the bastard who swindled hundreds of people in a Ponzi scheme and then committed suicide. A nasty piece of work by all accounts. And you're related to him? Bloody hell. How on earth did the family take that?'

Rob knew all about Seb's family, as on one drunken night, when they were both attending the same training course, they had a deep and meaningful heart-to-heart. Seb trusted him implicitly never to mention their conversation, the same as he kept to himself everything that Rob had confided.

'Let's put this way. It hasn't been easy, especially for Sarah. She doesn't believe it's suicide, and has asked me to investigate.'

'Oh, so now you're a private investigator? I'd swear that in the past you didn't have any time for them. Have you now changed your mind?'

'I'm doing this as a favour and certainly don't intend on becoming a PI, as my views haven't changed. Anyway, the point is that Andrea Wood invested some money with Donald, and I'd like to speak to her about it. I don't believe it's common knowledge, so I'm trusting you not to repeat any of this.'

'We're mates. My lips are sealed. I might be able to get you in there, not actually through my wife, because I don't know if she could, but I do have another contact.'

Excellent. He knew his friend would be able to help.

'Sounds interesting, who is it?'

'Just someone I know. Leave it with me and I'll see if I can arrange for an interview, but I can't promise anything, considering you're not actually police. You'll have to be prepared to go whenever it suits the woman.'

'Of course. Who's this person you know?' he asked, his curiosity getting the better of him.

'I'm not saying,' was the cagey response.

Seb didn't want to push it. It could have been anybody, ranging from an informant to a friend and if Rob wasn't prepared to tell him then it proved his general trustworthiness.

'If you can get me in there, I'll owe you one big time.'

'I won't let you forget it either,' Rob said, laughing. 'So you really like Market Harborough?'

'I've only been here a few days, but it certainly makes a change from London. It's quiet and pretty. There are lots of walks to go on, and the best thing is there's no rush hour traffic to contend with.'

He hadn't realised quite how much he liked the place until saying it out loud.

'You've only left the force a short while and now you're turning into a country bumpkin. Mind you, you were never suited to city life. Not with your background and all those country pursuits your lot get up to.'

'When have you known me to engage in *country pursuits*?'

'You might have done if it wasn't for the demands of the job, although ... maybe not. That aside, I still think you didn't fit in the force. Not in terms of doing the job because you were brilliant at that. But you never liked going out and letting off steam. I didn't ever witness you being loud and crazy like the rest of us.'

'We can't all be like you.'

'I'm not like that, now. That's married life for you. That and getting older. It's been great to hear from you. We'll catch up soon. I've got to go as I'm due in a meeting. I'll be in touch as soon as I've got any news.'

EIGHTEEN

13 May

Seb spent the rest of the morning researching Donald's social activities. There was plenty of recent publicity regarding the Ponzi scheme, but he was more interested in what the man did leading up to it, over the previous eighteen months and even further back. It seemed Donald was very active in the social scene and there were many photos of him attending events. Often Sarah was with him, but sometimes he went alone.

In particular, Donald was photographed at charity events and would always bid for items in charity auctions. Interestingly, although media stories mentioned bidding by different people for items, rarely did Donald win. He mostly dropped out towards the end. A clever ploy to appear benevolent without having to pay up, Seb suspected. Donald had cultivated an image of being very wealthy and philanthropic until such time as it all imploded. After his death.

Seb's phone rang, interrupting his deliberations. It was Rob. Had he worked his magic already?

'Clifford.'

'You owe me big time for this one, mate,' his friend said. 'It wasn't easy, but I've managed to secure you an interview with Andrea Wood.'

'I knew you could do it. Thanks.'

'The only problem is, it's tomorrow. She's on the telly from six until nine and after that she has a production meeting. But she can see you at midday. I've been told that the interview can only be for a short time, maybe fifteen minutes tops, as then she goes to her London flat to relax before going to bed early. She gets up at two in the morning every day to get ready for the show, so I'm reliably informed. It must pay well if she's prepared to do that. Anyway, that's what you've got to do. Okay?'

'How did you find out all this about her?'

'It's called knowing the right people.'

'Did you explain why I want to question her?'

'Um ... I implied that it was linked to a police matter.'

Damn. That could prove to be an issue.

'Why say that? You could get yourself in trouble if it gets back to the wrong people.'

'I'll deny it. The only person in trouble would be you for impersonating a police officer.'

'Except I'm not going in as an officer.'

'I was joking. Don't worry, it'll be cool. When you arrive at the studio, go to the front desk and ask to see her. Tell them you have an appointment and give my name as the person who organised it. There shouldn't be any issues.'

'So you will be incriminating yourself.'

'You worry too much. After you've seen her, let's meet up for lunch.'

'Can you spare the time?'

'Always, for you. There's a pub around the corner from the studio. Meet me there between half-past twelve and one. We'll have a good catch up.'

'Can't wait. Did you say it was just me, or did you mention that there might be two of us at the interview?'

'How can I mention what you didn't tell me? Who might you be taking?'

'It's a DC Bird, aka Birdie, from the Market Harborough force. She's helping me on the side.'

'I won't ask how you managed to get the police to assist, though I'm not surprised with your charm. I'm sure it won't be a problem and I'll see you *both* for lunch, then.'

Seb ended the call and sent a text to Birdie,

Interview with Andrea Wood tomorrow in London. Want to come?

After a few seconds, he had a reply.

Yes. Call me.

He called immediately. 'You wish to speak to me?'

'Well, yes, obviously.'

'Why didn't *you* call me then?'

'I can receive calls but don't want to be seen making a call because Sarge is hanging around and as I'm not working a case, he might try to listen in.'

'You know that makes no sense. He could still wonder what this is about.'

'Stop being so literal. I want to know what's happening. Thanks for arranging it on my day off. How did you manage to swing it?'

'I didn't know you weren't working. Our appointment's at twelve and I thought we'd take the ten o'clock train which arrives at St Pancras station a few minutes after eleven. That will give us plenty of time to get across town.'

'What shall I wear?'

He frowned. 'Smart casual. Why?'

'We're meeting a celebrity and I want to dress for the occasion. I might be spotted for some reality TV show.'

Was she being serious?

'This isn't an audition. We're going to be with her for fifteen minutes at the most. So wear what you want and remember you're not to ask anything other than what's absolutely relevant. This isn't a springboard for a career in TV.'

'You're so boring. Here was me thinking that my life was about to change and you're trying to ruin in.' She gave a loud sigh, followed by a giggle.

'Nobody's twisting your arm, you're welcome to leave me to go alone,' he teased.

'No chance, mate.'

'I'll pick you up at nine-thirty so we have time to buy our tickets, in case there's a queue.'

'You know we can get them online.'

He'd already planned on doing that, but he didn't want to tell her in case she thought they could leave arriving at the station until the last minute.

'I'm not prepared to risk missing the train, so I'm warning you now. Don't be late because I won't wait.'

'Not even one minute?' she taunted.

'Not even thirty seconds.'

'I'll be there on time. Just don't knock at the door,' she warned.

'I wouldn't dream of it.'

He ended the call and smiled to himself.

The reason he'd said nine-thirty was to allow for her inevitable lateness.

He was looking forward to meeting up with Rob for lunch and have a catch-up. It would be interesting to see his take on Birdie.

He suspected they'd get on very well.

NINETEEN

14 May

Birdie ran from the bathroom to her bedroom, quickly peeping out of the window. Crap. Clifford was there already. Typical. Just one day, she might actually be on time. It wasn't that she'd got up late, well, only a few minutes after falling back to sleep when her alarm went off. But even so, she thought she'd allowed herself sufficient time to get ready.

She ran back to the mirror, picked up the brush, and tugged at her hair. It was even worse than usual. She grabbed a hair-band and tied it back, as there wasn't time for her to coax it into shape. She'd made an effort with her make-up and worn a pair of dark flared jeans, with a short, ribbed cardigan over a white T-shirt. On her feet she had a pair of grey suede ankle boots with a two-inch heel. At least then she wouldn't look quite so miniscule beside Clifford.

She grabbed her handbag from the bed, ran down the stairs and out the front door. Glancing at her phone on the way, she was pleased to see that she was only one minute late. It had to be a record. She opened the door and got in.

'I made it on time,' she said, grinning at Clifford, as she fastened her seat belt.

'I was just about to leave.'

'Yeah, of course you were. I'm only one minute late. Not even that.'

'I told you I wasn't prepared to wait beyond nine-thirty.'

'And I knew you didn't mean it.' She didn't know that at all, but she didn't want him to realise that. 'Well, come on, let's get a move on.' He started the engine and headed down the road. 'Am I *smart casual* enough?' She ran her fingers down her jeans. They were new, and she'd been dying to wear them somewhere special.

'Spot on,' he said.

'You couldn't bring yourself to dispense with the tie, I see. Or is that your definition of smart casual?'

'It's what I would usually wear for work,' he said, shrugging. 'Plus, I hardly had any clothes with me when I arrived, as I had no intention of staying this long.'

'I'll take you shopping after the interview if you like? Make you all trendy?'

He glanced at her, an unreadable expression on his face. 'Thanks, but I'm okay.'

'I didn't have time for breakfast,' she said, changing the subject.

'That's a surprise,' he said, giving a wry smile. 'We don't have time to stop at whatever café you were thinking of.'

She laughed. It was going to be a fun day.

They made it to the station in under ten minutes.

'See, we've got plenty of time to park and get our tickets,' she said.

'Actually, I got them online,' he said. 'If I'd told you, you'd have been even later.'

'That's so not true,' she said, scowling and refusing to admit he was right.

'You've now got time to buy something to eat from the café while I park. I'll meet you there.'

She jumped out of the car and headed into the small café inside the station. She stood at the back of the short queue and opened her bag. Crap. She'd left her purse on the bed, after taking it out to make sure she'd got everything she needed.

She left the café and went towards the main station entrance to wait for Seb. After a few minutes, she could see him heading in her direction and so ran outside to meet him.

'I forgot my purse. Can you buy something for me, please?'

'That's a new one. How many more excuses do you have lined up to get me to pay for your meals?' He arched an eyebrow.

'Shut up,' she said, flicking him on the arm. 'You can charge it to expenses.'

'You do know that I'm not being paid, so who exactly will be paying these expenses?'

'Details. Come on, we don't have much time.'

He strode off in the direction of the café and she tried to keep up, but with his long legs it was impossible. She ended up jogging to catch him up. They went in and she picked up a bag of crisps and ordered a hot sausage roll. She caught the look in his eye.

'Don't tell me you had muesli with skimmed milk, topped with a couple of strawberries,' she said, tilting her head to one side. He looked away. 'Ha. You did, didn't you?'

'There's nothing wrong with fruit and muesli. Although I have to admit, it does smell good.' He nodded at the sausage roll which she was now holding.

They headed over to the platform. 'I'll eat it on the train,' she said, more to herself than to him.

She didn't want the other travellers staring at her chewing, not least because she was bound to make a mess. Eating a sausage roll wearing decent clothes probably wasn't the best of ideas. She'd have to cover herself with serviettes while eating.

The train came in on time, and when they got on it was full, as it had come from Nottingham via Leicester.

'Let's find a seat,' Seb said, as they walked through the first carriage but finding no empty seats.

'I have to sit facing the way the train is going, or it makes me feel sick.'

They ended up walking through three further carriages until finding two seats facing the front.

'This will do,' he said, stepping to the side so she could sit by the window. How did he know she wanted to sit there?

Once seated, Seb pulled out a book.

'You're going to read the whole journey?'

'Do you object?'

'I don't mind what you do. What book is it?' She peered at the book in his hand.

'The latest Harlan Coben. What about you, are you going to catch up on your sleep, as you had to get up early on your day off?'

'I might just do that. But first of all, it's breakfast time.' She held up the paper bag containing her sausage roll, pulled out the three serviettes she'd taken from the counter and covered herself with them.

They sat in silence while she ate, and he read. The journey into St Pancras took just over an hour, and from there they took the Tube to Sloane Square and then walked the fifteen minutes to Battersea, on the south bank of the Thames.

'We've still got plenty of time, let's go for a coffee,' Seb said.

'That works for me. The more caffeine the better.'

They found a small café close to the studio and ordered two coffees.

'Why are you always late?' Seb asked once they'd found somewhere to sit.

She was always getting bollocked for being late, but he was the first to ask why it happened.

'Habit. Leaving everything to the last minute. I don't know. It just happens. I don't deliberately do it.'

'What time did you get up this morning?'

'Eight forty-five. Why?'

'Even though you knew I was picking you up at nine-thirty? No wonder you missed breakfast. If you set your alarm half an hour earlier than you really need you'll never be late,' he suggested.

What he said made perfect sense. Except, knowing her, she'd sleep through the alarm.

'It's not such a big deal. I was ready on time, today, wasn't I? What's a few minutes, anyway?'

'I'm only trying to help. You've been getting in trouble at work for being late, don't you want to fix it?'

'It's just a thing. It doesn't affect how I do my job.'

She couldn't explain it, but she'd always been like that. When she did reflect on it, she'd decided it could be because her parents were always on time for everything, often early. In fact, they were obsessive about it. She wanted to be different. And it wasn't as if she could have inherited the we-must-always-be-early gene because she was adopted. Her timekeeping was proof.

'That's debatable. It might not have affected the way you do your job, but it's certainly affected you being allowed to do your job.'

Right again.

'It's something I do. Let's leave it at that.'

'I'd hate to see your talent go unnoticed because of this one issue.'

'I never miss anything, I'm just a bit late, sometimes.' He tilted his head to one side. 'Okay, most of the time,' she acknowledged.

'It can be frustrating for people. Take today, we only have fifteen minutes to interview Andrea Wood. If we're late for that, by even five minutes, that would cut down our time with her by thirty per cent. We could lose valuable information.'

'But we won't be late.' She tipped her head back and drew in a frustrated breath. 'We've got plenty of time. We're actually way early.'

'You're deliberately being obtuse.'

'Whatever.'

She folded her arms and looked away, not wanting them to fall out over her timekeeping as it was going to be a fun day. Informative, obviously, because they were working on the case, but as she'd never been to a TV studio before, or spoken to a celebrity, still fun.

At ten minutes to twelve they left the café and walked around the corner and into the studio.

'My name is Sebastian Clifford, and I've got an appointment with Andrea Wood at midday. It was arranged by Rob Lawson.'

'One moment, please,' the receptionist said. She made a call announcing their arrival. 'If you take the lift up to the fifth floor, it's the third room on the right. The Edison Suite. They're expecting you.'

She swallowed hard. 'Do you have stairs?' Birdie asked the woman.

'Yes, you'll find them just before the lift, but they're very steep.'

'I'm in training.' They walked away from the reception and when they reached the stairs, she turned to Seb 'I'll meet you up there.'

'It's five flights. Surely you don't have to train *now*.'

She sucked in a breath. 'I get a bit claustrophobic and only go into a lift if it's absolutely necessary.'

'You were fine on the tube.'

'Because it's more spacious. It's really lifts I can't stand. We don't have time to discuss this now. I'll meet you there.'

She jogged up the stairs. The woman wasn't wrong, they were steep and she had to stop several times before her legs gave way. When she reached the top Seb was waiting for her.

He knocked on the door, before she even had time to catch her breath, and a woman answered.

'Mr Clifford?' she said.

'Yes, and this is B ... Lucinda Bird.'

Seriously? She glared at him, but he didn't seem to notice.

They were ushered into a large room with a black leather three-piece suite on one side and a circular table with chairs around it on the other side, next to the window.

Andrea was seated alone at the table and standing in the corner was a thickset man dressed in a dark suit, with a shaved head, who stood with his arms folded. He looked to be in his late thirties or early forties. Was he security? He'd picked the wrong people to try to intimidate, if so. She'd handled much worse.

'This is Sebastian Clifford and Lucinda Bird. They've an appointment with you,' the woman who brought them in said.

Was she even aware they were going to interview her?

'Come and sit down,' Andrea said, flashing a set of perfect white teeth as she smiled and looked directly at Seb, totally ignoring Birdie.

'It was good of you to spare the time,' Seb said, as they sat opposite her.

'It's my pleasure. How may I help you?' Andrea said.

'We'd like to ask you about Donald Witherspoon.'

She cleared her throat, panic etched across her face. 'Who?'

'You know who I mean.'

'Are you from the press? I wouldn't have agreed to speak to you if I'd known.'

'No, we're not the media.'

'Aaron, I'm worried that the alterations on my dress for tomorrow won't be made on time. Could you go to wardrobe and check with Annie?'

'Okay.'

He scowled at Seb and Birdie before leaving the room. What was that all about?

'I don't know what you have heard, but my connection with Donald Witherspoon isn't public knowledge,' she said.

'I'm investigating his death, on behalf of his wife.'

'He committed suicide. What's there to investigate? He stole all that money and took the coward's way out rather than facing everyone.'

'His wife isn't convinced that's what happened, and I've agreed to investigate.'

'What do you want from me?'

'At the beginning of the year, you invested some money with him and we wanted to discuss it with you.'

'How do you know about this?'

'I've examined Witherspoon's financial records. How much money did you invest in his scheme?'

'A hundred thousand. It was what he recommended.'

'Why so much?'

'I'd decided to diversify and believed investing with him would be a good idea.'

'Did you take any financial advice before investing?' Seb asked.

'No, I decided not to involve my business manager in this particular investment.'

'Why not?'

'I wanted it to be kept under the table, in case my soon-to-be ex-husband got wind of it. We've separated and divorce proceedings have been decidedly acrimonious. I wanted this investment to be kept out of the equation. It's not like I have the money now, anyway.'

Something wasn't adding up. Unless ...

'Did you already know Mr Witherspoon before investing?' Birdie asked.

'Vaguely,' Andrea answered, her cheeks flushing.

'When you say *vaguely*, what do you mean exactly?' Birdie pushed.

'Our paths crossed a long time ago, and when I was looking to invest the money and his company's name popped up, I decided to go with him. That's all.' She waved her hand dismissively.

There had to be more.

'How did your paths cross?'

'We met at a charity event, if I remember correctly. It really was a long time ago and I can't remember exactly.'

'Between first meeting him, and then investing at the beginning of the year, did you see each other at all?'

'I meet a lot of people in this job. I really can't tell you.'

'Although it was because you knew him that you decided to invest on the side and not involve your business manager.'

'Partly. But I fail to see why this is relevant.'

'And—'

'How often did you receive your dividend payments from him?' Seb asked, interrupting Birdie.

Why? What was wrong with her line of questioning?

'Quarterly. I only received the first quarter because he'd died before the second was due.'

'There was no record of that. How much did you receive?'

'I don't remember.'

'What was your reaction when you learnt of his death and that you'd lost your money?'

'What do you think? I was furious. It was a lot of money to lose.'

'Where were you on Saturday 10 April?'

'I'd have to look in my diary.' She reached for her phone,

which was on the table, and unlocked it. 'I was doing a personal appearance in Bath and decided to make a weekend of it. I went there on Friday night and returned to my flat in London on the Sunday afternoon.'

'Can anyone vouch for you?' Birdie asked.

Andrea frowned. 'What's this? A police interview? I'm talking to you as a favour. I wasn't alone, and that's all I'm going to say on the matter.'

The door opened and Andrea's assistant entered the room. Andrea made a show of looking at her watch. 'Time's up. I've been up since two and want to go home to get some rest. Yvette, see these people out.'

She turned away and the assistant who'd let them in showed them to the door and out into the corridor.

Birdie glanced at Seb.

'What the fuck ...' She mouthed.

TWENTY

14 May

They left the studio in silence and once they were in the street Birdie turned to Seb.

'Well?' She hadn't liked to say anything until they were well out of the way in case they were overheard. 'A bit up herself if you ask me. But I suppose that's what famous people are like. You know plenty of prominent people. Is that how they all act?'

'I don't frequent red-carpet events, nor do I have celebrity friends, contrary to what you believe.'

He said that, but surely he must know some of the rich and famous. She'd get it out of him. Perhaps after a few drinks he might spill the beans.

'If you say so.' She waved a dismissive hand. 'On the telly, Andrea Wood smiles all the time, but apart from when she first saw you, she didn't smile once. Especially after we told her why we were there. Did you notice that? I suppose we weren't important enough to have the special treatment.'

'How would you feel if you were hoodwinked into an interview about something you thought was a secret?'

'True. If I'd lost a hundred grand I'd be crying non-stop for the rest of my life.' She pulled a face.

'We weren't there to be liked, or to like her. What we wanted was information about Donald. What did you deduce from that perspective?'

'She was certainly hiding something. All that business about keeping everything on the down-low so her ex didn't find out and also not wanting to involve her business manager. Why not? She was fobbing us off.'

'My sentiments, exactly. She said she'd only met Donald once before deciding to invest with him on the side. That doesn't ring true, not when there's so much money involved. The question we have to ask is, why?'

'Do you think she was having an affair with Witherspoon and he persuaded her to invest because he needed the money? That would give her a reason to be so secretive.'

'It's one avenue of thought, but are we making a big leap? And even if she was, then why would that lead to his death? As we've discussed before, why would anyone who invested with him want to see him dead? It would mean they'd lost their money forever.' Seb's brow furrowed.

'We should still look deeper into Andrea. Actually, we need to investigate all of his investors. There's got to be something that will help us.'

'Agreed,' Seb said nodding. 'We'll split the research. Can you check criminal records for all of Donald's investors? Say no if it might get you into trouble. I don't want that to happen.'

'As I'm the only one in the office most of the time, it won't be hard. I'm a dab hand at closing a screen if anyone gets too close.'

She'd had a lot of practice.

'Unless the IT department track what you do.'

She laughed. 'This is Market Harborough, not the Met. It will be fine.' She didn't bother to mention that she knew more than the IT person assigned to work with them and was well able to cover her tracks.

'I'll do more research into Donald, and identify which of his other investors were friends, and then take a look at them. Can you get your bit done by Friday?'

'Yes, boss,' she said, saluting. 'By the way, who's this guy we're meeting for lunch?'

'A friend of mine from the Met.'

'Not another aristocrat.' She smirked, and he rolled his eyes. 'I suppose that was a bit stupid. I mean, how many of your lot are going to be in the police?'

'He's a friend and ex-colleague. We trained together.'

'Was he in the disbanded squad with you?'

'No, he's a DI in the Homicide and Serious Crime Command Unit.' They headed into the pub. 'There he is, at the bar.' They walked over to him. 'Rob.'

The guy turned around and gave Seb a bear hug.

She stared at the pair of them, open-mouthed. She thought Seb was large, but his friend was even larger. Was that even possible? She'd need to stand on a box to even be heard.

'Drinks are on you, mate.' He glanced down at her. 'I'm DI Rob Lawson and you must be DC Bird. I've heard all about you.'

'Yes, that's me.' She held out her hand, and he clasped it so tight she had to fight the urge not to scream. 'Call me Birdie. Anything else and I won't answer.' Crap. He was a DI. Maybe she should change her tone. 'I'm off duty at the moment,' she added as if to excuse herself.

'It's okay, Birdie. I'm not going to pull rank,' he said, as if reading her mind.

'What would you like to drink?' Seb asked.

'Half a cider, please.'

'Half a cider and two pints of stout,' he asked the guy

behind the bar. He turned to Rob. 'I take it you haven't changed in your choice of beer.'

'No. Nor you, by the looks of things.'

'Are we going to eat?' she asked.

Seb laughed. 'What you need to know about Birdie is she's obsessed with food. Wherever we go, she has to eat. And if you're the person with her, you'll most likely to be the one paying.'

'I couldn't help forgetting my purse this morning,' she said.

'And the other times?' he asked, handing her the menu.

'I'm a lowly DC, hanging out with the higher-ups, so you've got no chance of making me feel guilty. I'll have fish and chips,' she said.

'Another thing you need to know is a salad would die alone on her plate.'

She elbowed him in the ribs. 'If you've quite finished, I don't recall ever seeing your plate covered in lettuce leaves. You're not giving a very good impression of me here. What if I decide to apply for a job at the Met and Rob here is on the interview panel, how's that going to look?'

'I believe he'll see for himself what you're like, without any input from me.'

'You two sound like an old married couple,' Rob said.

'Don't even go there,' she said, grimacing.

'Lunch is on me. Why don't you two go and get a table and I'll order? Fish and chips all round?' Seb said, looking at Rob.

'Yep, that works for me. There's a table over there. Come on, Birdie,' Rob said, pointing towards the back of the pub.

They left Seb at the bar, and sat at the round table Rob had spotted. The pub was typically Victorian with an open fire. It was large, and busy. She wanted to know more about Seb while he wasn't there and decided to take a chance by asking Rob.

'So how do you know Seb?' she asked even though she knew the answer.

'We trained together, and we've been friends ever since.'

'And what do you think of his background? Weird someone like that being on the force.'

'A man can't help his family. He's a good guy, and he has a special talent, which no doubt you've come across.'

She tilted her head to one side. 'Talent. What talent?'

'You haven't seen it in action.' He gave a belly laugh. 'You're in for a treat in that case.'

'Tell me.'

He did a zip motion across his lips. 'Not up to me.'

'Oh, you mean his HSAM,' she said suddenly remembering.

'The very thing. You seem rather underwhelmed by it. Maybe you haven't seen him at his best.'

'He rattled off some bank transactions without having them in front of him.'

'That he can do in his sleep. He can be much more impressive when the circumstances demand.'

Interesting.

'Okay, what else can you tell me? Is he married? Or has he been married? Or does he have a girlfriend ...'

'Birdie, stop. He's my friend and I'm not going to start blabbing to you. Ask Seb yourself if you want to know anything.'

'Know what?'

Shit. She hadn't seen Seb walk over to the table. Oh well, no point in lying.

'I was pumping Rob for info about you, but he won't tell.' She stuck out her bottom lip.

'Thanks,' Seb said, grinning at his friend. 'You're more than welcome to ask me anything you like. I won't guarantee to answer though.'

'I'll remember that. Except it's much more fun when you find out from someone else, and you get the true stuff,' she said, smirking.

'What do you want to know?'

'Nothing,' she said, waving a hand. She couldn't ask now, without appearing like a nosy parker.

'Tell me more about the case and Witherspoon's death,' Rob said.

'My cousin Sarah, who I mentioned, isn't convinced by the suicide verdict and believes that he was forced to write his suicide note. She said he left clues in there that only she would recognise.'

'If it's not suicide, it most likely would be murder. What are your views so far?' Rob asked.

'I'm not yet convinced by her view. Yes, there are some inconsistencies but they can be explained. We'll see where the investigation takes us.'

'Are you enjoying the case?'

'I am, but that doesn't mean I want to become a PI if that's what you're suggesting.'

'Why not? I'm sure you'd be really good at it with your memory,' Rob said.

'I haven't yet decided what I'm going to do next.'

'I suppose it won't hurt to wait a while longer if you've got enough money to keep you going.'

'I can manage for the time being.'

'Lucky you have a family who can help out,' she quipped. He arched an eyebrow. 'Sorry, that was out of order.'

She kept quiet after that and enjoyed listening to the banter between Seb and Rob during which she got to see a more relaxed and jokey side of him.

After lunch they said their goodbyes and went across London to catch the train. Was he annoyed with her for nosing into his life, and then what she'd said about his family? It was difficult to tell. She didn't want to bring it up in case he'd forgotten.

'What's puzzling me the most is, if Donald was murdered,

then what was the motive? Surely it can't be because he'd stopped making payments to clients because as soon as he was dead, they'd definitely not get their money. It doesn't make sense,' Birdie said.

'I agree, which points to it not being murder and was, in fact, suicide.'

'But that doesn't sit right either based on what we know from Sarah. Maybe he borrowed money from loan sharks and couldn't pay it back so they came after him.'

'That's also a possibility, except they don't usually kill because then they wouldn't get their money back either. If anything, they might have threatened the family but Sarah hasn't mentioned it and I'm sure she would have.'

'What about his children, could they have been involved?'

'They have twin boys who are both at university. I don't want to interview them because they're far too fragile at the moment. You know, despite there being some questions surrounding it, the verdict of suicide might be correct and we're looking for evidence which doesn't exist. Sarah could be wrong.'

'Are you saying you want to end the investigation? Earlier you decided we were going to do some more investigating into Donald and the other investors.'

'I'm going to think about it overnight. Let's meet up tomorrow to discuss it,' Seb said.

'I'm working during the day. Meet me in town at six forty-five in the Diablos bar. We'll have a drink and talk it through.'

TWENTY-ONE

15 May

Birdie had aimed to leave work dead on six and she almost made it. *Almost.* She drove home, quickly showered and changed and went to meet Seb for a drink at Diablos. She'd decided to walk so that she didn't have to worry about driving, and when she arrived, she glanced at her phone.

Seven-twenty. Not bad for her.

She walked in and scanned the room. Seb was sitting at a table by the wall with a pint in front of him. She stopped at the bar, ordered half a cider and a bag of crisps, and went to join him.

'Been here long?' she asked, sitting down and placing her glass on the table. She opened her crisps and took out a handful.

'You were meant to be here at six forty-five,' he said, drumming his fingers on the table impatiently.

'Come on, Seb, I'm only thirty-five minutes late. That's nothing for me. I made a real effort to get here on time and didn't even have anything to eat. Hence these.' She picked up the bag and shook them in front of him. 'Want one?'

'I couldn't deprive you of your food,' he said, a wry smile tugging at his lips.

'Wise man, because I'm not a pretty sight when hungry. Did you come to a decision regarding the investigation?'

She hoped he wanted to continue, although it wouldn't surprise her if he didn't, based on what they had so far. Although she'd never admit it out loud, she'd really enjoyed the time they'd spent together working. He'd have made an awesome partner. Nothing against Twiggy and the others, who were great, too. But this had been different.

'So far nothing has persuaded me that the police and coroner's verdicts were incorrect. Donald might have acted out of character in his suicide note, but that's not unusual for someone in his frame of mind. We have to accept that if he wasn't of sound mind, and in my view he wasn't, then it was suicide. Irrational thinking might have led him to not consider Sarah and what would happen after his death. We know that he wanted to be liked and admired, and that went hand in hand with having a successful business. He was depressed at his failure and couldn't face the consequences, both socially and economically. He saw ending his life as his only way out. An alternative to incarceration which he most surely would have got.' Seb picked up his glass and took a drink.

'He could have gone bankrupt, and then he wouldn't have been charged.'

'He would because the Ponzi scheme was illegal. Most definitely he would have ended up in prison.'

'Like that chap from America. What's his name?'

'You mean Bernie Madoff?'

'Yeah, that's the one. So you think that Donald committed suicide to avoid prison. What about the insurance policy?'

'All I can deduce is that he either forgot about the exclusion period or thought it was twelve months, which many policies are.'

'That makes sense, especially if he was depressed and not thinking straight. He might have got muddled about it.'

'Yes, that's what I believe happened,' Seb said.

'Which means Sarah really is left with nothing apart from the massive big house.'

She'd love to visit and take a look around. She'd gone onto Google Maps and checked it out, but it wasn't the same as seeing it in real life.

'Yes.'

'Does this mean you're going to call it a day on the investigation?' Her heart sank at the prospect. The last ten days it had given her a sense of purpose which she'd missed.

'We've done all the research we can, bearing in mind it was a stab in the dark. It would have been impossible to interview every single one of his clients, and we've spoken to those who stood out. All that's left now is to inform Sarah of our progress. Or lack of.'

'Are you going to leave Market Harborough and return to London after you've spoken to Sarah?'

'There's nothing to keep me here.'

'Why not stay for a few days and have a holiday? You like it here, don't you?'

'It's not a good time as I have my future to sort out.'

'Relaxing away from home in a different place might be perfect for making a decision about what to do next,' she suggested, noting the indecision in his eyes.

'It's not practical. I've got a flat in London that I need to get back to.'

TWENTY-TWO

15 May

Seb glanced at his phone. It was already nine-thirty. 'I'd better go. I don't want to leave Elsa on her own for too much longer.'

'Are you sure you don't want one more drink as you're not driving?' Birdie asked, holding up her empty glass. 'Are you?'

'No, I walked here, but two pints are enough for me. My book's calling.'

'I'd hate to keep you from Harlan Coben, although I could think of better things to be doing on a Saturday night, but each to their own. When are you going to see Sarah?'

'Tomorrow, then I'll leave for London first thing Monday.'

Her eyes widened. 'I didn't think you'd be leaving so soon. Does that mean I won't see you again? I suppose it does,' she said before he could answer. 'Well, it's been an experience, that's for sure.'

'Likewise. Although maybe not in the same way?'

'What's that meant to mean?' she asked, narrowing her eyes.

'Only joking,' he said, hoping he hadn't hurt her feelings.

'Usually I'm happier working alone, but you've added a certain *je ne sais quoi* to the whole proceedings.'

'Hmm, if you say so. Anyway, thanks for giving me something to take my mind off my current boring existence at work. It's a shame we didn't discover that Donald was murdered though, because that would certainly have livened things up, and I might have been allowed to work on the case.'

He frowned. 'I'm not sure that *livening things up* is what's best for Sarah. At least now she can put it to rest and try to get on with her life.'

'When you put it that way, you're right. Sorry, I didn't think about Sarah.'

'Shall I walk you back home?' he offered.

'No, thanks. I'm staying in town. I've arranged to meet my friends in an hour or so. Saturday night is clubbing night.' She did a dance move in her chair.

'What are you going to do in the interim, stay here on your own?'

'Don't worry about me, there are some people in here I know who won't mind me hanging out with them for a while.'

Worry about her was one thing he wouldn't do. He had no doubt of her ability to take care of herself in whatever situation she found herself. He was half tempted to stay a while longer, then remembered Elsa, so reluctantly stood.

'I've enjoyed making your acquaintance,' he said, holding out his hand.

'I think we know each other better than that by now,' she said, jumping up and standing on tiptoe to give him a hug. 'Next time you're in Market Harborough, make sure to look me up. You've got my number. We'll have a night out on the town.' She smirked. 'Or sit quietly in the pub talking about books, like other old people do.'

'I keep telling you, late-thirties isn't old. And ditto to you if you ever find yourself in London.'

He headed for the door, turning before he exited the pub and returning Birdie's wave. He walked along High Street, humming to himself, until reaching The Square where the church and old grammar school, an historic building which had been built to educate the poor in the 17th century, were situated. The museum had been temporarily closed, which was a shame as he'd have liked to visit before leaving town.

Shuddering as a gust of wind whistled around him, he zipped up his jacket and pushed his hands into his pockets. The stars were non-existent as the dark clouds blanketed the night sky.

He turned onto Church Street, where not a soul was in sight. It was eerily silent and so different from where he lived in London, where twenty-four-seven there were people milling around. As he continued walking, he heard a sound a few yards behind him. Glancing over his shoulder, no one was there. He must have been mistaken.

A little further along, after turning onto King Street, he definitely heard the sound of footsteps. They were from more than one person and were keeping in time with his own.

The hairs rose on the back of his neck and he clenched his fists in anticipation of being accosted.

He spun around.

Nothing.

No one.

Maybe they'd gone into one of the houses. He was being paranoid. Why? This was Market Harborough, not the back streets of London.

Relaxing a little, he turned left onto Doddridge Road, continuing until turning the corner onto Heygate Street.

He started. A steady pounding of footsteps on the pavement got louder and louder. Reverberating. Echoing.

He turned.

A man in dark clothing was hurtling towards him.

His heart pumped hard in his chest and he stepped to the side to get out of the way, but there was someone else there and as he attempted to move his legs were taken out from under him. Pain shot through his shin as he fell to the floor.

He tried to get up but a boot kicked him in the side of his face.

'Arrgghh' he groaned, clutching at his head.

He drew his legs up to his chest as a foot connected with his ribs. Again. And again.

Through slits in his eyes, he made out two men both wearing hoodies, one of whom was swinging a baseball bat. He sucked in a breath as it smashed into his head.

Blood splattered everywhere and as it dripped into his mouth, he spat it out onto the ground.

He rolled over on the pavement, and tried shouting for help, but the words stuck in his throat. A dark shadow loomed over him as the baseball bat was lifted and swung towards him, this time landing squarely on his back.

Pain ricocheted through his body.

Was he going to die?

'That's enough,' one of the attackers growled. 'He'd have got the message to back off by now.'

Message?

'I'll grab his wallet.'

Seb lay motionless while one of his attackers found the wallet in his back pocket, and the other one stood a few feet away. Out of the corner of Seb's eye he spied a tattoo of an eagle on his attacker's hand, between his thumb and forefinger.

They ran off and Seb tried to stand but fell back down. His whole body throbbed. All he could do was reach into his jacket pocket for his phone and call 999.

Then he lost consciousness.

* * *

Seb's head pounded as they wheeled him from radiology to accident and emergency and took him back to the cubicle he'd been in since the ambulance had brought him to the hospital.

Every part of him hurt.

'You're back,' the nurse who'd been looking after him said. 'We're waiting for a bed to come available, and you'll be moved to a ward. Sorry, I don't know how long that will be, Saturday night is always chaotic.'

'I've got to go. My dog's on her own.' His voice was hoarse and brittle.

He attempted to sit up and then dropped back down on the bed after only moving a few inches.

'You're not going anywhere tonight, so don't even try. You've taken a severe beating and have concussion. We need to keep an eye on you. The doctor will see you once the X-rays have come back and we can see if anything's broken.'

He didn't think he could get out of bed, anyway. He'd have to call Birdie, and ask if she could help as Elsa couldn't be left alone all night.

'What time is it?'

'Ten forty-five.'

'I need to contact someone. Where's my phone?'

'We put all your belongings in a bag at the bottom of your bed.' She opened it, pulled out his phone and handed it to him.

He hit the speed dial for Birdie.

'Missing me already? What do you want?' Her cheerful voice echoed in his ear, causing him to flinch.

'I'm in hospital. I was attacked.'

She gasped. 'What? Which hospital?'

He glanced at the nurse. 'Where am I?'

'Leicester Royal Infirmary.'

'I heard that,' Birdie said. 'Are you okay?'

'I'm alive.'

'Crap, Seb. I'll get to you as soon as I can.'

'Elsa's on her own. Can you look after her for me tonight?'

'Of course, you don't even have to ask. Just hang tight and don't do anything stupid like trying to leave.'

'I've already done that and wasn't able to move. I'm sorry to interrupt your evening.'

'Don't be daft. I'm still at the pub, anyway. I'll be with you soon. Don't give the nurses a hard time.'

He finished the call and dropped the phone next to him.

'Can I have some water?' he asked, his voice all croaky.

'Not until we get the X-ray results back I'm afraid, in case the doctors need to operate.'

'I take it that means no painkillers either.'

He touched his face. Was there any place they didn't get? He played rugby, for goodness' sake, so was used to getting bashed, but this was at a whole new level. And with a baseball bat, too.

Did they speak to him? He had a vague recollection that they did. It was all a bit hazy.

'I'll check if we can give you some IV pain relief.'

The nurse left the cubicle and he closed his eyes. He must have drifted off because when he opened them Birdie was standing by him, her mouth open wide.

'Oh, my God. Look at you.'

'Elsa. You said you'd take care of her.'

'I will. Give me your keys and I'll go after I've left here. I'll stay with her until you're well enough to go back to the house. Can you remember what happened?'

Even in this state, the memories were there waiting for him to access.

'I was walking home and after I went past the old grammar school, I thought I was being followed, but every time I turned there was no one there.'

'Were you followed from the pub, do you think?'

'Not that I noticed. But I wasn't looking out for it. I'd just turned into Heygate Street when I was attacked by two men. One of them had a baseball bat. They took my wallet.'

'It was a mugging?'

'I don't think so. They took it as an afterthought.'

'To make it look like you'd been mugged?'

'Yes.' He dragged in a breath. How could talking hurt so much?

'If you're right, do you think it's related to the case? Had we got close to uncovering something without realising?'

'I don't know.' He turned slightly and winced.

'Has anyone from the force been to see you?'

'Not yet.'

'What did the doctors say?'

'They're waiting for X-ray results to see what damage has been done. I've got to stay here until they can find me a bed on one of the wards.'

'I'm at work tomorrow so I'll come back and take a statement. Don't worry about Elsa, she'll be fine with me.'

'The food ...'

'I'll find everything. Where's the key?'

'Try the bag at the end of the bed. The address is on the fob.'

She opened it. 'Found it.' She waved it under his nose. 'Does Elsa get fed twice a day?'

'Yes.' He nodded.

'She'll be fed, watered, and walked. Remember, I worked at the kennels and know what to do, so don't worry.'

He'd forgotten, but now she reminded him he felt better about leaving her in charge of Elsa.

'Thank you. I—'

The curtain opened and the nurse walked in, interrupting him. 'All you have are broken ribs, the rest of you is fine, apart from the cuts and bruising. The doctor has prescribed some painkillers which I'll get for you.'

'Can I go home?' he asked, thinking that Birdie could take him.

'No, because of the concussion, as I've already told you. You're on half-hourly obs.'

'I'm going now. Take it easy' Birdie said. 'Don't take any crap from him,' she said to the nurse, grinning at Seb as she left.

TWENTY-THREE

16 May

Birdie tossed and turned all night, unable to get the sight of Seb's battered face from her mind. It could've been so much worse. The attackers must have been very strong to do something like that to someone of his size. Then again, it was two against one and they had a weapon. She couldn't sit back and let someone else deal with the case, she'd make sure it was hers. Before going to bed, she'd sent an urgent email request to the Leicestershire secure control room, which luckily operated twenty-four-seven, asking for access to all CCTV footage in and around the area where Seb was attacked. She assumed it would be there for her in the morning.

Finally, at six o'clock, she got up to see to Elsa, who she already adored. After feeding and walking her, Birdie headed home, where she had a quick shower and grabbed a bowl of cereal.

She then drove to work intent on checking the CCTV footage from the area to try to identify the attackers. She stopped at the machine in the corridor for a coffee and set to work. None of the team had arrived yet, which meant no interruptions or having to explain what she was doing. She also wanted to get to the hospital as soon as possible to see how he was. It was too early to phone in case it woke him up.

The link to the footage had been emailed to her and she called it up on her screen. She watched from when he'd left the pub, heading up High Street. The streets were fairly deserted, apart from two teenage girls, and a man in dark clothing on one side of the road. Was he one of the attackers? She peered closely at her screen but couldn't make out his face. She then noticed that on the other side of the road there was a second man, also keeping his head down.

They both walked quickly and kept a set distance behind Seb. When he turned into The Square, one of the men crossed the road and joined the other. They followed Seb onto Church Street, and that's where the footage stopped, because there were no more cameras. Damn.

It had to be them. There was no one else around, and Seb had said he thought he was being followed for a while.

She reran the footage to see if the weapon could be spotted. But they were both wearing hoodies. 'Easy to hide a baseball bat in there,' she muttered to herself.

'What are you doing here?' She started at the sound of Sergeant Weston's voice. How long had he been standing there? 'What are you looking at?'

'There was an attack in town last night, which I'd like to deal with. With your permission, Sarge. It's a bit complicated.'

'I'd expect nothing less,' he said, arching an eyebrow.

The door opened and Twiggy and DC Gemma Litton, aka Sparkle, walked in. 'Can I talk to you in private?' she asked quietly, nodding at the other officers, so he would realise she didn't want them to hear.

'Come with me.'

She followed him through to his office, sitting on one of the chairs in front of his desk while he sat behind it. The room was a mess. Folders piled high on every surface. Old police magazines in the corner on the floor. Several jackets were hanging on a peg on the back of the door. But no one would dare say anything. Crossing Sergeant Weston wasn't advisable, as she'd found out to her cost on more than one occasion.

She cleared her throat. 'Before I start, you're not going to be happy with what I've done, but—'

'What is with you? How hard is it to keep your nose clean? How many times have—'

'Let me explain,' she interrupted. 'I'll start at the beginning and it will make more sense. Do you remember the suicide of Donald Witherspoon?'

He frowned. 'Yes, of course. Why?'

'His wife didn't believe the verdict and so she asked her cousin, Sebastian Clifford, who's a former detective with the Met, if he'd look into it.' She paused a moment, bracing herself. 'I've been helping.'

'Helping? How do you know him?' He locked eyes with her, and she squirmed in her chair. She was convinced that he'd spent years perfecting that look.

She rubbed her hands down her trouser legs. 'I don't know him, exactly. Well, I do now. But we got to know each other after he phoned CID asking to see the police report, and I was the one to answer the call.'

'Of course, you said no because you're a stickler for rules and regulations.'

'Not exactly. I talked to him to find out what he was doing, and why he wanted the report, and he seemed to have a genuine case. And, you know, he's ex-job, and I was so fed up being stuck behind a desk doing nothing that—'

'Whose fault was that?'

'I know. Mine.' She waved her hand dismissively. 'Anyway, I told him that I'd get the police and coroner's reports if he let me assist in his investigation. I did it in my own time, though. I didn't do anything while at work.'

A slight distortion of the truth, but she wasn't going to admit that. It was bad enough that Sarge now knew she'd helped Seb.

'That makes it right does it?' He leant forward on his desk and she, involuntarily, backed away.

'No, Sarge.'

'During this *investigation* into Witherspoon's suicide, did you find anything other than what we already knew?'

'Seb ... I mean Clifford, was given access to Donald Witherspoon's computer and files. After he'd examined them, he isolated several people to interview, including friends and family, who had invested money. And, by the way, he has this weird memory thing where he can recall *everything* that has ever happened to him.'

'Like a photographic memory?'

'No. It's something else. He doesn't like to talk about it much. But it's bloody useful. Anyway, we met last night and decided that although Witherspoon was dodgy financially, which we all know, there was nothing that pointed to a suspicious death, and that it was most likely suicide.'

'That the police and coroner were correct, you mean.'

'Yes. But as Clifford was walking home last night, he was attacked by two men and badly beaten. He's now in hospital with concussion. I think it's related to our investigation.'

'You just said that you'd both decided the death was suicide.'

'So why was he attacked, then?'

'Was anything taken?'

'His wallet.'

'Which makes it a vicious mugging.'

'Clifford thinks they didn't take his wallet until the end, you know, as an afterthought.'

'How can he be sure of that, the state he's in? Look, Birdie, I know you're anxious to get back outside. I accept that. And I will let you out there. I think you've learnt your lesson and I've noticed you've come in early a few times, even if it was to work on this.'

She held up her hands in protest. She didn't want to get in more trouble. 'It wasn't—'

'We'll park that for one moment,' he interrupted. 'You're a good copper, no question about it, but this could have been kids on drugs. There have been some serious attacks recently, not dissimilar to this one. These attackers could have got carried away before taking his wallet.'

'On the CCTV footage, there were two men walking separately and then joining up as Clifford walked into Church Street where there are no cameras.'

'It could be coincidental?' His tone wavered. Did he now believe her?

'Maybe, but it still needs considering. Please may I be the one to investigate the attack? I already know the background on the case and if it doesn't turn out to be linked to Witherspoon's suicide, then it doesn't matter.'

'Okay, you can take it, but for now it's going to be classed as a mugging, unless we discover otherwise. We're certainly not going to open up a murder investigation on such flimsy evidence, especially as the death has already been investigated.'

'Got it. I'll interview Clifford this morning, he's at Leicester Royal Infirmary. If that's okay?' she added as an afterthought.

'Get a statement and we'll work from there.'

'Thanks, Sarge.'

She returned to her desk, happy to be back on the job, even though she thought Sarge should've been more receptive to her theory.

She looked again at the CCTV footage of the two men, paying particular attention to their clothes. They both wore hoodies and dark trousers, and one was wearing gloves. They didn't look like drugged up kids. Neither of them had their face captured on the camera. Was that a deliberate ploy? Had they checked in advance the camera angles and where they were placed? Being a small town, they didn't have that many, and they were easy to evade, unlike in the big cities.

She downloaded the footage of them turning into the street onto her phone to show Seb when she saw him later.

Surely if it was just a mugging, they'd have asked him to hand over his wallet and not wait until they'd beaten him to a pulp before taking it.

And if it wasn't a mugging, then what was it? Why had he been chosen?

If it was to do with Witherspoon, was she at risk, too? No one had come after her. Yet.

TWENTY-FOUR

16 May

At nine-thirty Birdie grabbed her bag from the back of the chair and slipped on her pink and white striped thick knitted cardigan. There had been a nip in the air when she'd arrived earlier, and it would keep her warm.

'Where are you going? If it's to get some breakfast, get me a sausage roll. I'll pay you when you get back,' Twiggy said, as she marched past his desk.

'I thought you were meant to be on a diet? I'll tell Evie,' she threatened, referring to his wife, and grinning in his direction.

'You can laugh, but it's driving me mad. The woman's emptied the house of anything decent to eat. No cakes. No biscuits. No crisps. I'm not even allowed brown sauce on my dinner. Can you believe it? A meal isn't a meal unless it's smothered in sauce. She says it's got sugar in it. But I don't know where. It doesn't taste sweet. Go on. Get me a sausage roll, please. I'll put in a good word with Sarge to get you back out there.'

'I don't need your help, thanks. I'm off to the hospital to take a statement from Sebastian Clifford. He got attacked last night in the town centre.'

He stared at her a broad grin on his face 'Good for you. What made Sarge change his mind? He'd seemed so determined to make you suffer a while longer.'

'He hadn't intended to, that was for sure. He's only letting me go because I know Clifford as we've been working together on a case.'

Crap. She hadn't meant to tell him about it just yet. Was he going to be upset that she'd kept it from him?

'What case and why don't I know about it? We're meant to be partners. When did Sarge give it to you?' His jaw clenched as he stared daggers at Birdie.

Twiggy was easy-going and was seldom annoyed, but this had clearly wound him up.

'That's the whole point. He didn't know about it because I was doing it on the side. I didn't want to involve you, in case Sarge found out, and then we'd both be in trouble.'

'What's the case?' Twiggy asked, his jaw relaxing and his usual expression returning.

'We've been investigating the suicide of Donald Witherspoon.'

'Ha. So that's why you wanted to know about the crime scene. All that crap about filing and coming across it. And I fell for it.' He smacked his forehead. 'I'm such an idiot.'

She felt the heat rush up her cheeks. Damn. She hated blushing. 'Sorry, I didn't mean to deceive you. Anyway, long story short, we looked into it, didn't come across anything to make us think the verdict was wrong, and then last night he was attacked. Sarge is classing it as a mugging, but I'm not so sure, and neither is Seb. We believe it could have been a warning for him to back off.'

'Who is this guy and how come he's investigating a case? Is he a PI?'

'He used to be a DI at the Met, and he's doing it for his cousin, who was Witherspoon's wife. He's a good guy, even if he is an aristocrat.'

'A what?' Twiggy spluttered.

'He's the son of a viscount, but he's not inheriting the title because he isn't the eldest son. But that doesn't matter. All you need to know is he was attacked last night and Sarge is letting me work the case.'

'Do you want me to go with you?'

His help might be useful, but she wasn't sure Seb would want anyone else involved. He'd already made it clear that he liked working alone and was only letting her help because he'd had no other option at the time.

'Thanks, but it's better if I go alone. He was badly beaten and won't be up to both of us visiting,' she said, using that as an excuse.

'Tell me more about your enquiry into Witherspoon.'

'I haven't got time now. We'll catch up later.' She didn't want to go into too much detail, until she knew more about what had actually happened and how it linked to Donald's death ... if it actually did.

'I'm here if you need me.'

'Sarge won't like that. Or have you now become an anarchist?' She smirked.

'Go.' He pointed at the door. 'But if you do need help, let me know. You know, you can't just don't go wading in single-handedly. If Clifford's incapacitated, he won't be much use.'

'I'm not going to do anything stupid. I'll find out in more detail what happened last night now he's had time to recover a bit. We've still got to find the attackers and learn their motive. I reckon one of the people we've interviewed set the whole thing up because they thought we were getting too close. Then again, it could be to do with his other work. But how likely is that?' she mused.

'Don't make it into something more than it is. Remember I was a part of the original Witherspoon investigation and it was all clear-cut.'

Was it? Was it really?

'I'm going in with an open mind. Oh and, FYI, Evie has asked me to report to her if you cheat ...' She stuck her tongue out and left the room before he could say anything else.

* * *

When she reached the hospital, she had to drive around the car park several times before finally finding a space. She had no idea which ward Seb was on so she headed to the reception desk and held out her warrant card. 'I'm looking for Sebastian Clifford. He was brought into accident and emergency last night.'

The receptionist stared at her computer screen. 'He's on the short-stay ward on level three. One of the nurses on duty will let you know which bed he's in.'

Birdie, avoided the lift and took the stairs, jogging all the way to the third level. She went over to the nurse on duty, holding out her ID. 'I'm here to see Sebastian Clifford about last night's attack. How's he doing?'

'He's improving, but I don't want you tiring him out. He still needs his rest.'

'He's a friend as well. I was here with him last night. I promise to be gentle, if he'll let me.' She smiled and the nurse's face softened.

'Head down the corridor and he's in the fifth room on the left. Bed number one.'

She followed the directions and on entering the room her stomach plummeted at the sight of Seb lying in bed, his face swollen and bruised. His eyes were closed. Was he asleep? She turned to the nurse who was close by.

'How is he?' she asked in a quiet voice, nodding towards him.

'I can hear you,' Seb said, his eyes now open.

'You're okay?' she said, smiling with relief.

'No, he's not *okay*,' the nurse said. 'We've already been debating the fact that he wants to leave.'

Why didn't that surprise her?

'What did the doctors say?'

'They want him to stay for another night because of the concussion, so we can continue monitoring his vitals.'

'I can't stay. We have things to do,' Seb said flatly.

'I'll talk to him,' she said to the nurse, in a low voice.

'Good,' the woman replied as she left the room.

Birdie glanced around the ward. There were four men, including Seb, and all eyes seemed to be on her. She pulled the curtain around Seb's bed and moved the chair until she could sit close to him. She took out her phone.

'I'm here on official business as Sarge has let me take your case,' she said, keeping her voice low so it couldn't be heard. 'I've got to take a statement and want to show you what I found on the CCTV footage. I admitted to him that I'd been helping you with your enquiry and told him your attack could be linked to it. He wasn't convinced and said it was an unrelated mugging. Particularly because we'd already decided Witherspoon's death was suicide.'

'If it had been my case, I might have thought the same,' Seb said. 'We don't have any proof.'

'How can you say that? It's too coincidental that you were singled out to be attacked out of everyone in town last night. By the way, how are you feeling? I forgot to ask.'

'I've been better. Is Elsa okay?'

'More than okay. We've had a lovely time. I even let her sleep on the bed next to me last night.'

'That's not allowed.'

'She was missing you. It was the least I could do. Have you looked in a mirror yet?'

'No. I avoided it when I went to the bathroom.'

'Wise move.'

'That bad, eh?'

'Worse. Wait a while before checking as you might not recognise yourself. Those film-star looks have disappeared.'

'Thanks for that. You really know how to make a man feel good about himself.'

'Have the doctors done their rounds yet?'

'Yes, you just missed them.'

'And?'

'They're happy with my progress. My ribs will take a while to heal, which I already knew because I've broken them before while playing rugby. A smaller man might not have come out of it so well. I'm going to be fine.' He gasped for breath.

'You don't sound it. You can hardly breathe. They still want you to stay in another night, though, don't they?'

'Not going to happen. Show me the CCTV footage.'

She called up the footage on her phone and showed him both men. 'They're separate at this point, but then join together. Do they look familiar?'

'I think it's them. One came at me from behind and one charged at me front-on.'

'Sarge thought whoever attacked you could be kids high on drugs and that's why they didn't get your wallet until they'd finished, but these two are definitely not kids, look at their build and the way they walk.'

'Agreed. They look like grown men.'

'Have you done anything in the past that might make people come after you?'

'At the Met, in the special squad, yes definitely. But why follow me here, and why now when I've left the force? I can't harm any of the people I used to be investigating.'

'Unless it was revenge.'

'Maybe, but I'm not convinced. Did I tell you about the tattoo?'

'No.'

'The man who searched for my wallet had a tattoo of an eagle on his hand. It might mean something significant, it's not an area I'm familiar with.'

'I'll research it when I get back to the station. Okay, let's recap. We've got two men, clearly not teenagers. We don't know if they were high, but from the way they were walking when following you there's nothing to suggest they were. You were attacked after we'd interviewed several people. Was anything said to you during the attack?'

'I was replaying the scene in my mind when you arrived.'

'Because of your memory thing ... of course. That's going to help greatly.'

'I hope so, but my HSAM suffered because of the beating. Last night I didn't remember, but now I can tell you that before they took my wallet one of them told the other to stop the attack because I'd have *got the message to back off by now.*'

'You could have told me this as soon as I arrived.'

Surely that made it conclusive. His attack was down to the investigation into Witherspoon's death.

'Cut me some slack, will you? I'm in pain here.'

'And here was me thinking you were tough. Was it the man with the tattoo who did the talking?'

'I believe so, but it was dark so I'm not a hundred per cent.'

'So what are we going to do now?'

'I'm going to discharge myself as I can't leave Elsa on her own any longer.'

'I can take care of her.'

'You're at work all day. If you can wait to take me home, I'd be grateful. I also need to see Sarah and update her. I don't want her to find out about the attack from the media, or she'll be worried sick. I'd rather see her in person than talk about it on the phone, or she'll imagine all sorts.'

'Not today. If you go in that state, she won't even recognise you.'

'Point taken. I'll go tomorrow and take it easy for the rest of today. I also think we should revisit everyone we've interviewed so far.'

'Is that a good idea, after the warning?' she asked.

'Do you have any other suggestions?'

'You could let the police handle it from here.'

She should report back to Sarge, but he might decide to pass the case over to Twiggy and she wanted to carry on with it. She should be able to keep it on the down-low for a while longer at least.

'You are the police.'

'True. And now I'm officially working the case, I'm not doing anything wrong. But what if these men come after you again?'

'I'll be prepared next time.'

'You have a gun?'

'No. But I'll be on my guard.'

'If you say so. I'll take you home, now, but I still need an official statement. Why don't I drive you to see Sarah tomorrow, to save you having to, and then we can go to the station and I'll show you the rest of the CCTV footage and not just the small amount I downloaded?'

'Will you be allowed to do all this? Won't your sergeant kick up about it, as he's viewing it as a mugging?'

'It doesn't matter what his opinion is, you can still look at the footage. It's part of my investigation and as I'm no longer chained to my desk, I can take you wherever you need to go.' She paused. 'Within reason, of course.'

'Of course,' he repeated, wincing as he grinned.

'I'll wait in the corridor while you get dressed.' She patted the bed.

'Ouch,' he moaned.

'Sorry. Shall I get a nurse to help you get dressed?'

'I can manage myself.'

'Suit yourself. I'll let them know you're leaving.'

TWENTY-FIVE

17 May

Every breath Seb took was a monumental effort. Thank goodness he'd arranged for Birdie to take him to Sarah's because he wasn't sure he'd manage to drive that far. It had been a mission to get up and feed Elsa. And as for the short walk he'd taken her on, the pain was still permeating throughout his entire body. She'd been playing in the garden for a while which hopefully would tire her out. He didn't want to take her to Sarah's because they were going to the station after.

Elsa seemed to understand that he was injured. Instead of sleeping in her bed in the kitchen, she'd insisted on coming upstairs and sleeping on the floor beside him, and he hadn't the heart to tell her no. She knew better than to try to climb on the bed, even though Birdie had allowed her to the night before.

After phoning Sarah to make sure she'd be there, he'd arranged for Birdie to pick him up at eleven, and he was now sitting in the kitchen nursing a mug of coffee he'd just made. He hadn't given Sarah an exact time, knowing what Birdie was like. It was already ten minutes past eleven and if she ran true to form, she'd probably be there in ten minutes. He lifted his mug to his lips to take a sip of coffee, when there was a knock at the door. 'It's me,' Birdie's voice called through the letter box.

He hobbled to the front door and opened it.

'You're early ... for you.'

'Still looking beautiful,' Birdie said, smirking.

'It's a good job we're not working together on a permanent basis. I don't think I could take your sense of humour.'

'Ouch. You know how to hurt. How are you doing?'

'My head hurts, I'm bruised all over, including places I wasn't even aware could bruise. Apart from that I'm fine.'

'You do actually look better than you did yesterday. But that wasn't hard. Are you ready?'

'I've got a coffee on the go. We'll leave when I've finished it.'

'It's after eleven, the time you wanted to leave.'

'I was working on Birdie time, so thought I had time to finish it. I wasn't expecting you for another ten minutes or so.'

'That's the last time I make an effort to be on time. Well, almost on time. But if we're waiting, have you got anything to eat? I'm starving because I didn't have time for breakfast.'

'*Mi casa es tu casa.*'

'What?'

'It's Spanish for *my house is your house.* So, come in and help yourself. I've got toast or cereal.'

'I'll have crisps and a couple of biscuits if you've got some.'

'I can do those, too.'

He'd bought them a couple of days ago, specifically for Birdie if she came around.

She marched past him and into the kitchen. 'Which cupboard?' she yelled.

'To the right of the fridge.'

She made herself a coffee and munched her way through a bag of crisps and then half a packet of biscuits.

'That's better, I'll be fine now until this evening.'

'You shouldn't eat rubbish like that all the time, it's not good for you."

'Yes, Mum,' she said, sighing. 'How many times do I have to tell you? I already have a mother.' Her face clouded over. 'Two even.'

'Two? I don't understand.' This wasn't Birdie's usual attempt at humour. Something was troubling her. 'Do you want to talk about it?'

She stared directly at him for a while, twisting strands of hair around her finger. 'I was dealing with this on my own, but ... yeah. I'll tell you, because it's eating me up inside.'

'Anything you say to me will be kept confidential.'

It had to be serious if it had caused her to go from her usual breezy, cheeky self to being so morose.

'I'm adopted and want to find my birth mother. I finally broached the subject with my adoptive parents who, by the way, are wonderful. I know it hurt them, I could see it in their eyes, but I can't stop myself. It's like part of me is missing. I know that sounds weird, but it's true, and I've felt like this for a long time.'

'I'm sure they'll understand if you explain your feelings to them.'

'Maybe,' she said, shrugging. 'I'm the only one who's adopted in the family. After they had me, my mum got pregnant. Twice. I've got two younger brothers. I've done my research and have applied to be added to the Adoption Contact Register to say that I'm happy to be contacted and now I'm waiting to hear if my mother is also on there. But it's such a slow process. If she is on there and has agreed to be contacted, then they'll put us in touch with each other. If she isn't on there, then I'll have to think again.' She let out a long sigh, the relief at having told him evident on her face.

'Do you have your birth certificate?'

'Yes. It has my birth mother's name, but no father's name, and shows that I was born in Leicester.'

'Surely you can search yourself as you have access to plenty of databases.'

'I can only see if she has a criminal record and I've done that already and found nothing. Also, she may have got married and changed her name. Or she could've moved overseas. There are so many things I don't know about her, including how old she was when she gave me up and exactly where she lived in Leicester at the time. It's not going to be an easy job, but I've got to do it.'

'If the Adoption Contact Register doesn't come up with anything, you could always try social media.'

'I will, but it's going to take a while and at the moment I don't have the time.'

'I'm glad you confided in me. I do understand your need to find your birth mother, as it will give you a sense of identity.'

'Yep,' she said, her eyes glistening with tears. 'Anyway, enough about me and my two mothers. Let's go see Sarah. I take it you told her what's happened?'

Her serious expression had disappeared. Birdie had hidden depths, which he was fortunate to have witnessed as he got the feeling much of the time she put on an act. A defence mechanism. It shows she must trust him.

'I didn't want to alarm her, so decided not to.'

'Seriously? So instead, we're going to turn up at her front door and she's going to see you looking like this. You used to be a DI which should mean you have some intelligence. I have to tell you that's not an intelligent way to behave.'

'Says the woman who gets grounded at work because she can't stop being late.'

'That's different.'

'I've been beaten about the head and I'm not thinking straight,' he said, by way of an excuse.

'You think? Maybe I should leave you in the car when we get there and warn her first.'

'I suppose that could work.'

'I'm kidding. We've known each other ages and you still don't get my sense of humour.'

'Just over a week, actually, even if it does seem longer.'

'That's charming, I ... you're joking, aren't you?'

'You're not the only person who can.'

'Enough. Let's go.'

'You drive a Mini, don't you?'

'Yes, a clapped-out old one.'

'In which case, we'll take my car.'

'Good idea.'

He gave her directions to Rendall Hall and as they drove through the gate and approached the house she slowed down.

'Wow,' Birdie said, letting out a low whistle. 'So this is where the money Witherspoon stole went.'

'Not in buying it, they've lived here for over twenty years and it was bought with Sarah's money, I believe. Donald used much of the money he'd embezzled for the upkeep, which is high. Old properties like this swallow the cash.'

She pulled up outside the house and they walked slowly to the front door and knocked.

'Stand behind me so I can warn Sarah when she answers. Turn around as well, or she'll see you over my head.'

After a few seconds, the door opened.

'Hello, Sarah, I'm Birdie. I'm a DC with the Market Harborough police force, and I've been helping Seb with his research into Donald's death. I wanted to give you a quick one second warning because he's decided to spring this on you. He was attacked on Saturday night and it's not a pretty sight.'

Seb turned and stepped to the side of Birdie so his cousin could see him.

'Oh, my goodness,' Sarah said, slamming her hand to her mouth, the colour draining from her face. 'What on earth happened?'

'Let me tell you inside as I could do with sitting down, it hurts to stand for too long.'

'We'll go into the kitchen, or would you rather sit on an easy chair in the drawing room?'

'The drawing room will be more comfortable.'

They followed her and Birdie looked at him and mouthed, 'Told you so.'

'Can I get you anything to drink, coffee, tea? A soft drink?'

'We've just had one, thanks,' Seb said.

'Would you like some cake?'

'We're fine, thanks,' Seb said.

'Tell me what happened.' Sarah said once they'd reached the drawing room and sat down.

'I was attacked after leaving the pub in Market Harborough town centre on Saturday night.'

'He ended up in the hospital at Leicester and he discharged himself yesterday against doctor's orders,' Birdie added. 'That's why I was the one to bring him here, because he wanted to see you and he can't drive himself, yet.'

'Do you know why you were attacked?' Sarah looked from Birdie to him.

'They took his wallet, but we think it might be related to your case,' Birdie answered before Seb had time to speak.

He hadn't intended to be quite so direct, but it was out in the open, now. 'But I'm fine,' he added.

'You don't look it. Stop the investigation straight away. They might come after you again if you don't. I couldn't have that on my conscience.'

'Let's not jump the gun. First of all, we've got to find out who did this to me and whether it was a random attack, or whether it's actually related to the investigation into Donald. Before this happened, we had intended telling you that we'd found nothing to make us think his death was anything other than suicide. Even the note we believed we could justify. But if this is to do with it, then that changes everything, and it points to you being right.'

Sarah bit down on her bottom lip. 'If you're sure, then carry on, but promise me you'll be careful. Both of you.' She looked across at Birdie and back at him.

He was in too deep now not to carry on.

'Oh, believe me, we will be. I was taken unawares on Saturday. That won't happen again, I can assure you.'

TWENTY-SIX

17 May

'Thanks for lunch, Sarah. And especially the chocolate cake, that was to die for,' Birdie said as they stood on the doorstep saying goodbye. She'd never been in such a large house before. It was beautiful, and she'd have loved to look around, but she didn't think Seb would be happy about her asking.

'You're welcome. It's nice to have someone appreciate my baking.' Sarah smiled, and it lit up her whole face. There was a definite family resemblance between her and Seb.

'You should take it up professionally. I'd be first in line to buy whatever you made.'

'Maybe I will.' Sarah turned to Seb, her face becoming serious. 'Please be careful, I don't want you hurt on my account. And don't forget to keep me updated.'

'I'll be fine.' He glanced at Birdie. 'We'll *both* be fine.'

They headed slowly to the car and Birdie opened the door for Seb to ease himself in.

'We'll go to the station so you can have a look at this CCTV footage and then I'm going to get you home because you're looking even worse than you did this morning,' Birdie said, once they were both strapped in and she had started the engine.

'I'm sure by tomorrow I'll be feeling much better.'

'Yeah, maybe. But you still had a nasty attack. How's your head? Do you want some headache pills?'

'I'll be fine.'

'Don't tell me you're one of those men who couldn't possibly take anything to help in case it made you seem weak?'

'I'm in no mood to discuss this.' He turned his head and stared out of the window.

That was the first time she'd heard him snap like that. Hardly surprising considering the state he was in, but it shocked her a little. He'd always given the impression of being so laid-back that nothing ruffled him.

She drove to the station and parked in the street, rather than the car park, concerned that someone might hit the BMW. It had been such a treat to drive it. The leather seats were soft and luxurious, and it was an automatic transmission, so all she had to do was sit back and stare at the road ahead. It would be a shame to go back to her old Mini.

They walked into the station through the front door.

'Afternoon, Bill,' she said on their way past the officer at the front desk.

He coughed and nodded at Seb. 'Signing in book.'

'Oh, yeah, sorry, I forgot.'

'No cameras or facial recognition?' Seb asked, looking all around.

'You do realise that we're in the sticks.' She rolled her eyes. 'Talk about you can take the man out of the Met, but you can't take the Met out of the man.'

After signing him in, she took him to the CID office.

'It's empty,' he said.

'Only me around today. It's Twiggy's day off. Rambo's on paternity leave, and Tiny and Sparkle are both in court.

Different cases. Sarge might be somewhere, I'm not sure. If I didn't know better, I'd say he lived here. He's never far away. With no one else in it will make our work much easier, as we won't be interrupted.' She grabbed a chair and pulled it along so he could sit next to her at her desk. 'I'll show you the CCTV footage that I didn't download to my phone.' She pulled it up on the screen. 'This is when you left the pub.'

'Can you pause it so we can take a closer look,' Seb said. 'I want to see if there was anybody else in the vicinity.'

'I've already looked and there wasn't. Not on this camera.'

'Did you look at any cameras further down the road, away from the direction I was heading?'

'No, I only checked the camera which followed you. There's one further down the street, let's take a look.' She went into the system and called up the particular camera she had referred to.

'See over there, standing in the shop doorway.' He pointed to the two shadows, who were clearly the men who'd been following him earlier.

'I'm such an idiot. Why didn't I think of going back rather than just looking at your walk home?' She stared at the two men. 'They're together now and split later. I'm guessing so they don't appear so noticeable to the public.'

'Is the entrance to the bar visible from there?' Seb asked.

'Yes, it is. The road isn't straight, and they can see diagonally across.'

'So they must have known I was in there and could see when I left. Maybe they'd been following me for longer, but if that's the case why didn't I notice?'

'You weren't looking for them. I wonder if they were watching your movements from the Airbnb. They could've parked up and then followed you when you were on your way to meet me.'

'How did they find me in the first place? And for how long
have they been following me?'

'Can't you use your superpower and call up everywhere
you've been and take a look around?'

'It doesn't work like that, Birdie. I can't recall anything that
didn't actually go in through my eyes. If I could, that really
would be a *superpower* as you called it.'

'Damn. Well, if it is connected to Donald, then the attack
was orchestrated by someone you interviewed. Clearly they
didn't do it themselves or you would have recognised them.
Unless, as I said before, this is nothing to do with the case and
from something you've been involved in when you were
working for the Met.'

'If someone wanted to either teach me a lesson or warn me
about something from the past, they could've done it in London.
Why wait for me to be in Market Harborough, especially as
they'd have no idea how long I would be here? Originally I only
intended being here for a couple of days, and that's all people in
London would have known. In fact, the only person who knows
I've stayed here for longer is Jill, my neighbour.'

'What about Rob?'

His brow furrowed. 'He knows I'm here. But ... no that's
ridiculous. No way would he set me up for a beating. He's my
friend, and we didn't even work together on cases at the Met.
It's not from the past, I'm sure of it. We have to focus on who
knows about our enquiry now.'

Birdie wracked her brain for something else for them to
consider. They had to be totally sure it was linked to the suicide,
or otherwise the attack would go down as a mugging.

'Could Sarah have confided in someone what we're doing?
She might have asked a friend for advice before asking you to
look into Donald's death, and that person was implicated in
some way. Oh ... I've had an idea ... What about this ... Donald
was having an affair with one of Sarah's friends and when you

started investigating his death, which really was suicide, this woman was worried that the affair would come out and wreck her marriage and friendship with Sarah. So she arranged for some thugs to beat you up as a warning to keep your nose out.'

'That's one scenario, I suppose, but nothing I've found has pointed to Donald having an affair. That doesn't mean Sarah didn't confide in anyone, though. We didn't discuss the need to be confidential about my work. I think we should focus on those who have been interviewed.'

'Okay,' she said, sighing. 'We know that these guys were together and then split up to follow you so they weren't so conspicuous. They met up again when you went into Church Street.'

'Can we see them any better on the other camera?'

'No, because they made sure to keep their heads turned away and they had hoods up.'

'What are you doing?' Birdie tensed. Crap. He was here after all.

'This is Sebastian Clifford, Sarge, he's the one who got attacked.'

'Yeah, I can see that for myself.' He turned to Seb. 'Sergeant Jack Weston. That was some beating you took, shouldn't you be home resting?'

'It's going to hurt wherever I am, so I might as well be here doing something useful.'

'I understand you used to be a DI at the Met.'

'Yes, that's correct.'

'That doesn't give you officer privileges here, it—'

'Sarge,' Birdie interrupted, worried about the direction the conversation could take. 'I've brought Seb in to look at the CCTV footage to see if he recognises the men who attacked him, so we can link it back to Witherspoon's death.'

'It was a suicide. We called it and the coroner agreed,' her boss said, his arms folded tightly across his chest.

'But what if we were wrong?' Birdie persisted.

'Have you found anything to indicate that it is?'

'This attack for starters, once we can establish a link.'

'Leave it. The wallet was stolen, and this has the hallmark of a vicious mugging.'

'But, Sarge—'

'*But Sarge* nothing,' he said, walking off and heading back to his office. Typical that he showed up when she didn't want him to.

'See what I have to put up with?' she said, nodding in her superior officer's direction, once he was out of the way and couldn't hear her.

'I also see that he has to put up with you,' Seb said, tilting his head to one side.

'He should listen to me because we could be dealing with a murder. But he doesn't want that outcome as we're understaffed and don't have the facilities to deal with anything big. Then again, why would we? This is Market Harborough, hardly the hub of serious crime, and anything big that happens gets taken over by one of the Leicestershire CIDs as we're all part of the same constabulary.'

'I see.' He exhaled a long breath and slumped in the chair.

He was flagging.

'That's enough for today. I'm going to take you home because you look about ready to drop.'

'I have to admit, you're right. I'll go home and get some rest. Tomorrow, I'm going back to speak to Edgar, Donald's brother.'

'Are you going to make an appointment?'

'Not this time. I'm going to turn up at his office in Leicester. If he was the one to arrange for me to be beaten up, I don't want to warn him in advance. Speaking to him at his workplace will offer a level of protection. No one is going to pounce on me there.'

'Do you want me to lend you some make-up?'

He frowned. 'Make-up?'

'Have you seen the state of your face? You'll need something to tone it down.'

'It will have faded a bit by tomorrow.'

'I'll drive you.'

Seb was quiet for a few seconds. 'Okay,' he agreed.

'Bloody hell, you must be feeling bad to agree straight away. I've just got to go to the loo and then I'll get you back to the house.'

* * *

Twiggy walked into the room and did a double take at the burly guy sitting at Birdie's desk. Was that the Clifford bloke? Judging by the state of him it had to be, but on principle he wasn't going to admit to knowing him. The man was no longer a copper, and he certainly wasn't going to kowtow to him because he'd been a DI.

'What happened to you?' he said, marching over and standing beside him. Even sitting down, the man was almost up to his chest.

'Beaten up on Saturday night. I'm Sebastian Clifford, you are?'

'DC Branch.'

'Aka, Twiggy.' He nodded knowingly. 'Birdie has mentioned you.'

'Where is she?'

'She's gone to the ladies.'

'What are you doing here? And how come she left you alone?'

'I'm looking through some mugshots, to see if I can identify the men who mugged me. As to your second question, she trusts me. I'm ex-job.'

'Birdie said that the attack was linked to the Witherspoon's death and not a mugging.'

'She told you that?' Seb frowned.

'Yep. We're partners, and that's what partners do. Confide in each other.'

'What else did she tell you?' Seb pushed his chair back from the desk and stared directly at Twiggy.

'That Donald Witherspoon's wife is convinced it's not a suicide, despite all the evidence pointing otherwise.'

'What's your view?'

'I was one of the officers at the scene and saw the body, the gun, and the note. There was nothing that pointed to it being anything other than suicide. And it wasn't just us who thought so. The coroner agreed.' Twiggy clenched his fists. He'd done a good job. He hadn't missed anything. This murder business was nonsense. Surely, it had to be. 'So are you just stringing this woman along to make some money out of her?'

He shouldn't have said that. Birdie had a nose for stuff and if she was convinced then maybe there was something in it.

'This *woman* happens to be my cousin and I'm not being paid. I'm doing it as a favour,' Clifford replied, his voice cold, and his lips set in a flat line.

'Even if what you say is true, I'm warning you … Don't you go getting Birdie into trouble.'

Clifford gave a wry smile. 'She can look after herself and as her partner surely you, better than anyone, would know that.'

'You're right,' he acknowledged. 'But if she gets into any trouble, you'll have me to answer to.'

'Noted.'

'Just because you used to work at the Met doesn't mean you can intimidate her into helping you. She …' His voice fell away. He should shut up. Even he could tell he was getting out of line.

'Do you know Birdie?'

'What's that meant to mean?'

'She's not going to let me intimidate her.'

'You say that, but she's still in awe of you, even if you did leave the force under a cloud.'

'Twiggy ... nothing I've done in the past will have any impact on Birdie. I promise.'

'Hey, what are you doing here? I thought it was your day off.' Birdie said as she headed over to them.

'I popped in to check something and was talking to Mr Clifford,' he said, taking a step away from where the man was sitting.

'What's in the bag you're holding?'

He hastily put his hand behind his back, not prepared to admit that he'd come in to eat the meat pie he'd sneakily bought while in town. He needed somewhere he wouldn't be spotted as Evie had her spies everywhere.

'Nothing important.'

'I'm about to take Seb back home to rest. We've looked at some mugshots but so far found nothing.'

'What about the CCTV footage?' he asked.

'Not much to go on there. These guys had obviously cased the street in advance and made sure to keep out of the way of the cameras.'

'Well, let me know if you want a hand. I know most of the young kids around here, especially those on drugs.'

'They weren't kids,' Clifford said, shaking his head. 'That I know for certain.'

'The offer's here if you want it,' he repeated.

'Thanks, Twig,' Birdie said. 'Come on, Seb, let's go.'

Twiggy watched as she helped the chap up from his seat and slipped her hand under his arm, guiding him out of the office. Surely he wasn't that incapacitated that he needed someone of her size to help him along.

There was something about the man that he didn't like, especially the influence he seemed to have over Birdie.

His partner.

TWENTY-SEVEN

17 May

Sarah stared at her phone for ages before finally plucking up the courage to call. She half-hoped it would go to voicemail so she could leave a message. Except after four rings it was answered.

'Hello, Auntie Charlotte, it's me, Sarah,' she said to Seb's mother. Would she hang up without talking to her?

After Seb and Birdie had left, Sarah had deliberated for ages whether to tell her aunt what had happened. She hadn't asked Seb whether his mother knew, but she was certain that he wouldn't have told her. In the past her aunt had moaned that he didn't keep the family informed of what he was doing, and it worried her because of him working for the police.

Sarah hadn't spoken to her aunt since before Donald's death, but she had to tell her about Seb. How could she not? If she was in her aunt's situation, she'd want to know.

'Sarah, good to hear from you. How are you?'

'Soldiering on, as one has to.'

'I'm sorry we couldn't come to the funeral, but with Uncle

Henry, as you would appreciate, we have to steer clear of awkward situations.'

'Yes, I understand. You weren't the only people who refused to attend. Thank you for sending Sebastian, though. He's been very supportive.'

'Is he still with you?'

'Yes, he's staying in Market Harborough.'

'Jolly good. I'm glad he's there to assist. Do you have a reason for phoning, only I'm due in a meeting shortly?'

'Um ... yes ... I do, actually.' How was she going to broach it?

'What is it?' her aunt's matter-of-fact voice echoed in her ear.

She hoped Seb wouldn't be too angry with her.

'Sebastian won't be happy with me telling you, but I felt duty-bound. There's been an incident and—'

'Incident? What sort of incident?' her aunt's worried voice interrupted.

'He's fine,' she reassured her aunt. 'But in Market Harborough on Saturday night Sebastian got attacked.'

There was a gasp on the end of the phone. 'Are you sure he's okay? Why did nobody tell me? I shouldn't learn about it several days later.'

'He visited me a short while ago and under the circumstances he's doing well. I thought to myself that if it had been one of my boys I'd have wanted to know. I know he's a lot older than them, but you never stop being a mother, do you?'

'No, you don't. Can you give me more information on what happened? I didn't even know he was still in your neck of the woods.'

She hesitated. She didn't want the family to know about the investigation, because all they wanted was for Donald's death and business practices to be forgotten.

'He was helping me with a few things. He went out with a

friend on Saturday night and as he was walking back to the
Airbnb he's renting he got attacked by two men. He was very
badly beaten up.'

'Oh, my goodness. How badly? Will he need surgery?'

'Nothing's broken apart from a couple of ribs, I understand,
but he's very bruised and swollen all over. His face especially is
a bit of a mess.'

'What's he doing now? He should come back home.'

'I think he's taking it easy and resting. It wouldn't be a good
idea for him to drive back yet.'

'Oh, this is dreadful. And you say he's staying in an Air
something. What's that?'

'It's an online place where people rent out their homes.
Sebastian is staying in a little house in the town centre.'

'But why did they attack him?'

'They took his wallet.'

'So it was a mugging?'

'Yes, I believe so.'

'But surely at his size he could have stood up for himself.'

'They caught him unawares.'

'Why doesn't he stay with you? Surely that's better than
being on his own.'

'I did offer, but he's happy where he is, and he's got his dog
with him.'

'I'll telephone him.'

'He might not be pleased that I told you but, as I said, I'd
want to know if it was me.'

'Thank you for letting me know, Sarah. I appreciate you
doing this, under the circumstances. I'll speak to him later as
soon as I come back from my meeting. I'm glad you're well, and
I'm sure we'll get together soon. We've just got to let the dust
settle for a little while longer.'

'I understand. Thanks, Auntie Charlotte.'

She ended the call but continued staring at the phone. Her aunt had seemed upset at the attack, yet she wasn't going to phone Seb straight away because she had a meeting to go to.

Sarah shook her head. Most bizarre.

TWENTY-EIGHT

17 May

Seb woke up with a start when his phone rang. He must have fallen asleep on the sofa after Birdie had dropped him off. It already was dark outside, what time was it? He picked up the phone and looked at his screen. It was his mother.

What did she want?

Had something happened to a member of the family?

They usually spoke every couple of weeks, and he'd called her the other night. Everything had been fine then.

'Hello.' He gasped as pain shot through his jaw which had locked while he'd been asleep.

'I've just heard.' The worry in his mother's voice echoed in his ear. 'Sarah called me. How are you? What on earth happened?'

He could cheerfully throttle Sarah. His mother was anxious about him at the best of times, and this would only add to it.

'It was an accident,' he said, downplaying it, not wanting her to worry further. 'Sarah shouldn't have contacted you. There was absolutely no need, as I'm perfectly fine.'

'That's not what Sarah told me. She said you were attacked, and your face is a mess. Why are you still there? Come home and let me take care of you.'

Or, supervise the staff doing the caring. His mother wasn't hands-on at all.

'Thank you for being concerned but it's not necessary, I'm not a child. What else did Sarah tell you?' He forced his voice to sound calm, despite being annoyed at Sarah's actions.

Had she told his mother about her suspicion regarding Donald's death? He hoped not, if there was going to be more scandal, he needed to break it to them gently, and also be there to help work out some strategy for dealing with it.

'To be honest, she was a little bit strange and cagey, which is most unlike her, though under the circumstances it's understandable. She told me that you were helping her with something but didn't elucidate. Why didn't you tell me you were still in Market Harborough when we spoke? I thought you were in London. Shouldn't you be at work?'

He drew in a breath. He didn't want to tell her about his job yet because she'd want to tell his father, and he needed to be more prepared for that. 'I agreed to stay a while after the funeral as a favour for Sarah. She asked me to investigate into Donald's suicide because she's convinced that it wasn't the correct verdict.'

'Is she right?'

'I don't know. Possibly. I'm working with a member of the Market Harborough CID on it.'

'How is Sarah coping, it must be very difficult for her?'

His mother and cousin had always been close and kept in regular contact, until Donald had died. Now it was difficult. But Sarah had still felt able to phone his mother and tell her about the attack.

'Not good. She's being shunned by most people and has money issues. It would be hard for the toughest of people, of which she isn't. Hardly anybody attended the funeral and that upset her greatly.'

He hadn't intended to apportion blame, but he hated seeing Sarah suffer. He also knew that given the chance, his mother would have most likely been there, except she didn't want to rock the boat with the rest of the family.

'You know what the situation is like with your father, it wasn't possible for us to attend.'

'Hence why I was instructed to represent the family as I don't have his social standing to worry about.'

Thank goodness.

'It wasn't an easy decision to make, and it pained me greatly not to be there for her.'

'In which case, maybe you can make it up to her. She's going to need support, especially now.'

'I will try my best. Why wasn't Sarah convinced by the suicide verdict?'

'Several reasons, the most worrying for her was that the note Donald left, although written in his own hand, wasn't worded in the way she'd have expected. She believed he might have been forced to write it and in there he left clues which only she would recognise.'

'Did she inform the police of this?'

'Yes, but they weren't convinced.'

'But you are?'

'Initially, no. But I'm leaning towards agreeing with her now.'

'If it isn't suicide, what happens next?'

'It would be classed as a suspicious death, most likely murder, and then needs further investigation.'

'Were you attacked because you were getting too close?'

'It's a possibility and what we're currently investigating.'

'Surely if it's murder you need to pass it over to the local police and not get involved. Although would you still be involved because you are the police?'

'Ex-police.' Damn, he hadn't intended to tell her.

Silence hung in the air, while his mother processed what he'd said.

'Does that mean you've left the police force? Why? Is it for good?' There was a lightness to her voice. Was she pleased?

He let out a sigh. 'After my unit was disbanded, all that was available for me was to return to working in uniform. I wasn't prepared to take such a step, so I resigned from the force.'

'Why didn't you tell your father and me?'

'I wanted to tell you face-to-face. Please don't mention it to Father. As soon as I'm back in London I'll make a time to visit and explain everything to you both.'

'What are your plans for the future?'

'I've yet to decide. The plan had been to use my few days here to think about my future and the direction I wanted to take. Then Sarah approached me and so I've ended up spending more time here than originally anticipated.'

'I think you should come back home and speak to your father straight away. He'll find you something on the estate. I'll worry a lot less about you now I know you're no longer in the police force. We were never happy with your choice of career, as you know. Working here is a far better option for you.'

He sighed. 'I'm sorry, Mother, but that's exactly what I don't wish to do. I had no desire to work on the estate when I left university, and nothing has changed. I will find another career in due course.'

'Not one where you get attacked and disfigured, I trust.'

He'd been hit a number of times since being in the police, especially during the short time when he was in uniform and on the beat, but she needn't know that.

'I haven't been disfigured, just badly bruised. I won't remain looking like this for long.' He moved slightly as he was getting stiff. 'Ouch.'

'What's wrong?'

'Nothing to worry about. I knocked my face with the phone. It's still very tender.'

'Sebastian, please come home now. I don't like to think of you being alone there when you're injured. I accept that you don't wish to work on the estate, but that doesn't mean you should avoid us at all costs.'

His insides clenched at the hurt in his mother's voice, but it wasn't possible for him to leave at the moment, and he wasn't ready to face his father, especially as he wasn't fighting fit.

'I can't leave here until the investigation is over. Plus, there are other things needing my attention,' he lied. It had always been the same. He much preferred to be in what he called *the real world* away from the aristocratic existence the rest of his family were a part of.

'Please be careful and don't be attacked again. I'd rather you had let me know yourself instead of having to hear about it from a third party.'

'I understand, Mother. I'll be in touch when I get back. Remember, please don't tell Father. Leave that to me.'

He ended the call and turned to Elsa.

'That was tricky. I'd like to think she'll do as I ask, but I wouldn't bet money on it. Can you imagine having to work on the estate all the time?' Elsa looked up and wagged her tail. 'You'd probably like it. Having those grounds to play around in. Come on, let's get you outside for a quick run around. Then it's time for me to go to bed, as tomorrow is going to be a big day.'

TWENTY-NINE

18 May

'Come in,' Seb said, when Birdie arrived. 'I'm almost ready.'

He was glad he'd agreed for the officer to take him. Although he was feeling much better, he didn't fancy driving to Leicester and back, even if it was only thirty minutes away. His body still ached, and he knew from experience that the broken ribs would give him hell for a while longer.

She followed him through to the kitchen and pulled out a make-up bag from her handbag, resting it on the table. 'You're going to need this,' she said, as she opened it up.

He held up two hands to block her from getting any closer, not liking where this was heading. 'If you think I'm going to wear make-up you can think again.'

'Look, I'm not going to plaster you with blue eyeshadow and red lipstick. Just some concealer over those bruises and a bit of powder. Trust me, by the time I've finished no one will be able to tell. You'll thank me when you see it.' She pulled out one of the chairs from the kitchen table and placed it in front of her, gesturing for him to sit.

He did as he was told, not having enough fight in him to refuse. He was saving his energy for the interview with Edgar. 'Okay, but if I end up looking like a painted doll then you can take it off again. I expect it to look natural.'

Please don't let him live to regret this.

'Deal,' Birdie said, pulling out what he assumed was the concealer. She removed the top and gave the tube a twist and then dabbed his face with the sponge end.

'That's enough,' he said after a few seconds and she hadn't stopped.

'Shut up,' she said, although she did stop and replace the cap.

Then with her finger she gently rubbed all the places she'd been working on.

'Ouch. Be careful,' he said when she hit a painful spot to the side of his left eye.

'You're such a baby. I've almost finished. I'm just going to add some of this amazing setting powder. Don't panic, it's perfectly natural-looking.' She took out a small black compact, and a large brush which she swished around in the powder and applied to his face.

'How do you know all this? Have you done a course?'

Birdie snorted. 'It's just make-up and it's no big deal. I learnt the same way as most other people, from reading magazines and copying.' She continued brushing his face and he bit down on his bottom lip to stop from moaning when she touched a tender area. Finally, she stepped back and scrutinised him. 'Much better. Go and take a look.'

He left the kitchen and went into the hall where there was a large mirror on the wall. He stared, turning his face from side to side so he could check from all angles. She was right, it was an improvement.

'Thank you,' he said, returning to the kitchen.

'See, I told you. You should learn to trust me.'

'I do. Sometimes.' He arched an eyebrow in her direction. 'Come on, it's time to leave.' He sorted out Elsa and they left the house.

'What's the address?' she asked, as they got into the car.

'King Street, in Leicester. Edgar's a partner at Cross, Barker and Witherspoon Accountants.'

'I know the street. He must be making a packet if he's a partner, so why is he claiming to have lost everything?'

'He has hefty outgoings. School fees, a big mortgage and fancy holidays. None of which he can now afford. That's why his kids are going to have to come out of school.'

'I'm sure they'll manage just fine having a state school education like the rest of us.' She looked at him. 'Well, most of us.'

They drove to Leicester and parked outside the Victorian three-storey terraced house where Edgar's company was situated.

Seb pulled down the visor in front of him and checked his face, wanting to reassure himself the make-up wasn't obvious. It wasn't.

'Okay, let's go inside,' he said.

'Will he see us without an appointment?'

'We'll soon find out. If he says no, we'll play the police card, assuming you've got your ID with you.'

'Of course, I always have it with me. Unless I'm going out on a real bender.' She grinned. He had no idea whether she was telling the truth or not.

They walked up the three stone steps and through the dark brown painted door into a rectangular-shaped vestibule. The reception desk was in the centre. 'I'd like to see Edgar Witherspoon. I'm Sebastian Clifford,' he said to the woman seated behind the desk.

'Is he expecting you?'

'He's not, but I'm a member of his family, if you wouldn't mind asking him if he would see me.'

She picked up the phone. 'I have Sebastian Clifford here.' She paused. 'Yes, of course.' She ended the call. 'He has fifteen minutes before his next appointment, if you'd like to go along to his office. It's down the corridor and is the first room on the right. He said to just walk in.'

'Thank you.'

They headed to his office, a square room with high ceilings and cornices, which was painted off-white. On one wall hung a painting, which Seb believed was a Turner print. Edgar was seated at his desk, but he stood as soon as they'd entered.

'Good God, man, what on earth happened to you?' He walked around to where they were standing and stood in front of Seb, shaking his head.

His shock appeared genuine. And clearly the make-up wasn't as efficient at hiding his bruises as he'd hoped. Then again, without it he'd look even worse.

'I was attacked on Saturday night.'

'Attacked. Where and by whom?'

'Market Harborough town centre, when I was walking back to the place I'm renting. I was mugged and beaten up.'

'What did they take?'

'My wallet, but it didn't have much in it. Five pounds and a credit card, which obviously has now been cancelled, so they can't use it.'

'Who'd have thought it would happen there, of all places. And you are?' he nodded at Birdie.

'This is DC Bird. 'She's assisting me looking into Donald's death.'

He scrutinised Edgar's face after announcing there was a police officer in the room, but it didn't change. Unless it didn't register. He hoped the man wasn't going to clam up, as he often did when there was more than one person talking to him.

Although being at work he might be better. He'd have to be, or how would he be able to conduct his business?

'Oh, you're still on that, are you? I'm surprised as I didn't think you'd find anything. The suicide seemed pretty clear cut to me.'

'I have a few more questions about your relationship with Donald, if you don't mind.'

'We've already discussed this, and I told you everything. Nothing has changed since then.'

'It won't take long.'

'That's good because I don't have long. Okay. Take a seat.' He gestured to the two chairs in front of his desk, and he returned to his.'

'First of all, did you tell anyone of our chat in the pub and the questions I asked you about Donald?'

'Only Celia. You didn't say not to. Shouldn't I have?' He fidgeted in his seat.

'It's not a problem. What did she say?'

'She thought Sarah was clutching at straws but did say she felt sorry for the woman. Which is an improvement on her feelings before. I'm hoping she won't mind if I contact Sarah now.'

'She must still be very angry about what happened to you?'

'Of course she is. It will take years for us to recover from the losses, if we can at all. We've sat down and made some preliminary budgets. Our top priority is keeping the house.'

'Prior to you finding out about the Ponzi scheme, would you say you had a good relationship with your brother?'

He cleared his throat. 'Obviously, because I invested money with him.'

'That doesn't necessarily compute. You might have invested with him because you thought he was good at his job and put your personal feelings aside.'

'Did you like him?' Birdie asked.

Seb nodded his approval at her getting straight to the point.

'Everyone liked him. He was outgoing, funny, popular, and a smooth talker. That's how he persuaded Sarah to go out with him. Before that she was with me.'

He exchanged a quick glance with Birdie. That was news to him. Did he still have a thing for Sarah?

'I didn't know that.'

'Not many people do. When we started dating Donald was at university. He arrived home for the summer holidays and totally won her over. I didn't have a chance ...' A pained expression crossed his face. 'That doesn't mean I'm not happy with Celia. Of course I am. When Sarah and I were together, we were young. It's all water under the bridge, now.'

Really? Did he still have feelings for Sarah?

'When Donald died, how did it affect you?' Seb asked.

'He was my brother. It was a terrible shock.'

'Was there anything going on between you, did you have a falling out before he died?'

'No more than usual ... I mean ... We were brothers and sometimes there were issues.'

'I'd like to discuss your investments with Donald. It seems perfectly understandable that you made the first investment. But why invest again if it meant using all of your money and leaving you with nothing. It doesn't make sense. You're an accountant and know better than to spread yourself so thinly.'

He slumped in his chair. 'I can't stand this any longer. It's been eating me up inside. I'll tell you because it's going to come out sooner or later, the way you're investigating.'

Seb leaned forward in his chair. Now they were getting somewhere.

'Continue.'

'There was a reason for the second investment. I made the first because I thought it was prudent and would give me a healthy return. Which it did. But the bottom dropped out of the financial market and Donald couldn't keep on top of everything.

He came to me and asked for a further investment into his scheme. I had no idea it was a Ponzi scheme. He neglected to tell me that. I said no because we couldn't afford it.' He let out a long breath.

'Then what happened?'

'He blackmailed me. Me. His own brother. Can you believe it? His own flesh and blood.'

'What did he have on you?' Birdie asked.

'He knew about the affair I'd had with my secretary a year ago and threatened to tell Celia.'

'How did he find out?'

'He saw us together in a pub and asked me. I admitted the truth, thinking I could trust him, and he promised to keep my secret. I believed him. Then the moment he needed money he made those threats. Dead or not, I'll never forgive him for that.'

'Why didn't you tell Celia yourself and then he'd have had no hold over you?' Birdie asked.

'I couldn't. It would destroy our marriage. It had happened once before, fifteen years ago. Celia found out and gave me another chance. She said if it happened again that was it. If she'd found out about this, my marriage would have been over.'

'Did you tell Celia about the new investment?' Seb asked.

'Not until after Donald had died, and we'd lost all the money. I had no choice.'

'Did you tell her about the affair then?'

'Absolutely not. It would have only added to the awful situation we're in.'

'When you invested, did you assume it was a legitimate scheme and that you'd be getting dividends on your money?' Seb said.

'Yes. And when there were none, I asked him to return the money. But he just laughed and said no.'

If he blackmailed his brother to invest, did that mean others were blackmailed?

'Do you know if Donald had engaged in blackmail before?'

'If you'd have asked me before he did it to me, I'd have said no way would he stoop that low. He did sail a bit close to the wind occasionally. But as for blackmail, no. He had some morals. Or so I thought. I believed he did it to me because I was his brother. You do things to family you wouldn't to other people.'

'Are you familiar with his friend Tony Yates?'

'I met him a few times. They went to university together. We've never socialised, but I do know him. Was he being black-mailed, too?'

'We don't know.'

He glanced at his watch. 'My next appointment is due here any minute. You're not going to say anything to my wife about the affair, are you? It only lasted a short while and the woman in question has left the company.'

'No, but it may come out if the suicide verdict is overturned and the police are officially involved. In that instance, I will be handing over all the information I have.'

'If that happens, I'm finished.' He rested his head in his hands, and they left his office.

'At last, we're finally getting somewhere,' Birdie said once they were back in the car.

'He's certainly given us more information. If he was the one to arrange for me to be attacked he must be a bloody good actor because he seemed genuinely shocked.'

'I agree. Do you think Donald was blackmailing others as well as his brother?'

'It's quite likely, that's why I want to interview Tony Yates again. His investment was not only large, but he'd never gone in with Donald before and it was also fairly close to when Edgar invested.'

'What about Andrea Wood?'

He frowned. 'You think she might have been blackmailed, too?'

'She invested a large sum of money around the same time the others did. Coincidence?'

'I agree it's worth investigating further. Let's interview Tony Yates first. He works here in the city. He's a quantity surveyor and has his own practice.'

'Another person with his own company. Then again, they're the ones who can invest large sums of money.'

'Donald's investors weren't all like that. Some, like Bert and Pearl, invested money from the sale of their houses.'

They drove to Yates's workplace and hurried to the reception.

'Sebastian Clifford to see Tony Yates. Is he around? I'm a friend of his.'

'I'm sorry, he's off today. I believe he's at home.' She covered her mouth with her hand. 'Oh. I shouldn't have said that.'

'It's okay, I won't say anything. Thank you.'

They left the building.

'Do you know where Yates lives?'

'Yes, a village called Clipston, near Market Harborough, which I'm sure you must be familiar. His address was in Donald's records.'

THIRTY

18 May

Birdie drove them into Clipston village along the windy Naseby Road until they reached the large L-shaped barn conversion, set back from the street, belonging to Tony and Pauline Yates. A separate three-car garage had been built next to it.

'Nice house. Being a quantity surveyor must be very lucrative,' she said, as she pulled into the circular drive and stopped outside the front of the house.

The door was answered by a tall, elegant woman in her fifties, with dark hair cut into a short bob with a fringe, and wearing a blue and white dress patterned with geometric shapes teamed with a pair of white trainers.

Birdie stood up tall, but the woman was still intimidating.

'Yes,' she said.

'I'm Sebastian Clifford and this is my colleague. I'm looking for Tony Yates, is he available?'

'I'm his wife, Pauline. I'll get him for you.' She disappeared for a few minutes, leaving the door open so they could peer inside. The large entrance hall had a flagstone floor and on the wall to the side hung a massive painting of the woman with, who Birdie assumed, was her husband Tony.

'Look over there,' she whispered, giving Clifford a nudge.

He turned and stared. 'Hmm,' he muttered.

'I think, *yikes* might be a better response,' she said. 'You couldn't hide your spots on a painting that large?'

'Shhh,' he said, nodding his head.

Heading towards them was the couple, with Pauline leading the way.

'What do you want?' he said, an angry expression on his face, as he glared at Seb.

'Tony,' his wife admonished. 'That's no way to speak to our visitors.'

'Sorry,' he said. 'How can I help you?'

'We have some further questions, if you don't mind?'

'What about?' his wife asked, looking at Seb and then back to her husband.

'Mr Clifford came to see me at work to ask about Donald Witherspoon's suicide.'

'Him,' she spat. 'What's this all about? Are you from the press and doing some *exposé* on him? If so, you can keep our name out of it. He's made us suffer enough. We don't wish to be ridiculed by everyone we know. We've managed to keep what he'd done quiet, so far.'

And if they were reporters, the silly woman was giving them even more to write about. Birdie could just imagine the heading.

Naïve victim of Ponzi scheme monster fails in attempt to keep hidden their downfall.

'No, we're not part of the media,' Seb reassured her. 'His wife had questions regarding the suicide verdict, and she asked us to look into it.'

'Why are you speaking to Tony? He had nothing to do with his death.'

'He was a close friend of Donald's and we thought he could give us an insight into him as a man.'

'A friend. Is that what you call the bastard? You don't steal money from a friend ...' She paused, staring at Seb's face. 'What happened to you?'

'I was mugged in Market Harborough on Saturday night.'

'Mugged, and you end up looking like that. Were they on something? I've said for a while that place is going downhill. That's why we live out here.'

'May we sit down somewhere?' Birdie asked, curious to see more of the house to find out if there were any more portraits of the pair of them.

'Yes,' Tony said. 'We'll go into the day room.'

They followed him through to the large rectangular room with beams going across the vaulted ceiling and a large open fireplace on the far wall. Birdie and Clifford sat on two tan leather easy chairs and Pauline and Tony sat next to each other on the matching sofa.

'I discovered during my investigation that Donald had been blackmailing one of his investors and I wondered if he'd approached you, Tony?' Seb asked.

Nothing like getting straight to the point. Why didn't he lead into it gradually?

'What a ridiculous thing to suggest,' Pauline said, answering for her husband. 'What could he possibly blackmail us about? We've done nothing. Tell them, Tony.'

'Pauline's right, Donald didn't try to blackmail me. The only reason I helped him out was because he was a friend in trouble and desperate for money.' He glanced at his wife; trepidation etched across his face.

Was he telling them the truth? Or was it just he was scared of admitting it in front of her?

'I wish you'd asked me first, though,' his wife said, turning to him. 'I'd have said no because it was too risky. And I would've been proved right because now he's gone, along with his business and our hundred thousand pounds. What if he'd taken our entire savings, where would that have left us? We're lucky to have the business and enough to cover our losses.'

Seb stiffened beside Birdie. She was sure Tony had given Witherspoon two hundred grand, and judging by Seb's reaction she was right.

'What else could I do, Pauline, he was my oldest friend?'

'A fair-weather friend, if you ask me. He rarely came to see you and when we went out with him and his wife, it was all *him him him.* He wasn't interested in anything you were doing. Do you remember the time we had a problem with some shares we bought? We went to him and he said he couldn't help us, even though he had all the right contacts. *Wouldn't help,* more like.'

'He had his reasons.'

'Hmmph.' She folded her arms tightly across her chest.

'He came to me and I was in the position of being able to help, but there's no point in rehashing it now. It's over.' He turned from his wife to address Seb. 'If you've come across a case of blackmail why are you still investigating? Shouldn't you be going to the police?'

'Actually, I am the police,' Birdie said.

His eyes widened. 'So, now it's a police matter. Does that mean you definitely think it wasn't suicide?' he asked her.

'That's not what I said. I'm here to help Seb with the investigation and now we've uncovered one case of blackmail we need to find out if it was a one-off or something Donald Witherspoon regularly engaged in, before we make any decisions regarding the verdict,' Birdie said.

'I can't help you ...' He started coughing. 'Could you get me a glass of water, Pauline? I've got a tickle.' He continued coughing, unable to talk.

'I'll be back in a minute,' she said, jumping up from the sofa and hurrying out of the door.

Once she'd left the room, his coughing subsided. 'I don't want you talking about these things in front of my wife, she's upset enough as it is about the money we've lost. Not to mention, as I'm sure you've worked out, she doesn't know how much I lent Donald.'

'I sense there's something else you'd like to tell me,' Seb said, leaning forward in his chair.

Was he being blackmailed, too?

'There is, but not here. Meet me later at the Fox and Hounds in Great Bowden. Come alone, I don't want the police involved.'

'I'm not here in my capacity as an officer, as I've already told you,' Birdie said.

'I don't care. If you want to know more, make it just you,' he said, staring directly at Seb.

'That's fine,' Seb said, nodding. 'What time shall we meet?'

Yates looked at his watch. 'Give me an hour. I'll make up an excuse to go out. But—' He clamped his mouth shut as there were footsteps on the floor outside the room.

'Here's your water,' Pauline said, walking in.

'Thanks,' he said, taking a sip from the glass she'd handed him.

'We'll be going,' Seb said, standing.

Birdie did the same.

'I'm sorry we can't help you further,' Tony said. 'Donald was a good friend, and I helped him out because he was desperate. I'm sorry to learn about the blackmail, but there was nothing like that between us.'

'Thank you for your time and assistance, we appreciate it,' Seb said.

'I'll see you out,' Pauline said.

They followed her to the door and left.

'Very interesting,' Birdie said once they were back in the car and driving down the road. 'I bet he was being blackmailed and his wife doesn't know. And, by the way, he was scared of her. It was written in his eyes.'

'That makes two of them,' Seb said.

Birdie frowned. 'Two of who?'

'Edgar and Tony are both wary of their wives.'

'Do you think it's connected? Did Donald blackmail them because he saw them both as soft targets?'

'Maybe. I'll know more once I've met with Tony.'

'I'm not happy with you going alone. What if he's the one who arranged for you to be attacked and knowing I won't be with you he sends someone along to finish you off?' She shuddered at the thought.

'That makes no sense, because not only does he know that you're aware of the meeting, but he knows your occupation. I don't believe it's going to be a dangerous situation. I'll be perfectly safe.'

'Says the man with a smashed in face. Do you think he could've sent those guys to beat you up? Because I do.'

He gave a sigh. 'I don't know. Anything is possible, but the fact that he wants to meet in a pub fairly close to where he lives doesn't seem like someone wanting to silence me. Plus, if he'd have wanted to do that, he'd need to silence you as well, yet he didn't want you there. I genuinely don't believe he's out to get me.'

'Even so, it would be good to have me close by. What if I stay in the car and wait for you outside? If you're not out by a certain time, or you don't send a text letting me know you're okay, I'll come in looking for you.'

'I'm perfectly capable of going to meet him alone. I'm feeling a lot better.'

'That's not what I mean. This is just a precaution. Anyway, how can you go on your own if you can't yet drive?'

'I'm sure driving won't be an issue now. We'll go back to Heygate Street, so you can collect your car, and then I'll drive to Great Bowden to meet Tony.'

'Only if you're a hundred per cent sure because I really don't mind waiting in the car while you meet him.' It was his decision, but she really wished he'd change his mind.

'Don't you have work to do?'

'Yes. I suppose I should go in, or Sarge will start breathing down my neck again. Although as far as he's concerned, I'm still investigating the mugging. Which reminds me, I still haven't done your official statement yet. We must do it soon, in case he asks to see it.'

'Tomorrow. Definitely.'

She drove them back to Market Harborough and pulled into a parking space outside the front of the house he was staying at.

'Before I leave, I'll come in to say hello to Elsa,' she said following him to the front door.

'She'll be happy to see you.'

Seb unlocked the door and they headed towards the kitchen where they were greeted by a very excited Elsa.

'Hello, girl,' she said, rubbing behind the ears, the spot which she knew the dog loved. Elsa pressed into her legs and stared up at her, her brown eyes excited and happy.

'She's such a poppet. I'll look after her any time you need someone,' she said to Seb, who'd gone back into the hall and was staring at his face in the mirror. 'Would you like me to top up your make-up?'

'No thanks.'

'Phone me as soon as you're back here and fill me in on what Yates tells you. Remember, if there's any sign of trouble call me. We can have a word or sentence, that tells me you're in trouble.'

'What do you suggest?'

'I don't know.'

'How about *make sure you're early*.' He arched an eyebrow, and stared at her, his eyes twinkling with amusement.

'You're so funny. But if that's what you want to use then those words it is.'

THIRTY-ONE

18 May

Seb arrived at the Fox and Hounds ten minutes before he was due for his meeting with Tony Yates. The pub wasn't busy. An elderly man was sitting on a bar stool talking to the bartender and a young couple sat close to the door. He scanned the room and noticed Yates had already arrived and was sitting at a table close to the fireplace. Seb ordered himself a half pint of beer and wandered over.

Yates was sitting ramrod straight with his arms resting on the table, his fists clenched. What appeared to be a whisky with ice was on the table in front of him.

'I'm not happy about this,' Yates said, not even giving a greeting.

'I realise that, and I'm sorry to be dragging everything up again, but it's done out of necessity. I take it there are things you've been keeping from your wife.' He got straight to the point, there was no need for niceties.

He nodded. 'I don't want what we discuss getting back to her. Everything I'm about to tell you is off the record.'

'I will endeavour to keep our conversation confidential but, as you know, we're investigating Donald's suicide and if it transpires that the verdict was incorrect, then I'll be discussing with the police all the evidence I have relating to him. Do you understand?' He waited for Yates's acknowledgement before continuing, but the man was silent. 'Tony?'

The man thumped the table, and his drink shook. 'Yes, I understand. Not that I have a choice. You know too much already. Just ask your questions and let's get this over and done with.'

'As I mentioned earlier, Donald had been blackmailing another person, and I suspect he might have been blackmailing you, too, otherwise you wouldn't have asked to meet me. Am I correct?'

Yates picked up his whisky and downed it in one, the ice cubes rattling in the empty glass when he banged it down on the table. 'What do you think?' His eyes were glassy.

'You know my answer to that,' Seb said, keeping his tone calm.

'Yes, Donald did blackmail me into investing with him. Okay. Now you know.' He bowed his head and sighed.

'Why don't you tell me exactly what happened?'

Yates picked up his glass and stared inside, twirling the ice cubes.

'Would you like another?' Seb offered.

'As much as I'd dearly love to say yes, I'll have to refuse. I'm driving and already had one before you arrived.'

At least he was being responsible.

'Please continue.'

'Donald came to me desperate for money and while we were talking, he suggested that I should invest with him, to give him a helping hand. I refused, saying I hadn't got any spare cash. Then he told me I should borrow it. He wanted two hundred grand. I laughed, thinking he was joking. I mean, who has that sort of money hanging around?'

'Then what happened?'

'He repeated his request, only this time there was an edge to his voice. It was then that I realised he meant it. I was stunned. When I told him no, he said refusing wasn't an option.' He paused, a faraway expression in his eyes.

'And then?' Seb pushed.

'I asked him what he meant, and he said if I didn't comply, he'd make sure everyone knew. It was then that I understood exactly what he meant. He was blackmailing me.'

'What did he have on you?'

Yates leant back in his chair, breathing in and out several times, seeming to be plucking up the courage to admit to what he'd done.

'It was something that happened when we were at university over thirty years ago.'

It must have been bad if the man had been carrying it with him for that long. He waited a few seconds for him to continue, but he'd clammed up.

'Had Donald ever tried to blackmail you over this issue before then?' Seb asked, leading him.

'No, never. We made a pact to never bring it up again, and we both stuck to it. It's what bound us together. We might not have remained friends if it hadn't been for this. In fact, I'm sure of it.'

'Can you tell me what it is?' Seb asked, encouraging him to continue.

Yates nodded. 'When I was at university, I used to drink quite heavily. We all did. We were binge drinkers, as it's called nowadays. My parents had given me a car and I would often drive us when we went out, not caring if I was over the limit which I often was. In fact, most weekends I wouldn't have passed a breath test. One time I got done for drinking under the influence and lost my licence for twelve months.' Yates ran his finger around the top of his empty glass. 'Look, I'm not proud of this, but ... even though I'd lost my licence I still drove. I know it's bad and I regret it. It's not something I'd ever contemplate doing now.'

'You were young and didn't think through the consequences of your actions. We all did things at that age that we later regretted. Is that what Donald blackmailed you over?'

Seb sucked in a breath. Extracting the information was proving much harder than he'd thought it was going to be. He was having to go through it one piece at a time.

Yates shook his head. 'If only. It's much worse than that. Much, much, worse. We were out one night, just me and Donald, and had both been drinking. I was tipsy, not totally out of it, but had drunk enough not to be fully in control. We were on our way home from the pub when I hit something. Initially, we thought it was a cat, so I stopped the car further up the road and we went back to look.' Tears formed in his eyes, and he blinked them away. 'It wasn't an animal at all. It was a person. A young woman. She was still alive. We could hear her moaning. It was dark, though, as it was a country road with no lighting, and she couldn't see us.' Yates leant forward and rested his head in his hand. 'I panicked. I'd just hit a person and could've killed her. I was way over the limit and couldn't afford to be caught because I'd go to prison. Drunk, knocking someone over, and driving without a licence. They'd throw the book at me. We ran back to the car and drove off, stopping at a phone box a mile down the road and phoning for an ambulance.'

Nausea pooled in the pit of Seb's stomach. How on earth did the man manage to live with himself after doing that?

'Do you know what happened to the woman you hit?' he asked, forcing his voice to sound calm and non-judgemental.

'Yes. She was a student, and news of what had happened to her was all over campus. She ended up in a wheelchair and came back to uni the following year to continue with her degree.'

'You should have gone to the police,' Seb said, his voice flat.

'It's easy for me to admit that now, as a responsible adult, but I didn't and although they interviewed lots of students at the time, they didn't ever question me or Donald.'

'There was hardly any CCTV back then, or smartphones which could be tracked. You wouldn't have got away with it now. You were lucky,' Seb said.

'If you can call it that. I've lived with what I'd done my entire life. I can still hear her moaning in pain as if it happened yesterday.' He gave an empty laugh. 'It's actually cathartic to tell somebody about it now. I ruined that poor girl's life and I'll never forget it. But at the time, I was young and all I could think of was what would happen to me. What my parents would say if I ended up in prison. How my life would be over. At the time, it seemed like I had no choice.'

'This type of crime might well have been tried in a magistrates' court, and not the Crown Court, which means the statute of limitations on the crime would most likely have expired and Donald couldn't have done anything to you, if he tried.'

Yates's eyes widened. 'But even if I couldn't be prosecuted, just bringing it out into the open would have damaged my work. I'd have lost clients. My marriage might have ended. My kids would never have spoken to me again. Everything I'd worked for over the years would have been destroyed. I had to do as Donald asked and lend him the money, but you've got to believe me, I had nothing to do with his death. I promise you.'

Seb was inclined to believe him. It would have been hard to fake the reactions he was having.

'After you paid Donald this first amount, did he come to you for more?'

'No. He knew it would have been impossible for me to get it. He realised I couldn't just give him a never-ending supply of money as it had to come from somewhere, and I wouldn't have been able to get another loan from the bank for that amount. My business is doing well, but not that well. I assume that's why he started blackmailing other people. I asked when I'd receive dividend payments on the money I'd invested, and he made up some excuses as to why I wasn't going to get any. I didn't bother to pursue it. There was no point.'

The man had visibly relaxed in his chair. He'd been holding this inside for decades, and now it was out. But Seb couldn't feel sorry for him. What had happened was inexcusable at whatever age the man had been.

'Did you discuss why he used the money to invest, giving you documentation and dividends, rather than just taking it for himself?'

'Oh, yes. Donald was very clever about it. He said that by doing it that way it meant he could claim it was a legitimate investment, should I threaten to go to the police about him. Then it would have been his word against mine.'

'Although if you had reported him, the police might have looked closely at Donald's business and the whole Ponzi scheme would have been discovered sooner rather than after his death.'

'I wasn't to know that. Donald must have done it as a scare tactic. And it worked.' He hung his head.

'Why did you tell Pauline that you only gave Donald a hundred thousand pounds?'

'I hadn't planned on telling her at all, and it was only after his death that I admitted it, in case it came out that we were creditors. Telling her I'd lent him a hundred grand was bad enough. If I'd told her the truth, she'd have made my life hell. It was bad enough anyway.'

'Couldn't she find out from the bank statements how much you were paying back to the bank each month and put two and two together?'

'I made sure she didn't see the loan documents.'

'Did she ask what Donald wanted the money for? Did she think that you were part of the Ponzi scheme he was operating?'

'I told her I knew nothing of his illegal activities, and I was helping him out because he was desperate. She believed me, even though she was angry about it.'

'Did she ask where you got the money from to lend him?'

'I told her I'd taken out a loan, but said I'd offset it against taxes for the company, so it wouldn't cost us much.'

The whole thing was complicated and didn't quite ring true. But Seb couldn't put his finger on it.

'Didn't your accountant have something to say about the loan you took out?'

'No, because he didn't know.'

'How can you take out a business loan without him knowing?'

'It was a personal loan.'

'But you said it was a business loan.'

'That's what I told Pauline.'

'In case she saw the business bank statements. But they would be on personal bank statements, not business ones.'

'I opened a separate bank account which she knows nothing about, and I get online statements only, so she won't get to find out.'

Talk about burying his head in the sand. Was he being deliberately obtuse, or did he genuinely believe that it would all remain hidden?

'Tony, you need to think this through carefully. There's a possibility that everything that happened between you and Donald will come out in the not-too-distant future. I advise you to speak to Pauline and tell her about the blackmail and the reason for it. At least then she'd be forewarned of any bad publicity and will be able to come to terms with the situation.'

'It's easy for you to say, you don't live with the woman. I'd much prefer to say nothing. It's not like I had anything to do with Donald's death.'

'That will be for the police to decide, if it turns out they become involved.'

'What are you going to do now?' He stared anxiously at Seb.

'I'll go back and discuss it with my colleague, and it will inform the rest of our investigation.'

'But she's a police officer. Even if she is helping you on the side, it doesn't mean that she won't go back to her superiors and report what I've done.'

'I've already told you the statute of limitations would most likely have passed. Our interest is in learning what, if anything, happened to Donald.'

'I promise you, I had nothing to do with his death.'

'It's up to you whether you discuss it with Pauline, you know what I'll be doing with the information you've given me.'

Tony slumped in his chair, and a twinge of pity coursed through Seb's veins. Until he remembered what the man had done.

THIRTY-TWO

18 May

Seb left the pub and returned to his car, immediately phoning Birdie because he knew she'd be anxious to find out what Yates had told him.

'Well?' she said the moment she answered.

'I've just come from my meeting with Tony Yates. He opened up and told me everything. He, too, was being black-mailed by Donald, as we suspected.'

'So, if he's blackmailed two people there's every chance that he's blackmailed more. I think that now confirms his death was suspicious. He's blackmailed someone who wanted to get their own back. But was it Edgar or Yates? Or someone else?'

'In theory, perhaps. But the nagging question is, why was he murdered so long after the blackmail? Also, if they wanted their money back, then murdering Donald wouldn't help them. The money they gave him was treated like an investment with all the paperwork and promised dividends.'

'Why did he do that?'

'According to Yates, as a precaution in case he decided to

go to the police, so it didn't appear to be blackmail. Also, it then would seem legitimate to his accountant and the tax man.'

'Maybe Witherspoon went back to someone demanding more money and it was the last straw, so instead they killed him.'

'Neither Edgar nor Tony had the funds to pay him any more money, and Donald was fully aware of that. According to Yates, Donald didn't ask for more.'

'He would say that if he killed Donald.'

'True. That's assuming Donald was murdered. We still don't have any concrete evidence.'

'Why do you keep saying that? We have the suicide note, which Sarah claims is suspect. We also have your attack, and the fact he was blackmailing at least two people, to our knowledge. That, to me, is evidence enough.'

Why was he resisting going with the obvious? Was it because of Sarah? How would she cope with being, yet again, the centre of what would inevitably be a barrage of media interest? The family would continue to desert her, and the boys would find being at university a nightmare.

'I want to be sure before doing anything rash.'

'What about Andrea Wood? Do you think she might have been blackmailed, too? She's another who made a large investment at the time when Donald was struggling. And if he was blackmailing her, he could have demanded more money, and she had him killed. Or killed him herself. And ...' She paused. 'You didn't get attacked until after you'd spoken to her, remember?'

Birdie had a point.

'We shouldn't discount Yates, Edgar, or the Blacks either. They were all interviewed before I was beaten up. But one thing to consider is we know that the person with Donald on the day of his death was male.'

'We need to pass this over to CID. We've gone far enough with it,' Birdie said.

'Not yet. I want to wait until we're sure.'

'Really? Aren't you keen to get away from here and back to the bright lights of London?'

He hadn't even thought about it.

'Where did you get that idea from?'

'I don't know. I just assumed. I'm more than happy for CID to take this over, especially if the sarge lets me in on the case.'

'And what's the likelihood of that if he believes you've been working on something you shouldn't? It wouldn't be beyond the realm of possibility that he'll exclude you.'

Was that what he truly thought, or did he say it so she'd agree to continuing with their investigation?

'Crap. I hadn't thought of that. Why are you right all the time? Did Yates say what he was being blackmailed over?'

'He asked me not to tell you because you're a police officer.'

'And you're going to let him dictate what you do, are you? Because if you do—'

'I was telling you what he'd said,' he said laughing out loud. Birdie was very easy to wind up.

'Ha. Ha. Very funny. Now tell me,' she demanded.

'One night when they were at university, Yates and Donald were out together drinking. Yates was driving even though he'd been banned following a drink-driving charge. He was involved in a hit-and-run incident, leaving the victim in a wheelchair. He didn't get caught, and only the two of them knew about it. They swore themselves to secrecy.'

'What a bastard. I could tell he wasn't a nice person,' Birdie snapped.

'You've got to remember he was a kid when it happened, and it's haunted him ever since.'

Why was he sticking up for chap when he thought the same as she did?

'Sorry, but he wasn't much younger than I am now, so that's no excuse. I don't dispute that he felt guilty about it. But not guilty enough to make amends and admit to what he'd done. So, it sounds like Donald had him over a barrel. He got money out of him once and wanted more.'

'Except, as I've already said, Yates said not. He had to take out a bank loan to cover the first amount, he had no way of accessing more money, and Donald was fully aware of this.'

'He would say that. And if it was Yates, he must have arranged for someone to beat you up. What now?'

'I want to pay another visit to Andrea Wood and question her about being blackmailed.'

'Would someone famous like her admit it, even if she was? Not to mention, will she even see us again, considering you had to ask Rob to arrange our first meeting?'

'Not us, this time. Just me. I'll take the train to London tomorrow and wait for her outside the studio at the time we know she usually leaves. I don't want to go inside as it's too public. This is the best way, as we don't even know if she'd agree to another meeting, especially if she's the one involved. It's more low-key if I go alone. And if I don't see her at the studio, I can go to her London flat and wait there.'

'How do you know where she lives?'

'Donald's records. He had the addresses of both of her residences listed.'

'What if she refuses to speak to you?'

'Then that might be the time to officially involve the police. At the moment, I'm going to make it informal. A further chat on the QT and we'll take it from there. Low-key for now is the best option.'

'I'm not happy about this. If she's the one who murdered Donald, then she could come after you, especially once she finds out you know about the blackmail.'

'I'm not going to put myself in a compromising situation. I

know what to look for. Nothing's going to happen to me, I promise.'

'So you say, and I hope you're right, but I don't like it when I'm not with you, because that's when you end up in trouble.'

He laughed to himself. He was twice her size, yet she thought she could protect him.

'Honestly, Birdie, I'll be fine.'

'Keep in touch and let me know what's happening. What about Elsa, do you need me to check on her?'

'She'll be okay. I'll only be gone a few hours, but thanks for offering. You go to work and let Sergeant Weston see how committed you're being. That way when the case gets passed over to them, he'll consider letting you work on it.' His phoned pinged, letting him know Sarah was calling. 'I've got another call, I'll speak to you soon.'

'Okay, be careful.'

'Hello, Sarah,' he said after ending the call with Birdie.

'I called to tell you that I have Donald's phone.'

'Where was it?'

'The people who bought the car found it hidden under the passenger seat and they returned it to the auction rooms who then gave it to the man who does my lawns and he's just given it to me. I've no idea how it got under there, even if it did fall out of his pocket.'

Was it Donald leaving another clue?

'I'm on my way back from Great Bowden. I'll be with you shortly.'

He took the quickest route, and was there in less than fifteen minutes. As he pulled up the door opened and Sarah stood waiting for him.

'You're looking better than the last time I saw you,' she said, staring at his face.

'I'm feeling better, thanks. I had a call from my mother.'

Sarah's cheeks turned pink. 'I had to phone her. All I could think of was how I'd feel if it was one of the boys. I'd want to know. Sorry if it caused you any problems.'

'None I couldn't deal with. I can't be too long as Elsa's been on her own for a while now, so if you could fetch the phone for me.'

'Come in, it's in the kitchen.'

He followed her and on the table was a phone. She passed it to him.

'Do you know his passcode, by any chance? It wasn't in his password notebook or I'd have seen it.'

Sarah shook her head. 'I've no idea. You could try his birthday, it's the tenth of November.'

Seb keyed in 1011 but it didn't open. 'That's not it.'

'Try my birthday the twenty-fifth of July.'

He tried 2507 but still nothing. 'No, it's not that either. I'll take the phone and see if Birdie knows anyone who can get it unlocked. There might not be anything of use on here, but it's still worth checking. I'll be in touch soon.'

He left the house and on his way back to Market Harborough he called Birdie.

'You've changed your mind and want me with you tomorrow,' she said by way of any answer.

'Nice try but I'm still going alone.' He laughed. 'I called into Sarah's on the way back because she has Donald's phone. The people who bought his car from the auction found it hidden under the passenger seat and managed to get it returned to her.'

'What was it doing there ... unless ...'

'My sentiments exactly,' he said pre-empting her response. 'If we say, for argument's sake, that we believe Donald was murdered, then by hiding the phone it would be yet another clue he was leaving.'

'Is there anything on there we can use?'

'That's the issue. I can't get into it. Sarah doesn't know the code and it isn't in the book Donald kept of all the passwords. I was hoping you might have a self-service kiosk at the station and you could open it for us.'

'You've got to be kidding. This is Market Harborough CID we're talking about. We don't have such luxuries. But … there's a guy in forensics who owes me one … don't ask why because I won't tell you.'

'Excellent. Meet me at my place in fifteen minutes and I'll give it to you.'

THIRTY-THREE

19 May

Seb bought a coffee to go from the café close to the TV studio and positioned himself against some railings so he could see the entrance. Several people who walked past him stared at his face. He wished he'd asked Birdie to put some make-up on him again, but he hadn't thought of it. Nor had she, or she'd have said. She'd already texted four times wanting to know where he was and whether he'd seen Andrea Wood yet. She also told him that the guy she knew in forensics had agreed to unlock the phone, but she wasn't sure how long it would take.

He waited for over half an hour and was about to give up, thinking Andrea had left early or out of another entrance, when he caught sight of her coming out of the double doors.

She was alone.

Perfect.

He walked purposely in her direction. She was wearing a cream shirt and dark blue trousers, with a long gold necklace, and was fully made-up.

'Andrea?' he called as he got close.

She stared at him, narrowing her eyes slightly. 'I know you. We met the other day, didn't we, in my dressing room?'

'Yes, that's correct I'm Sebastian Clifford.'

Her eyes travelled from his feet to his face. 'How could I forget someone of your size? What have you done to your face? It looks dreadful.' She grimaced.

'I was mugged several nights ago.'

He scrutinised her facial features for any telltale signs of already knowing what had happened but it was difficult to gauge.

'Oh dear, how awful. Did they catch the person who did it?' She rested her hand on his arm.

'I was attacked by two men and, no, they haven't been apprehended yet. But I'm sure it's only a matter of time before the police find them, they have some strong leads.'

Again, he looked to see if his words made any impression on her, but they didn't appear to.

'I hope so. They shouldn't get away with it. Is there a reason for you being here, or just a lucky coincidence?' She gently squeezed his arm.

'I'd like another word with you about Donald Witherspoon.'

She bit down on her bottom lip and withdrew her arm, taking a step backwards. 'I have nothing else to add to what I've already told you.' Her body tensed, and she glanced anxiously from side to side.

'My investigation has progressed since we last spoke and I'd now like to talk to you about something we've discovered regarding Donald.' He paused. 'He blackmailed several people, and we believe you might have been one of them.'

Colour drained from her face, and she blinked furiously. 'I'm not prepared to talk about it here in the street,' she said, her voice barely above a whisper.

'Where can we talk?'

'My driver, Aaron, has gone to fetch the car. You can travel with me and we'll talk on the way. Then—'

'Andrea, Andrea. I'm such a fan,' a middle-aged woman said as she ran up to them waving her phone in the air. 'I record your show every day and watch it when I get home. I'd love a selfie to show my daughter that I've met you. She'll be so jealous.'

'Of course,' Andrea said, smiling, but it didn't reach her eyes, which remained troubled.

'I'll take the photo for you,' Seb said, holding out his hand.

'Thanks. Are you famous, too?' the fan asked as she gave him her phone.

'No, I'm not.' He stifled a chuckle.

He took a couple of photos and returned the phone to the woman. 'Thank you so much, Andrea. I knew today was going to be good, it said so in my stars.' She left them, and as she headed down the street, she kept turning back to wave.

'It must be extremely frustrating if this happens all the time,' he said, once the fan had done her final wave and was now out of sight.

'I don't mind,' she said, giving a small shrug. 'Most fans are very nice, like she was, and don't outstay their welcome. But it can get frustrating, like when they follow you into the ladies' loo and want a photo when you're desperate for a pee.'

'Seriously, people do that?'

'I wish I could say it's a rare occurrence, but it isn't. There's no such thing as privacy when you're on the telly. You become the property of the public. I'm used to it now. Mostly.'

'How long is your driver going to be?' Seb looked up and down the road, unsure the direction he'd be coming. Or the car he'd be driving.

'I'm not sure where he parked. When we arrived this morning, there were no spaces in the studio car park, so he dropped me off outside.'

'Don't you have your own space?' Surely a star like her wouldn't have to chance her luck when parking.

'You'd think I should, but only the top management are so lucky. I'm a self-employed presenter and don't count. He shouldn't be too much longer.' She tapped a foot impatiently on the ground. 'He's taking me back to my flat as I need to get some sleep. I'm usually in bed by seven-thirty because I have to get up at two-thirty in the morning, but last night for some reason I couldn't sleep and now I'm exhausted. And there's only so much the make-up artist can do.' She stared up the road. 'Ah, here he comes.'

Was this nervous chatter, or what?

A black Mercedes E-Class Saloon drew up beside them and the driver jumped out to open the back door. Andrea got in first and moved along to make space for Seb.

'Thank you,' he said as the driver closed the door behind him.

'Mr Clifford is coming with us, Aaron,' she said to the driver who nodded.

'Where do you live?' Seb asked, wanting to make sure it was the address he'd seen in Donald's records, and he wasn't being taken somewhere else.

'In Battersea, close to the docks.'

Yes, that was the same.

'It's a nice area.'

'If we don't finish talking in the car, maybe you'd like to come inside, and we can finish up there.' She placed a hand on his knee and squeezed.

Was she coming onto him? He glanced at her and she smiled. What was going on? Only a few moments ago she was shocked and panicked about him wanting to discuss Donald and blackmail.

Her driver pulled out into the heavy traffic and headed south.

He gently removed her hand from his leg and placed it on her lap. 'As I said, we've found out that Donald was blackmailing some of his clients, in particular those who made a large investment recently. Were you one of them?'

Andrea nodded slightly at the driver whose head was tilted as if he was listening to their conversation. 'I don't think this is the right time and place to discuss that,' she said quietly. 'Wait until we get back to my place.'

Seb glanced again at the driver and caught his eye, as he was staring back at him through the rear-view mirror. His eyes were narrowed, and he looked away. Seb continued staring at him and then he glanced down at the steering wheel. The driver was gripping it so tightly his knuckles were white.

Seb did a double take.

On the man's hand was a tattoo of an eagle.

The same eagle that was tattooed on the hand on his attacker.

Fuck. Was this a trap?

Was Andrea in on it?

She had to be.

How could he have been so stupid as to get in the car with the pair of them? He could just imagine what Birdie would say when she found out.

He averted his gaze from the driver to Andrea, not wanting him to suspect that he'd recognised him. She stared back at him with a smile on her face. But what sort of smile? Sly? Complacent? Knowing? Machiavellian? It could be any of these.

He had to get out of the car. And fast. Without letting them know he'd sussed them.

They were coming up to some traffic lights. He had a plan. If they stayed red until the car reached them, he could use it to his advantage. He sucked in a breath as they approached, bracing himself to jump out of the car, but they turned green and the driver continued driving.

Damn.

There had to be more lights coming up, London was littered with them. He'd be more prepared the next time.

'Tell me about today's show,' he said, deciding the best course of action was to take Andrea's mind off the blackmail and act as if he was talking normally, while he edged slightly over to the door, and positioned his arm so his fingers were close to the handle. It helped that he was so large because it made it more difficult for her, or the driver, to see what he was doing, as he already filled the space.

'We had Hugh Jackman on via satellite to talk about his new film, and Graham Norton came in to talk about his latest book. Have you read it? I loved it.'

'No, I haven't, but I've heard he's an excellent writer. I'll look out for it the next time I'm in the bookshop.'

'And, of course, we had our usual cookery spot,' she continued, seeming happy to discuss it. 'Today they made a vegan chocolate mousse. I could've eaten the lot, it was so delicious, though jam-packed with calories. Then Sam Smith came in and sang his latest. I do love his voice, it's so haunting.'

'Do you always enjoy the show this much?'

'Most days, especially when we have guests like today. Sometimes it gets a bit repetitive, but the pay's good and I enjoy the perks, of which there are many.' She paused and pulled a face. 'Please don't mention that to anyone, it wouldn't look good for my image.'

'My lips are sealed. We can't be expected to enjoy our work all of the time.'

Through the front window he could see that they were approaching another set of lights and they were red.

'I knew you'd understand,' she said, smiling at him. It was weird that now she was acting as if he hadn't even mentioned the blackmail. Why? Part of her plan to disarm him? Too late, as he already knew what was going on.

But he had to be careful how he played this. He couldn't just jump out when the traffic lights had just turned to red in case the driver was able to get out and stop him. Or he might turn on the child lock. Whenever Seb decided to make a run for it, it had to be done quickly and take both the driver and Andrea by surprise.

He'd wait for that split second when he thought the lights would go from green to red. He'd watch the lights for cars crossing in front of them, and wait for those cars to stop which would give him a couple of seconds to make his move.

The cars coming across them came to a halt, and he made a show of looking at his watch.

'Crap. I'm meant to be somewhere. Got to go.' He opened the door and jumped out just as the lights went to green and the driver drove forward.

'What?' he heard Andrea say.

He tried to land on his feet, but his legs gave way from under him, and he fell forward, doing a roll on the pavement. He grimaced as every movement sent pain rocketing through his already battered body. But he couldn't dwell on it. He needed to get moving and with great determination he pulled himself up and took off down the street, in the opposite direction from where the car was heading, to give him as much time as possible before they could turn around and come after him. *If* Andrea was in on it as she wouldn't want him getting away.

He half-ran, half-jogged down the street, looking for somewhere safe to stop, so he could call Rob and ask him to get in touch with his contact at the TV studio to find out what he could about Andrea's driver.

THIRTY-FOUR

19 May

Seb stopped at the entrance to a Tube station and dragged in some raspy breaths. There wasn't a part of him which didn't hurt. He wasn't unfit, but having to run after rolling out of the car, on top of his other injuries, was pushing him to the limit. But he'd had no choice other than to escape from the car. If Andrea Wood and her driver were in it together, his life could've been in danger.

He pulled out his phone from his pocket and gave Rob a call.

'Clifford, what the hell are you doing phoning again? You disappear without a trace for ages and then, all of a sudden, I'm being inundated with calls,' Rob said, giving a deep belly laugh.

'I urgently need your help.'

'What is it?' Rob's voice immediately became serious.

'The investigation I'm undertaking, the one I told you about concerning Donald Witherspoon, has turned nasty and I thought you could help me. I need to know the full name and address of Andrea Wood's driver. He also does other work for

her, security, I think. All I know is his first name is Aaron, and
he's around six foot tall, well built, shaved head, with a tattoo of
a bird on his left hand.'

'What do you mean by turned nasty?'

'Briefly, I got badly beaten up on Saturday night in Market
Harborough, and I believe that one of my attackers was her
driver. I only just discovered it was him when I was in Andrea's
car a moment ago and saw his hand, showing the tattoo, on the
steering wheel.'

'What were you doing in her car?'

'I'd waited outside the studio for her, so I could ask more
questions about Witherspoon, because we suspect he might
have been blackmailing her. She'd only talk to me in her car.
What I don't know is whether her intention had been to get me
in the car so she could get rid of me, or whether or it was
genuine that she wanted to talk. As soon as I spotted the driver
was my attacker, I jumped out at some traffic lights and made a
run for it.'

'What the fuck, Clifford? Why are you still handling this?
Turn it over to the police, for God's sake, before it anything else
happens to you. You should know better.'

He was right but Seb still wanted to make absolutely sure
the evidence stacked up before he gave up the case. It was now
a matter of principle.

'I will do, but first I want to find out who he is and where he
lives. Will you do that for me?'

'I suppose so. But I'm not happy about it.'

'Noted. Your help is appreciated.'

'Leave it with me and I'll get back to you as soon as I can.
Don't hold your breath, though. I might not be able to get
anything.'

Seb ended the call and headed down the street in search of
a café so he could wait for Rob to get back to him. He stopped at
the first one he came to and ordered a triple shot espresso. He

sat at the back facing the door so he could see who was coming in and out, as he wasn't going to take any further risks. Though he doubted they'd find him.

He took out his phone and called Birdie.

'DC Bird,' she answered, sounding very formal.

'It's me.'

'I know. I'm at work, so this conversation might be a little bit one-sided if anyone gets too close to me and can overhear. How did the meeting with Andrea go?'

He'd have to play it down, or she'd start getting onto him and her colleagues would soon realise that she wasn't on normal police business.

'First of all, you're not to react to what I'm going to tell you. However much you want to shout and scream in my ear, unless you don't mind everyone in the office realising that there's something wrong.'

'What?' she hissed.

'I wanted to warn you, so you weren't taken by surprise.'

'For fuck's sake just tell me.'

Clearly his plan to calm her first wasn't working.

'Okay. One of the men who beat me up was Andrea Wood's driver, Aaron, I saw his tattoo. Do you remember him, he stood by the window staring at us when we interviewed her, until she sent him away.'

She gasped. 'Him? How do you know?'

'I was in her car and spotted the tattoo on his hand. He saw me looking, but I'm not sure if he realised I'd identified him. I couldn't take the risk so I jumped out of the car at some traffic lights.'

'*Jumped?* What the hell were you thinking? Did you hurt yourself?'

'It was a tricky move because I waited until a moment before the lights turned to green. I didn't quite land right and ended up rolling a bit.'

'Bloody hell, Seb. Are you okay?'

'A few more bruises, that's all,' he said, forcing a laugh.

'Did you ask Andrea whether she was being blackmailed?'

'I mentioned it to her when we were standing in the street waiting for Aaron, but she wanted to speak about it in private, which is how I ended up in her car.'

'Or she engineered it and had planned to kidnap you, and do God knows what to you. What the fuck were you thinking when you agreed to get into the car?' Her voice was low and expressionless, but he could sense her annoyance.

'I didn't know about the driver until we were moving. He could've put the child locks on the back doors and then I'd have been in trouble. But thankfully he didn't. I've already got Rob onto it. I've asked him to find out the full name of this Aaron and where he lives so I can stake it out and see what else I can discover.'

'What if he sees you?'

'I'll make sure he doesn't.'

'Because you're so small and inconspicuous that you'll easily blend into the scenery. I seriously think you've lost the plot.'

'Trust me, I know what I'm doing. I have no intention of doing anything to endanger myself. As soon as I've got something I'll come back. At least now we're getting somewhere.'

'At what expense? You getting beaten up and still putting yourself in harm's way. If I'd have known you were this stupid, I'd have insisted on going with you. How you ever got promoted to DI at the Met is totally beyond me.'

'Stop overreacting. I'm going to be fine. London's a busy place and no one will be able to walk off with me. I'll let you know as soon as I'm back at the house which should be this evening.'

'Just keep in touch.'

He ended the call and picked up a magazine on the table

and flicked through it, except he wasn't taking anything in. He was now one hundred per cent convinced that Sarah was right. Donald's suicide had been staged to hide his murder and it was most likely to do with the blackmail. What was Andrea Wood being blackmailed over? He sensed that was the key to all of this. But how was he going to find out? He strummed his fingers on the table deliberating.

His phone rang, interrupting his thoughts. It was Rob.

'What have you got for me?' he said, not bothering to say hello.

'I've found your man. He's Aaron Dunkley and he's been working for Andrea two years.'

'Thanks. Where does he live?'

'If I tell you I don't want you going there alone to accost him. That's not going to help.'

'I don't intend to approach him. I want to watch and see what he does. I'll also take a few photos. Did you check whether he has a record'?

'I didn't have time. You'll have to do that yourself.'

'How did you find out who he was?'

'The same way as I got you in to see Andrea Wood in the first place. I used my contact. And, no, I'm not going to tell you who they are.'

He hadn't intended asking. Rob didn't want to divulge his contact before, so he was hardly likely to do so now.

'I understand. Thanks for your help, I really appreciate it.'

'You're welcome. He lives in the flats at 104 Lee High Road in Lewisham. Let me know how you get on.'

'I will.'

'After this is over, we'll get together for a drink. No excuses.'

'It's a deal.'

Seb took the train to Blackheath and positioned himself on the opposite side of the road to where Dunkley lived, so he had a view of the car park. He waited for over an hour and finally saw the Mercedes driving in. He crossed the road until he could see Dunkley get out of the car. After taking out his phone, he zoomed in and took several photos. The man went into the back entrance of the flats. Seb checked he'd got a good set of photos and then decided he'd leave. He didn't want to be spotted.

He hailed a taxi to take him to St Pancras. The way he was feeling, there was no way he could face walking the couple of miles back to Blackheath. On the way he texted Birdie with Dunkley's full name and address and asked her to find out what she could about him.

* * *

Birdie stared at the unopened email in her inbox. It had arrived fifteen minutes ago, and she'd been doing everything other than open it. It was from the Adoption Contact Register.

What were they going to say?

Did they have her mum on the database?

Were they going to tell her where she lived?

Or were they emailing to say they had no record of her? People only go on the register if they want to be found. That's if they even know it exists. Birdie had been researching the adoption process when she came across it. She'd never heard of it before.

'Are you okay?' Twiggy said, coming up beside her.

'Yeah, fine. Just preoccupied.'

'By what? Not this suicide investigation still? Have you got anywhere with it?'

She couldn't tell him, or he'd wonder why it wasn't now a case with CID.'

'It's still progressing,' she said, shrugging. 'Nothing to report yet.'

'If you do have anything, you need to tell Sarge.'

'What made you say that?' He wouldn't meet her eyes.

'You've been talking to him, haven't you? I bet he told you to check up on me.' Twiggy still didn't speak. 'I knew it. He doesn't trust me. And now you, *Mr Suck Up*, are spying on me for him.'

'Hey. That's not fair. I admit he did mention it to me, but I haven't been reporting back to him. Not that there's anything to report that I can see.'

She could see the hurt expression in his eyes and guilt flooded through her. It wasn't his fault that she was walking a tightrope.

'Sorry. I'm preoccupied with a family issue. It's nothing to do with Clifford and his cousin's dead husband.'

'Want to talk about it? You know you can, and I won't say anything to anyone.'

'Thanks, Twiggy, you're a good mate. But no, it's nothing I want to share with anyone. Not yet.'

Except she already had done with Seb.

'Okay, no pressure. Want anything to eat? I'm going to grab a muffin. I need something to fill me up as my stomach's been rumbling like a train for ages. Hardly surprising after the minis-cule bowl of Bran Flakes I was allowed for breakfast. Evie reckons I'm not losing enough weight and she's planning on some fucking detox thing that she's seen on the internet. The woman will kill me at this rate.'

Birdie laughed. 'Whose fault is that? If you stopped cheating on your diet, then you'd lose all those extra pounds you're carrying around.' She patted him on the stomach. 'She's got your best interests at heart.'

'Yeah, if you say so. I just think she likes seeing me suffer.'

He walked away and Birdie returned her attention to the unopened email. Her hand hovered over the mouse beside her keyboard. She sucked in a breath and clicked on it.

Dear Miss Bird,

Thank you for your application to join the Adoption Contact

Register. According to our records, the mother listed on your birth certificate has written to us requesting that she isn't to be contacted. We understand this may be distressing for you, however, we are duty-bound to keep her information confidential. We will keep your registration on record in case there is any change.

Kind regards

Birdie stared at the words dancing in front of her eyes. All the time she'd thought about getting in touch with her birth mother, never once had the scenario gone through her mind of her actually requesting *not* to be contacted. Birdie had thought she might not be on the register, which meant that the register couldn't help. But she'd actually contacted them to say there was to be no contact ...

Tears stung her eyes, and a single one rolled down her cheek, which she brushed away with the back of her hand. What was she going to do? Giving up wasn't an option. There could be a genuine reason for her not wanting Birdie to contact her. Would the registrar tell her the date when her mother had contacted them? Surely that wasn't a breach of confidentiality.

Her phone pinged and she glanced at the screen. It was Seb. She opened it.

Found anything on Dunkley yet?

No. Because she hadn't even started to look. She'd been sidetracked by the email from the Adoption Contact Register.

I'm on it at the moment.

She didn't want to admit she hadn't done anything yet. After what had happened to Seb she owed it to him to give the case one hundred per cent attention. It would do her good to take her mind of her birth mother. She'd revisit everything once the case was over, and she could fully focus on it. She'd lasted twenty-six years without knowing her mother, a little while longer wasn't going to make any difference.

THIRTY-FIVE

20 May

Seb opened one eye and winced as he moved and caught one of his bruises on the edge of the pillow. He checked the time on the small travelling alarm clock he kept next to the bed. Ten o'clock. Shit. How on earth had he managed to sleep in so late? Then he remembered. He'd put his phone on silent late last night not wanting to be disturbed.

Had anyone tried to contact him? He fumbled for his phone on the bedside table and looked.

There were five texts, and a voice mail from Birdie that had been sent over an hour ago. He sighed. She wouldn't be happy. He pressed to listen.

Where are you? Are you okay? Why aren't you answering your phone? If I don't hear from you soon, I'm coming over.

He hurriedly texted her back, expecting to hear the front door being kicked in at any moment. *Sorry, phone on silent. I'm at home. Taking Elsa for a walk soon.*

His phone pinged only seconds later. *I'll be over in an hour.*

I'll take your statement while I'm there, as we still haven't done it.

A Birdie hour most likely meant an hour and a half, but he couldn't risk it. He eased himself out of bed and hobbled to the shower, then went downstairs to see Elsa. He grabbed her collar and took her in the car for a walk down by the river. Once they'd returned, he fed her and then put on the kettle.

A few minutes before eleven-thirty there was a knock at the door. He'd been right about the ninety minutes. He'd left the door on the latch and he heard it open. Birdie walked in carrying a tray with two coffees and a bag of what smelt like doughnuts. His stomach rumbled.

'Have you had breakfast?' she asked.

'Not yet.'

'Neither have I. So here we are, coffee and doughnuts, and then we can discuss what happened yesterday and what we're going to do next.'

She placed everything on the table, and he pulled out a couple of plates from the cupboard.

'This isn't what I usually have for breakfast,' he said.

'You can always have a bowl of muesli, or some toast if you'd prefer. But I'm eating these.' She took a doughnut out of the bag and took a large bite, catching the oozing jam with her finger before it landed on her shirt.

'How could I resist,' he said, reaching in the bag and pulling one out, the smell causing his stomach to grumble again.

'I was worried about you,' she said, between bites.

'Sorry. I thought you knew I was okay because I'd emailed with my attacker's name and address while I was on the way to the station to catch the train back here,'

'Well, I'm not a mind reader. You didn't say where you were, or where you were going. For all I knew, you could have approached this Dunkley chap at his house and he'd locked you up somewhere.'

'I'm not that stupid. What did you find out about him?'

'Nothing, other than a couple of parking tickets. No record. No nothing. I was surprised, considering what he did to you.'

'I'm not convinced that he doesn't have a record.' He helped himself to a second doughnut. Birdie was right, these made a much better breakfast than his usual cereal. 'I've got an idea. I know someone who may be able to help with some more digging.'

'Who? I have access to the police databases and can usually find stuff.'

'I'm sure you can, but there's a DC who works at the Lenchester force, whose skills are extraordinary. I've no idea how she does it, but if there's anything to find on Dunkley she'll find it.'

'Well, ask her then. What are you waiting for?'

'It's not that simple. I can't contact her directly, I'll have to speak to her DCI first, but it shouldn't be a problem.'

Birdie shook her head, disappointment shining in her eyes. 'And you reckon this DCI will let you use her DC? I'd put money on her saying no, especially as you're no longer a DI and this isn't an official police investigation *yet*. Note the emphasis on the word *yet* as we're at the stage of passing it on.'

'Don't waste your hard-earned cash, I see no reason for her refusing to help.'

'Are you friends?'

'No.' He grinned.

'What then, and why are you making this so mysterious?'

'We worked together on a case before I left the force. You'd get on with her, there are certain similarities between the two of you. She's not your average DCI.'

'I don't know whether to take that as a compliment or what?'

'I'll leave that for you to work out.'

He pulled out his phone and pressed DCI Whitney

Walker's number which he still had on speed dial, even though they hadn't spoken since he'd left Lenchester rather abruptly.

'Walker.'

'It's DI Clifford. I mean ex-DI Clifford.'

'Seb, how are you? I was only talking about you the other day to George, wondering how it turned out for you. You said ex, so now I know.'

'You didn't follow it in the media?'

'I did, but everything reported was about the squad generally. Nowhere was there anything published about you specifically.'

'I had no choice but to leave the force as the only job left open to me was going back in uniform. I couldn't do it.'

'That sucks. I'm sorry.'

'Don't be, it's fine. How are you and George, and Tiffany?'

'We're all doing well. What can I help you with?'

'I'm phoning for a favour.'

'Go on,' she said, hesitancy in her voice.

'I'm in Market Harborough doing a bit of PI work for my cousin. Long story, but her husband's death was recorded as suicide and we now think it could be murder. My enquiries got too close to the truth, and I was beaten up as a warning. I have the name and address of one of the men, but records are coming up with zilch.'

'I'm assuming you mean police records, in which case, how are you manging to access them?'

'I'm working with a DC from the local force.' He started as Birdie nudged him, and she did a zip sign over her mouth. He mouthed 'it's okay.' He wasn't about to let Whitney know Birdie's name, even though he trusted her.

'Surely this should be a police matter now?' Whitney said.

'Agreed, but initially the attack on me was classified as a mugging, because as an afterthought, they took my wallet. I wanted to investigate a little more myself before handing it over and seeing what the police think.'

'I never had *you* down as a rebel. What do you want from me?'

'Ellie's help. Is there any chance she could check this man out for me?'

'We've hit a lull at the moment ... Crap why did I say that. Now I'll be jinxing it. Text me his details and I'll get her onto it. But not a word to anyone at the Market Harborough force, I don't want them thinking I'm treading on their toes.'

'My lips are sealed. How soon will Ellie be able to get the details for me?'

'So now you want to put a deadline on it?' Whitney sighed. 'No need to answer. If she starts now, she should have something soon. I'll give you a call later.'

'Thanks, guv, I owe you one.'

'Whitney, not guv, now you're not in the force.'

'Thanks, again, *Whitney*.' He ended the call and grinned at Birdie.

'I take it your friend came through.'

'I told you she would, you should have trusted me. I'll text her the details. Ellie won't take long.'

'Fingers crossed she comes up with the goods. Show me a photo of your attacker so I can remind myself what he looks like.'

Once he'd finished texting, Seb held out his phone, showing Birdie the photo of Dunkley. 'Now do you remember him from when we spoke to Andrea?'

'Yes, but I didn't pay much attention to him other than noting how he stared at us trying to be intimidating, but failed as I wasn't bothered. Are you sure he was the one who attacked you? It was dark, remember, and you'd been drinking.'

'I'd only had two pints and yes I'm sure. Not just the tattoo on his hand, but the icy expression in his eyes when he noticed me staring at him in the mirror was further proof.'

'You said you didn't think he'd realised that you recognised him?'

'That didn't stop him from glaring at me in that insidious way. I expect he assumed that I wouldn't recognise him because it was so dark. He wasn't to know that I'd seen the tattoo or that I was able to recall the incident later in glorious technicolour.'

'Let's hope you're right. Did Andrea say anything in the car that implicated her?'

'This is what I can't quite sort out in my mind. If anything, it was the opposite. She wanted to talk in private and lowered her voice when I mentioned other investors being blackmailed. If she was in cahoots with Dunkley, then why talk in hushed whispers? It doesn't make sense.'

'I know I've mentioned this before, but what if the attack on you was nothing to do with Andrea being blackmailed? I'm not saying that Donald wasn't murdered, but could we be looking at two separate things and the murder and the attack aren't connected.'

'What other reason can you think of for me being beaten?'

'Your work at the Met. Could Dunkley have been involved in something illegal that was linked to you in some way, and when he saw us during our interview with Andrea, he believed he'd been recognised?'

'Until we hear back from Walker, we won't know, but I doubt it because, as I keep on saying, that work is over for me.'

'Would he know that?' Birdie persisted. 'He could have thought you questioning Andrea was a ploy we'd pulled off in order to see him.'

'Okay, I accept that it could be possible. Someone from my past could've seen me at the funeral, if I'd been caught in any of the photos, but I'm still of the opinion that it's less likely than our investigation into Donald. But that doesn't mean we won't keep the other possibility on the back burner.'

'Good. Because we shouldn't narrow our focus until such time as we're convinced one way or the other.'

'Agreed. But, assuming for the moment that they are linked, I think that if Donald was murdered and it was to do with the blackmail then it's most likely my attacker was also the murderer. In which case we—' His phone rang. 'It's Walker.' He answered. 'Whitney, you have something for me already?'

'And hello to you, too. Yes. Ellie has come up trumps. I'll pass you over to her.'

'Hello, guv,' Ellie said.

'Seb will do fine, I'm no longer in the force. How are you, Ellie?'

'Very well, thanks. You wanted more information about Aaron Dunkley. Well, there's nothing to be found regarding anyone of *that* name and address, other than minor infractions.'

'I'm sensing a *but* ...' He gave a nod in Birdie's direction.

'You're right. He—'

'Wait a moment, Ellie. I'm going to put you on speaker so my colleague here can listen.' He rested the phone on the kitchen table. 'Fire away.'

'Aaron Dunkley legally changed his name four years ago. He was previously known as Ross Burns and he comes from Coventry. He has a long record sheet under that name and was in prison three times for grievous bodily harm. He was married and several times was accused of domestic violence, but his wife wouldn't press charges, so it never got any further.'

'Do you have her details by any chance?'

'Yes, her name is Katy Burns, formerly Peters before she married him. She lives in a flat in Windsor Street, Coventry.'

'Thanks, Ellie. I knew you'd be able to help. Thank the DCI also, for allowing us to borrow you.'

'It's my pleasure. Let me know if I can help further.'

'I will do, but not without running it by the DCI first.'

He ended the call.

'The girl's a genius,' Birdie said.

'The best I've come across. And she's only your age, maybe a little younger, I'm not sure.'

'I'm impressed. We might have got there eventually, but to find all that out in such a short space of time, is ridiculous. So, what's our plan?'

'I'm going to see Dunkley's ex-wife in Coventry.'

THIRTY-SIX

20 May

'What do you mean *you're* going to see her,' Birdie said. 'I'm coming, too.' Why was he continually trying to exclude her? Did he want her off the investigation all together?

'You're on duty.'

'That doesn't matter. I can take your statement on the way in the car. I'll record it and then transcribe it later.'

'I don't want to get you in trouble. I'm happy to go see Katy Burns on my own.'

'I'm meant to be assisting with this case, and if I go back I'll be stuck in the office because Sarge hasn't given me anything else as he thinks I'm working on the mugging.'

'Has he asked you how it's going?'

'I told him I've still got to take your statement, because you weren't up to it before now, and that we're continuing to look at photos. He seems to have left me to my own devices for some reason, which I'm pleased about.'

'Okay, you can come with me.'

'Shall I drive?' It wouldn't be a hardship, she'd enjoyed her time behind the wheel, and it wasn't like she'd get another opportunity to drive such an awesome car once he'd gone back to London.

'Not necessary, I'm able to drive now.'

He was looking a lot better than he had, but there were still purple and yellow bruises on his face which didn't look good. 'Want some more make-up? I could put a bit more concealer on the bruises?'

'No thanks. I got it all over the pillowcases when you plastered me in it before. They were an awful mess, and are currently soaking in the sink.'

'That's very domesticated of you.' She arched an eyebrow. 'But first of all, you weren't *plastered* in it, it was a light covering to hide the state of your face, which it did. And second of all, you were meant to wash it off before going to bed. I can't do everything for you.' She gave an exasperated sigh.

'Point taken. I didn't think about it as I was too tired. It's not like I'm used to wearing make-up on a regular basis.'

'You'll know for next time. Shall we bring Elsa with us? She might like the drive.'

'No, she'll be fine left here. I'll let her out before we go and give her a treat. She'll most likely sleep until we get back.'

'How did you manage with her when you were at work all day or if you were away on a case?'

'I have a very understanding neighbour, Jill, who's always happy to look after her.'

'I'm not surprised, she's such a lovely dog.'

'By the way, have you heard anything yet from your friend in forensics regarding Donald's phone?'

'Nothing. I can't push him, though, because he might have lots of other legitimate work. I told him we needed it as soon as possible, so we'll just have to wait.'

'Damn. I have the feeling that they'll be stuff in there which will assist us.'

'I can speak to him again in the morning, but I don't want to harass him as he's doing us a favour.'

The drive to Coventry took forty-five minutes and when they reached the flats in Windsor Street, they parked in the small visitors' car park.

Birdie pushed open the entrance door and wrinkled her nose. 'Someone needs to clean in here, it stinks of stale urine and weed.'

'I've been in a lot worse. Surely you must have, too, being in the job for a few years,' Clifford said.

'Yes, but that doesn't mean I like it.'

They walked up the stairs to the third-floor flat and she knocked on the door. There was no answer, but the door adjacent opened and a young woman in her late teens poked her head out. 'You looking for Katy?'

'Yes. Do you know where she is?' Birdie asked.

'Who are you?'

'Friend of a friend,' Birdie said, not wanting to admit who they were for fear of her clamming up.

'I saw her go in a few minutes ago and she looked all right.'

'What do you mean?'

'She wasn't off her head or pissed or anything. Try knocking again,' she said going back inside and closing her door.

Birdie banged hard on the door.

'Hang on,' a voice called. The door opened and there was a woman who was only about five foot tall, in her late thirties. Her face was thin and drawn, and she had straight mid-brown hair which came to her shoulders.

'Katy Burns?' Seb asked.

'Why?'

'I'm Sebastian Clifford, and this is Birdie. We'd like to talk to you about Aaron Dunkley.'

'Are you police?'

'I'm an investigator,' Seb said.

'I'm an officer,' Birdie admitted. 'But not here in an official capacity.'

Katy eyed them suspiciously. 'Oh, well, I suppose I'll talk to you. Come on in.'

The flat was practically bare, apart from a worn green sofa, a television, a wooden chair, and a small dining table in the corner. There were no photos, ornaments, or anything personal on show.

'I was in the kitchen making myself a coffee, would you like one?'

'No thanks,' Seb said.

Katy disappeared for a few minutes and came back with a mug in her hand. Birdie got a whiff of whisky as the woman walked past her to sit on the chair.

'What do you want to know about Aaron?'

'A bit of background would be good. When you were together, he was known as Ross Burns. Do you know why he changed his name?'

'To get away from you lot,' she said nodding at Birdie. 'He thought with a different name no one would know about his past.'

'He did it after you divorced?'

'Yeah.' She took a large swallow of coffee and visibly shuddered.

'Do you see much of him now?'

'Not if I can help it. Sometimes he visits.'

'What for?' Birdie said.

'I don't know. A reminder of his old life, maybe. I wish he wouldn't bother as it always ends up in a fight.'

'What can you tell us about the woman he works for now? Andrea Wood. Do you know her?' Seb said.

'Yeah, of course I do. We all went to school together.'

Birdie exchanged a glance with Seb. His eyes reflecting her thoughts. They hadn't expected that.

'You, Aaron, and Andrea Wood, aka Ann Smith, went to the same school ... Where?' Birdie asked.

'Here in Coventry.'

'She doesn't have a Coventry accent,' Birdie said.

'Not now, but at school we all sounded the same. She must have had elocution lessons or something. Andrea was clever and stayed on to do her A levels. I don't know for definite, but she might have gone to university after that.'

'Were you friends at school?'

'She was one of the popular kids and out of my league. Ross always had a thing for her and liked to think they were friends.'

'Did they ever go out together?'

'He wished. But he was always there to do her dirty work. He beat up a few boys in his time if they were annoying her too much.'

'In other words, she used him,' Birdie said.

'You got it in one.' Katy looked at Seb. 'She's smart, that one.'

'When did you last see her?' Seb asked.

'Not since I left school at sixteen and got a job at Primark. Apart from on the telly sometimes, but she looks nothing like she did when I knew her.'

'Tell us about your relationship with Aaron Dunkley.'

'He left school the same time as me and worked at a tyre factory. We were going out together then and drifted into marriage.'

'Do you have any children?'

Her face clouded over. 'We had a little boy, Jeremiah, who died when he was two. Ross was looking after him at the time. That's what caused the split between us.'

'How did he die?' Birdie asked, gently.

'The coroner said it was an accident, but I didn't believe them. Ross used to lose his temper so easily, especially when JJ was being naughty. It all happened a long time ago. Eighteen years. But you don't forget. You never forget ...' Her voice faded away.

'What exactly happened?'

'JJ drowned in the paddling pool when Ross was meant to be taking care of him. He told the police that he was playing hide and seek with JJ and that he must have run into the garden to hide. Ross found JJ lying face down in the water.'

'And you're not convinced that's what happened.'

'Ross was beside himself when JJ died, and I know his grief was genuine, but the way he told the story to the police seemed made-up. He'd never played hide and seek with JJ before. He hardly ever played with him at all.'

'What do you think might have happened?'

'I have no proof, and I didn't accuse Ross because if I had he'd have leathered me. But I think JJ was being naughty and Ross put him outside in the garden and locked the door so he couldn't get back in. He'd threatened to do it in the past but I wouldn't let him. JJ went to go into the paddling pool and slipped. It had rained the day before and there was a few inches of water in the bottom.'

'I'm so sorry,' Birdie said. What else could she say? It was such a tragedy.

'Did Aaron keep in touch with Andrea over the years?' Seb asked a few moments later.

'Not that I know of. He might have followed her career, the same as I did. As soon as she was on the telly, we knew it was her, even though she'd changed her name.'

'What about the job he now has working for her? Do you know how that transpired?' Seb asked.

'Ross, or Aaron as he was by then, bumped into Andrea in Coventry one day out of the blue about two years ago. She'd returned for a funeral. One of her parents, I think. I've no idea where they met, but they did, and they chatted. She told him she'd been looking for a driver and someone to do odd jobs. He said he wanted to apply, and she told him the job was advertised online. He came straight round here and wanted me to help with the application form. He applied, went for the interview with Andrea and someone who works with her. On his way back home he received a call from her offering him the job. She told him that she could trust him to take care of her. It was like being back at school all over again.'

'She definitely said *to take care of her*?' Birdie asked.

'According to him.'

'Did she mention that she needed protection from anything?'

'You'll have to ask him, I don't know.'

'When did you last see Aaron?' Seb asked.

'I can't remember. One good thing about this job is I hardly see him at all, now, which I'm extremely grateful for.'

'Do you know the name Donald Witherspoon?'

She shrugged. 'No. Never heard the name in my life. I'm going out again soon, so if you're done, I'll see you out.'

'Thank you very much for your help,' Seb said, standing up.

'I'll tell you one thing, if you suspect Ross of anything then you're probably right. He's always been on the wrong side of everything.'

She showed them to the door, closing it behind them.

'Very informative. Do you think Andrea and Aaron are in it together?' Birdie asked.

'Possibly. Or he's doing it to protect her and she doesn't know. If he's seen himself as her protector ever since they were at school, then he could easily have done this off his own bat. It makes more sense because, as I said, based on the conversation in her car, it was like she wanted to keep the blackmail quiet and not let him know. We'll drive back to Market Harborough, via Foxton Locks. I want to show the manager of the pub the photo of Dunkley to see if he recognises him as the man who was with Donald on the day he died.'

THIRTY-SEVEN

20 May

It was almost six o'clock when they arrived at the Foxton Locks pub and as they pushed open the door the low hum of voices and the smell of beer invaded Seb's senses. It was much busier than the last time they'd visited. He was sure he could smell chips, which reminded him he could do with something to eat.

They headed towards the bar and as they approached, Seb signalled for the bartender to come over. 'Is the manager, Freddie Evans, available?'

'It's his night off,' the bartender said.

'Do you know where he is?'

'He's upstairs and doesn't wish to be disturbed, can I help? I'm in charge this evening.'

Birdie stepped forward and held out her warrant card. 'I'm DC Bird from Market Harborough police, please contact Mr Evans and ask him to come down to speak to us immediately.'

The bartender glanced from Birdie back to Seb, his brow furrowed. 'I'll phone upstairs and let him know.'

As he disappeared to the rear of the bar and picked up the phone, Seb turned to her. 'Hasn't your shift officially finished?'

'We'll call this overtime. I didn't have a choice in making it appear as a police matter as it was the only way we were going to get to see Evans this evening.'

'Let's order a drink,' Seb said as he stepped up to the bar. One of the guys standing behind the bar came over. 'I'll have half a pint of stout and ...' He glanced at Birdie.

'It'll have to be lemonade now I'm back on duty. And a packet of cheese and onion crisps. We haven't eaten since the doughnuts this morning.'

'No wonder I'm feeling hungry,' Seb said. 'Make that two packets.'

'Shall we stay here for a meal?' Birdie suggested. 'Their lasagne and chips is to die for.'

'Not this time. I want to get back to the house after we've spoken to the manager.'

'Perhaps a drive-through burger on our way then?' she suggested.

'Let's see what time we get out of here,' Seb said.

'Okay, but—'

She stopped as the bartender arrived back. 'Freddie said would you mind going upstairs to his flat as he's in the middle of cooking his dinner.'

'No problem,' Birdie said.

They picked up their drinks and crisps and followed him through the pub, to a door marked *private*. 'Go to the top of the stairs and into the flat. The door's unlocked so you can go straight in.'

They headed up the narrow, dark wooden staircase typical of buildings of this age, and into the flat.

'Hello,' Seb called out.

'I'm in the kitchen,' Evans called out.

They went in the direction of the voice and into the kitchen, where the manager was standing at the hob. Two saucepans were on there, a delicious smell of tomato sauce coming from one.

'I remember you from before, but you were off duty then, is this about something else?' Evans said.

'Same investigation. We won't keep you too long,' Birdie said. 'We're here to check whether you recognise this man.'

Seb took out his phone, pulled up a photo of Aaron Dunkley and showed it to the manager, who took it and stared for a few seconds, nodding his head.

'He's definitely familiar. Definitely. I'm trying to think from where.' He slapped his forehead. 'I remember, now. He was with Donald Witherspoon the day that he died. How could I have forgotten that?' He narrowed his eyes, while continuing to stare at the photo. 'I think it's because there's something different about him in this photo, but I'm not sure what it ... Oh, I know, he had a beard when I last saw him. He must have shaved that off, but yeah, it's definitely him. He wasn't friendly, in fact he appeared sullen.'

'Are you absolutely sure he was with Donald Witherspoon?' Seb asked.

'Yes.' He turned to give the sauce a stir.

'Did they come in together or separately?'

'If I remember rightly, they met in here. Witherspoon arrived first, ordered a drink and made sure he could get a table at the back of the restaurant, and then he was joined by this man, about ten minutes or so later.'

'Did they have a meal?'

'I believe so, yes.'

'Who paid?' Birdie asked.

Seb nodded his approval at her quick thinking, it could lead to a paper trail.

'I couldn't tell you, sorry.'

'Is there any way of finding out? Can you track which credit card was used?' she continued.

'I'll have to go through the records. Can I do that later and let you know?'

'Yes, that's fine,' Birdie said, giving him her card. 'What time did they leave?'

'Now you're asking. I honestly don't know.'

'Can you remember whether they were they arguing, or chatting in a friendly way?' Seb asked.

'Definitely no arguments, or it would've made me take notice. I'd assumed he was a prospective client because Witherspoon got out some leaflets. He'd often do that when he was here with clients so he could explain various investments.'

'How do you know that's what he did?' Seb asked.

'Sometimes I'd listen to see if I could pick up any tips.'

'Didn't Witherspoon mind?'

'I'd position myself in such a way that he couldn't see me.'

'Did you take any of his advice?'

'I couldn't afford to, but it was useful to know for when I decide to invest my money, if I ever have any spare. Though, seeing as his whole business was a sham, it's probably not a good idea to take notice of what he said.'

'Are you sure the meeting he had with this man was the same as the others?' Seb asked.

'It didn't seem any different.'

'And you definitely don't remember the time they left?'

'I've already said that. All I can tell you is they left together because I was standing behind the bar when Witherspoon called out goodbye. I glanced over and saw the man was with him.'

'What sort of frame of mind would you say Witherspoon was in? Did he look scared, or under duress?' Seb asked.

'The exact opposite. He seemed happy and I remember

thinking that he must've got the man to invest. When I found out about the suicide, I thought it was strange.'

Birdie's eyes widened. 'Yet you didn't tell the police any of this.'

'I would've done if they'd asked me, but as I told you last time, no one came to see me about it. I thought that meant it wasn't important.'

'Thank you, for your help. We'll leave you now to get on with your dinner,' Seb said.

They returned to the pub and found a table in the corner where they sat with their drinks and crisps.

'Now the manager has confirmed the connection it's an official police matter. We know Dunkley attacked you and we know he was seen with Donald on the day he died,' Birdie said.

'If only the police had spoken to the manager and found out more about Donald's movements before his death, it might have changed things.' Seb picked up his drink and took a sip.

'It still could've led them to the verdict of suicide. Although they might have listened to Sarah a bit more. And if they'd discovered who Donald was with it could've raised alarm bells. But this is all *coulda, woulda, shoulda*. Even if I'd been on the case, I can't say for certain that I'd have followed up on everything. You know what police work is like. We know now, and that's the main thing.'

'You're right. We'll go back to my place, pull everything together and you can take it in.'

They finished their drinks and got back in the car and headed towards Market Harborough. As he was driving, Seb's eyes were drawn to his rear-view mirror.

'Is there anything wrong?'

'I think we're being followed by a silver Volkswagen Golf. In fact, now I'm aware of it, I've seen this car a few times today. I can't believe it hadn't registered before now.'

'Can you see who's in it?'

'Not clearly. I'll slow down so they can get closer.' He released his foot from the accelerator. 'Damn. They've slowed down, too, and are keeping their distance. But I think it could be Dunkley, and there's another male with him.'

THIRTY-EIGHT

20 May

'What are we going to do?' Birdie asked, staring at the intense concentration etched across Seb's face as he drove them towards Market Harborough.

She glanced in the wing mirror at the Golf, which was still quite a way behind them. If only she could see the number plate, she could call it in.

'Nothing, other than keep an eye on them.'

'We should go straight to the station. It could be dangerous.'

'They're hardly going to follow us there and give themselves up. Let's bide our time and see what happens. I want to make absolutely sure they're the ones who attacked me and murdered Donald.' His lips set in a flat line. He was determined.

She shouldn't let his age and experience get in the way. Going to the station was the right thing to do. Should she pull rank? He was no longer a DI so her being a DC put her in charge.

'You said you recognised him. How much surer do you have to be?'

'I *think* it's him and that he's been following us, but I want to play it out and see if they follow us all the way back to town and then to my place.'

'I'm still not sure that's the right thing to do, but okay. I suppose it's not taking us out of our way.'

They continued along the Gallow Field Road, turning right onto the Harborough Road, towards the town centre. She kept her eyes constantly on the car behind. There was now a vehicle between them. Perhaps Seb was mistaken. But would he be, with his memory?

'What if they try to run us off the road?'

'There aren't a lot of places around here that they can do that,' he said, cracking a smile.

'I suppose not. It's not like in parts of America. Surely they must know you've clocked them.'

'They've been keeping well back, so they might not. I'm sure they won't try anything at the moment because my car is much more powerful than theirs, and I could lose them easily enough if necessary.'

They reached the outskirts of the town centre and turned into Bowden Lane but the car behind them went a different way.

'They've gone,' she said, glancing in the wing mirror. 'Maybe it wasn't them after all and you were mistaken. They could have just been coming back from Foxton after being in the pub or looking around the locks.'

'The driver did look like Dunkley, but as it was from a distance you could be right. And I didn't recognise the man with him.'

'Then again, what if it was them and they've gone to your house to wait for you? They know the area you're staying in because they followed you, even if they don't know the actual house, although I expect they do if they've been keeping an eye on you for a while.'

'They're not heading in the right direction. I was most likely wrong.'

'And if they do turn up at your place?' Birdie pushed, still uncertain.

'I'll call the police. If they're after me, wherever I go they'll find me. You're worrying unnecessarily.'

'Am I? What if they don't give you the opportunity to call the police? They could beat you up again. They could murder you. I mean, they've already done it to Donald, haven't they? Or they could kidnap you. It's going—'

'Birdie, calm down,' Seb interrupted. 'It's not going to happen. I need some time to get everything together so I can hand it all over. I'll do that this evening. You can let your sergeant know where we are with the investigation and tell him that tomorrow morning I'll bring everything in and we can go through it with him. My concern is that we don't have concrete proof Donald was murdered. The coroner's report, the police report and the fact the case hasn't been reopened all goes against us.'

'But we now know about Donald blackmailing Edgar and Tony, and it looks likely that Andrea was being blackmailed, too.'

'That's all very well, but whether any of these people will admit to it in a police investigation, is a different matter. I suspect they won't, and then what do we have? Our word for it?'

For the remainder of the journey, she was silent. He might be confident that he wasn't in any danger, but she wasn't so sure.

When they arrived back at his place, she scanned the street and couldn't see the car which had been following them. Seb pulled in outside the front of his house and she drove off in her Mini towards the station. As she got to the end of the street, parked in a side road was the silver Golf.

Crap.

She stopped in a nearby street and called Twiggy.

THIRTY-NINE

20 May

Twiggy had put his jacket on to leave the station, already late for dinner, when his phone rang. Surely it wasn't Evie again, he'd already told her he wouldn't be much longer. He'd been behind on his paperwork and he'd been informed by Sarge that he wasn't to leave the station until it was all up-to-date.

He glanced at the screen. It was Birdie. What did she want? She hadn't been seen or heard from for much of the day and it hadn't gone down well in certain quarters.

'Now you choose to let us know where you are,' he said, without even saying hello. 'Sarge has been breathing down my neck wanting to know what you're doing. I tried to cover for you, but I didn't have a clue what you were up to. What shall I tell him?'

'Nothing. Actually ... Yes ... He needs to know. There's a situation. I need you urgently and bring backup. I think the men who attacked Clifford are at the house he's renting in Heygate Street, waiting to confront him.'

'Are you close by? Can you see them?'

'I was on my way back to the station when I saw their car parked up. They'd been following us most of the day, but then they disappeared.'

'Are you sure?'

'Positive. They must have taken a shortcut.'

She caught him up with everything that had happened, and mentioned that these men might have murdered Witherspoon.

'What the fuck, Birdie? Why didn't you let us know you were in danger? And why did you let him go back to his place on his own? That's police work 101.'

'Okay, stop having a go. They stopped following us so Clifford thought it would be okay and that he might have been mistaken about it being his attackers. I didn't really agree, but I was overruled. Meet me on the corner of Heygate and Doddridge and we'll go in together. These men could be armed.'

Twiggy gripped hold of the desk, so tightly his knuckles went white. He couldn't believe that she could be so reckless as to allow Clifford to put his life at risk.

'Okay, but stay where you are, I don't want you making any moves without me.'

'I won't, I promise.'

He ended the call.

'What's that all about?' Sarge said.

Twiggy hadn't seen the officer come up behind him.

'The men who attacked Clifford are after him again. Birdie saw them parked near the house he's staying at and she thinks they might be inside waiting for him. It's possible that these men murdered Witherspoon. At least, that's what Birdie and Clifford believe. Birdie's waiting for me. These men are dangerous and could be armed.'

'You go to Birdie, and I'll bring backup. I'll let the DI know what's going down and get his permission to use firearms and

Tasers before signing them out. He's at the Wigston station all day, but he'll no doubt come straight here, as he'll be senior investigating officer. Don't do anything until we get to you.'

'Yes, Sarge.' Twiggy grabbed his jacket, hurried out to the car park and drove as fast as he could.

FORTY

Seb stuck his key in the lock, while scanning the street to see if he could see the car that had been following him. It wasn't there. He must have been mistaken. He opened the door and went inside, expecting Elsa to come and greet him, as she usually did. But she didn't

'Elsa,' he called, his heart pounding in his chest. 'Where are you?'

His eyes were drawn to what looked like a half-eaten lump of steak on the floor. He bent down to check and gasped. There were grains of white powder on it.

Had Dunkley and his mate got inside and drugged her?

If they'd harmed so much as one hair on her head, then so help him, they wouldn't live to tell the tale.

He grabbed hold of a large china figurine of a 1920s woman, which was situated on the hall table, and headed down the corridor. Lying just inside the kitchen door on the floor was Elsa. He bent down and felt her pulse.

It was steady.

She was alive.

He let out the pent-up breath he'd been holding. It must have been a sedative. Thank God.

Where the hell were the bastards?

If they weren't in the kitchen they had to be hiding somewhere.

He wasn't going to search for them because that could put him on the back foot. He'd wait for them to come to him. It gave him more of an advantage.

He needed a more effective weapon than an ornament. Not a knife. That would mean getting up close to them. He remembered the walking stick in a bucket by the back door and grabbed it.

He pulled the phone out of his pocket, hit the record button, and then replaced it. Whatever happened, he wanted to make sure that Dunkley would be caught.

He stood stationary in the middle of the room.

Waiting.

The only sounds were his ragged breaths.

He was about to move, when footsteps pounded on the wooden floor in the hall.

His grip tightened around the stick and he sucked in a breath.

Two men burst into the kitchen, narrowly avoiding Elsa. No hoodies this time. He could see as clear as day that one of them was Dunkley.

'Don't you ever learn your lesson? You were warned to keep away,' Dunkley said. 'And did you? No. Well, now you're gonna regret it.'

'What warning?' Seb said. 'You beat me up, without saying a thing. What was I being warned about?'

'Don't play dumb with me. You couldn't leave her alone, could you? You're going to pay for that, make no mistake.'

'What are you going to do about it?' Seb said, standing his full six feet six inches and staring down at the pair of them.

'What are you going to do about it? *Old bean.*' The guy with Dunkley, who was stockier and shorter than his colleague, said imitating Seb's voice.

Normally, Seb could take on the pair of them, as he worked out on a regular basis, but he wasn't fighting fit. That didn't mean he wouldn't put up a good fight if he had to. His phone rang.

'Don't answer it,' Dunkley said.

He hadn't intended to in case they spotted him recording the conversation. He had to get them to admit to the murder.

'Did Andrea Wood put you up to this?' He locked eyes with Dunkley. 'Your old school friend ...'

Dunkley stiffened. 'How do you know?'

'It doesn't matter. The fact is, I do. And I'm not the only one. I also know you used to be called Ross Burns. So, whatever you think you can do to me now isn't going to change that. Did Andrea ask you to attack me and come here today?'

Dunkley, clearly agitated, hopped from foot to foot.

'She knows nothing about it, so don't try to frame her.'

'Why don't you tell me everything. I know you murdered Witherspoon. You've been identified as being in the pub at Foxton Locks on the day he died. Why did you do it?' Because he was blackmailing Andrea? Were you protecting her? You've always had a thing for her, haven't you?'

'You know nothing,' Dunkley snarled.

'I know you've been in love with her since school and she used you to do her dirty work.'

'You call it dirty work. I call it helping a friend.'

'A friend who you happen to be in love with. Except she didn't love you back, did she?'

The lines tightened around the man's eyes. He'd touched a nerve. 'I look after her so she ain't bothered by the likes of you.'

Under her authority?

'Is Andrea happy with you interfering in her life like this? Because even if she wasn't physically involved in what you've done, you do realise that she's an accessory and will go down for a long time.'

Fear flashed in his eyes. 'What I did was my decision and not hers. It's my job to protect her and I decide how.'

'Even if that protection involved murdering Donald Witherspoon. Don't deny it. You've been identified and we know you had lunch with him on the day he died and were pretending to be interested in investing with him. You might have thought you'd made his death appear a suicide, but he tricked you. The note he left. The one you forced him to write, was full of clues.'

'You're bluffing. What clues?'

'Clues that his wife was able to spot a mile off. Admittedly, you had the police and coroner fooled, but not now. We have all the evidence we need to prove that you're guilty of Witherspoon's murder. And the expression on your face is an acknowledgement of that fact. Admit it. You murdered him, didn't you?'

Seb stopped talking. He'd learnt long ago that after giving enough information to draw a suspect in, the best course of action was to wait for them to speak.

'It was his own fault. I don't care if he needed money, he shouldn't have gone after Andrea like that. She's been through enough over the years. If he'd have kept his nose out he might still be alive.'

'Did Andrea tell you about the blackmail?'

'I overheard a conversation between her and Witherspoon and realised what was going on. She'd given him money once and he was after more. I had to save her.'

'Do you know what she was being blackmailed over?' he asked, curious as to how much he actually knew.

'No, and I don't need to. All I knew was that he'd blackmailed her once and wanted more money out of her.'

'So you went in on your white charger, like you did at school because you were in love with her. You sorted out anyone she didn't like. She knew how you felt about her, and used you, just as she's using you now, even if she isn't aware of exactly what you've done.'

'You bastard. You're dead.'

'I don't think so.'

Dunkley lunged towards Seb, and he pulled back the walking stick and swung it hard into the man's face. His nose cracked and blood came pouring down. His hand flew to his face, and he groaned.

'You'll pay for that.'

The other guy ran from where he'd been standing close to the door and Seb stuck out his foot and tripped him. While the man was righting himself, Seb grabbed his arm and twisted it up his back and held him so he couldn't move.

'Get off me.'

The front door opened, and Birdie ran in, closely followed by three other officers holding Tasers.

'I've got it under control,' he said, grinning at Birdie.

'Arrest him for murder.' He nodded at Dunkley. 'And this one for GBH.'

Birdie turned to Dunkley who was still clutching his nose. 'Aaron Dunkley, I'm arresting you on suspicion of murdering Donald Witherspoon, and for grievous bodily harm to Sebastian Clifford. You do not have to say anything, but it may harm your defence if you do not mention when questioned something which you later rely on in court. Anything you do say may be given in evidence. Do you understand?'

He grunted his reply.

She turned to the other one and arrested him.

'Take them away,' she said to the officer with her. 'Where's Elsa? Did they hurt her?'

'She's behind you,' he said, nodding at the floor. 'They

sedated her. I found a half-eaten piece of meat in the hall. They must have shoved it through the letter box before breaking in, to make sure she wouldn't attack them. Don't worry, she'll be fine.'

Birdie rushed over and bent down beside her, pulling her into her arms. 'Elsa, wake up. It's okay. Those arsewipes have gone.' A tear rolled down her cheek and she sniffed.

'She'll be okay,' Seb said, squatting down beside her. 'Won't you girl.' He stroked her head and Elsa stretched her legs out. 'See, she's coming around already.'

'Thank goodness,' Birdie said, smiling through her tears.

He stood, as his eyes had begun to fill up, too and he didn't want Birdie to see.

'How did you get in without breaking down the door?' he asked, as he replayed the scene in his mind.

'You left the keys in the lock.'

He smacked himself on the head. 'I was so busy looking for Elsa I forgot them. I'm such an idiot.'

'You'll get no argument from me about that,' Birdie said. 'I'm going back to work. You stay here with Elsa and come in to the station tomorrow morning to make a statement.'

FORTY-ONE

Seb arrived at the station first thing in the morning. He glanced around the interview room where Birdie had left him as she went to track down her sergeant and, he hoped, a coffee. The room was basic, with a table, four chairs, and some recording equipment. None of the fancy stuff they had at the Met.

Being at the station the last hour had highlighted to him that he didn't miss police work, despite him thinking that he would. He hadn't realised how constrained he'd been at work until undertaking this investigation for Sarah. He'd been able to make his own decisions without having to report back to a superior officer. There was a lot to be said for that sort of autonomy.

The door opened and Birdie walked in carrying two plastic cups, which she placed on the table. She pulled a packet of biscuits from her pocket and sat opposite him.

'Machine coffee only, I'm afraid, but it's drinkable and better than nothing. With a bourbon biscuit or three to help wash it down. I keep asking for an espresso machine, but you can imagine the response I get to that request.' She opened the packet and took out a couple of biscuits. 'These will have to do until lunchtime. Though God knows what time that will be. Want one?'

He shook his head and took a sip of his coffee. Warm, and just about passable. 'Did you find Sergeant Weston, is he going to be long?'

He really wanted to get back to be with Elsa. When he'd left the house she was fine, and had suffered no ill-effects from the sedation but the whole scenario kept playing around in his mind. What if Dunkley hadn't sedated her and instead put a bullet in her head? He shuddered at the thought.

'He's on his way. Be warned, he—' The door opened, and she clamped her mouth shut, pulling a face which only Seb could see.

'Clifford,' he said nodding, and sitting beside Birdie. 'Is one of those for me?' he asked, looking directly at the cups on the table.

'Sorry, Sarge, I could only manage two. But help yourself to a biscuit.' She slid the packet towards him.

He ignored the biscuits and stared at Clifford. 'You have some explaining to do. Why wasn't this handed over to us as soon as you suspected foul play?'

Seb had no idea what Birdie had already told him, so he had to be careful. If he kept his eyes on her, she might give something away. He didn't want to land her in trouble, and not just because Twiggy had threatened him the other day.

'It was mentioned to you at the time of my attack, but you insisted it was a mugging, if I recall correctly.'

Birdie grimaced. That hadn't come out exactly as he'd planned.

'That was a mistake,' the sergeant admitted. 'But once you knew about the blackmail, you should've come to see me and explained.' He turned to Birdie. 'You should've insisted that's what he did.'

'It's what I had planned to do, but first I needed to connect the dots. It wasn't until I saw the tattoo on Dunkley's hand two days ago that I realised he was one of my attackers. That was the only clue I had to his identity. I wanted to make sure all the evidence stacked up in case they slipped through the net. You know what barristers are like, they'll get people off on the most ridiculous technicality.'

Sergeant Weston nodded. 'You can say that again.'

'I want to make it clear that DC Bird had nothing to do with any decisions made during this investigation,' Seb continued. 'Once we'd confirmed with the manager of the Foxton Locks pub that Dunkley had been with Witherspoon on the day he died, I intended to share with you everything I had. Birdie wanted us to go straight to the station after I thought we were being followed, but once they disappeared it seemed I'd been mistaken. I didn't expect them to turn up at the house. But it did mean I was able to record our conversation and we have a confession from Dunkley.'

The sergeant clenched his jaw. 'You were bloody lucky not to have been killed. What would you have done if they'd been armed?'

'Luckily for me they weren't.'

'But it still could've turned out very different.'

'Actually, Seb had it all under control by the time we got there, Sarge, as you saw for yourself,' Birdie said.

'That doesn't make it right. And you,' he jabbed his finger in Birdie's direction. 'Should've known better than to engage in this investigation at all.'

'What else was I to do? You wouldn't listen to me about the mugging. I knew something wasn't right. If I hadn't helped Seb, then this murder could've gone undetected and—'

'I think your sergeant understands,' Seb said.

'See what I have to put up with? If I had any hair, I'd be

tearing it out by now. I swear I've aged twenty years since you joined CID.'

There was a twinkle in his eye.

'What are your next steps?' Seb asked Sergeant Weston.

'Dunkley and his accomplice have been charged and, as we speak, officers are going to the TV studio to bring Andrea Wood in for questioning. Do you believe she was involved?'

'It's unlikely, for several reasons. First, she didn't want to talk to me about the blackmail while Dunkley could hear, even though she'd known him for many years. Second, if you listen to the recording of my discussion with Dunkley before you arrived to arrest him, he specifically denied she had anything to do with it. He also had no idea of what Witherspoon was blackmailing her over. Any chance I can observe the interview with her?'

'In what capacity?' Weston asked.

'Interest. To close my investigation and be able to report back to my cousin, Donald Witherspoon's wife, who was the person who asked me to look into his death.'

Weston frowned. 'You're now a private investigator?'

'No. Although in the spirit of openness, my cousin did offer to pay me, but I declined. Her situation is dire enough after what Donald had done, without me adding to it.'

He was about to say more, then realised he'd be doing Sarah a disservice by airing her dirty laundry in public, to quote one of his mother's favourite sayings.

'I don't see why not, so yes, I will allow you to observe.'

FORTY-TWO

21 May

Seb sat on a stool in the observation area and leant forward, resting his arms on the bench. He stared into a room that was very similar to the one he'd been sitting in only a few hours ago. Andrea Wood was seated at the table with her hands in her lap, her face drawn and pinched. She stared ahead into space, looking nothing like the vivacious woman he'd interviewed a while ago.

Did she know why she'd been brought in for questioning? Had she any idea of what Dunkley had done on her behalf?

The door opened and Birdie, followed by DS Weston, walked in. He was holding a thick Manila folder which he placed on the table in front of him as they both sat opposite Wood. Standard procedure in investigations, to make the person being interviewed believe the police had lots of information on them. He'd done it himself, many times.

Weston pressed the button on the recording equipment which was mounted on the wall.

'Interview on Friday, 21 May. Those present: DC Bird, DS Weston, and ... please state your full name for the recording.' He nodded at Wood.

'Andrea Wood. Will someone please tell me why I'm here? And why I was escorted out of the studio immediately after my programme had aired, not even being given time to take off my TV make-up.' She glared at both Birdie and Weston in turn. 'In case you didn't realise, I don't usually go around with my face this orange colour.'

A slight exaggeration although he had to admit the make-up was a lot different in colour from the last time he'd seen her.

'We'll get to that shortly,' Weston said.

'Not only that, the officers were in uniform, so everyone knows that the police have arrested me. Can you imagine the headlines in tomorrow's papers? It's probably already spread over the internet. The paparazzi won't leave me alone after this.'

That was going to be the least of her worries when she discovered why she was there.

'You weren't arrested,' Weston said. 'You were brought in to help us with our investigation.'

'Trying telling that to the public after they see photos of me with your *PC Plods*.' She folded her arms tightly across her chest. 'What am I meant to be helping you with? Do I need my solicitor?'

'You're welcome to call your solicitor, and you can remain here until they arrive, but as you're only here to help us with some facts regarding the death of Donald Witherspoon you might decide it's not necessary.'

'If it's only helping, and I'm not being accused of anything, then okay, as I don't want to be here any longer than necessary.' She stared directly at Birdie. 'I know you. You came to see me at the studio with that other guy, really tall. Clifton.'

Was she pretending not to know his name as a way of

distancing herself from the situation? She knew all about the investigation because he'd told her, but she might not realise the police were fully acquainted with all of the details.

'Clifford,' Birdie said.

'When he was in my car he suddenly jumped out. It was it was all most strange.'

'Back to the interview,' Weston said. 'You're friends with Aaron Dunkley.'

'I wouldn't say it's a friendship, he's my employee and drives me around and does odd jobs for me.'

'How long have you known him?' Weston said.

'He's been working for me for two years now.'

'That's not what Sergeant Weston asked,' Birdie said. 'How long have you *known* him? We believe it goes back a lot longer than that.'

Wood flushed. 'Um ...'

'To save time, I'll tell you,' Birdie continued. 'You went to school with him in Coventry when you were known as Ann Smith and he was Ross Burns. Is that correct?'

The woman drew her lips into a thin line. 'If you already knew that, why didn't you say, instead of asking me? Are you trying to catch me out? Because if you are, you're not succeeding.'

'We want to establish the truth from your perspective,' Weston said. 'Tell us about your friendship with Dunkley.'

'We knew each other at school, but after he left I didn't see him again until I was in Coventry attending a funeral. I bumped into him in the city centre. I happened to mention that I was looking for someone to work for me and he asked if he could apply. I said yes. That's all there is to it.'

He believed her. There was nothing in her body language to indicate otherwise.

'When you were at school, would you say you were close friends?' Weston asked.

'No, we weren't.'

'He used to have a thing for you, didn't he?' Birdie said.

The woman shrugged. 'He might have done. It was a long time ago and I can't really remember.'

'Would it be fair to say that because of his strength and violent nature you used him to sort out any kids at school who were bothering you?' Birdie said.

Wood glanced down at her lap, clearly embarrassed. 'I'm not sure what you mean.'

'If boys were pestering you, or doing things that you didn't like, you got him to beat them up. Is that clear enough?'

'I admit he might have helped me out, the odd time.'

'I'd say it was more than *the odd time*.' Birdie made quote marks with her fingers. 'I think you knew about his feelings for you and took advantage of them.'

'Look, we were young and, yes, I might have been a bit of a queen bee at school, but so were lots of others. You know what girls can be like at that age. Aaron left school at sixteen and I didn't see him after that, as I've already told you.'

'Did you leave at the same time?'

'I stayed on to take my A levels, and then went on to university and studied journalism. I got a job on a local paper and from there worked for a magazine in London. After that I got into TV work.'

'And you didn't have anything to do with Dunkley in all that time?'

'How many times do I have to tell you? There was no contact between us. Not at all, I promise. I can't make it any plainer.'

'Did you take him on to work for you because of your history, and you knew he'd do whatever you asked of him?'

'I was looking for someone to drive me and someone to do odd jobs and act as security if I ever needed it. It's not often we get accosted, but occasionally someone might take it too far. I remembered how Aaron was at school and thought I could trust him because of our past.'

'Did he turn out to be a good choice for the job?' Weston asked.

'He's been an excellent employee and will do everything asked of him, and more.'

'Mr Dunkley has been arrested for the murder of Donald Witherspoon,' Birdie said.

Wood's mouth dropped open. 'I didn't ask him to do it, if that's what you're thinking.'

'Did you tell Dunkley that Donald Witherspoon was blackmailing you?' Birdie asked.

Wood glanced away. 'I—' She hesitated.

'He was blackmailing you, wasn't he?'

'Yes,' she said, her voice a low whisper and her head bowed.

'Over what?' Birdie asked.

'I can't tell you. Just know that I had nothing to do with his murder, and I certainly didn't tell Aaron about it. No one else knew.'

'That's not good enough,' Weston said, leaning forward slightly. 'You can tell us now why Witherspoon was blackmailing you and, if it was the motive for his murder, we want to know your part in it.'

Wood glanced up to the ceiling, her fists clenched tight as they rested on the table.

'You have to believe me. I had no part in Donald Witherspoon's murder. I didn't even know it *was* murder until you just told me.'

'Why was he blackmailing you?'

'I can't say.'

'As it stands Ms Wood, we know that Donald Witherspoon was killed by your employee, Aaron Dunkley, who used to *sort people out* for you at school, because he discovered you were being blackmailed. As far as we're concerned, you put him up to it. Without any additional information, we have no choice but to charge you as an accessory to murder. How do you think the paparazzi and your fans will like those headlines? Or would you prefer them to say you helped us solve a heinous crime and lock up a dangerous man instead?' Weston snapped.

Wood shuddered. 'Okay, but this is to go no further.' She looked from Weston to Birdie. 'I'll be ruined if it gets out.'

Could there be a better motive for murder?

'We can't promise anything, but if it's possible, we will keep it quiet,' Weston said, his voice much gentler than before.

She cleared her throat. 'Many years ago, when I was at university, money was tight. My parents weren't rich, and they couldn't help me financially. I had a part-time job at a local pub but got fired over some missing money. It wasn't me who took it but they wouldn't believe me, and I lost my job. I was desperate and when somebody approached me to do some modelling work, saying it would be easy money, I jumped at the chance. Who wouldn't? Stupid me didn't realise the sort of modelling they meant. It turned out to be an *adult film*. I should have walked away as soon as I found out, but they offered me five grand for doing it. Five grand. That was a huge amount of money all those years ago, especially to a student who could barely feed herself. I accepted the job, and it was the worst experience of my life. I'll never forget it for as long as I live. But I forced myself to get through it and the money I earnt helped me through university and paid off a lot of my debts. Afterwards, I put it to the back of my mind and never thought about it again. Until ...'

'Witherspoon saw it?' Birdie asked.

'Yes. He came across the film and thought he recognised me from the TV. I had no idea it was still out there. I really thought it had just gone away. I'm still not sure how he made the connection as I don't look anything like I did eighteen years ago. My hair was a different colour and much longer. I was also ten pounds heavier. But recognise me, he did, and he got in touch.' She bit down on her bottom lip.

Donald was a conniving bastard. How could he have done something like that? Sarah might not agree, but the more Seb got to learn about the man the more convinced he was that she was well rid of him.

'How did he contact you?' Birdie asked.

'He emailed, making a very clear reference to the film, and asking to meet. I went into a mad panic and had to agree. I had no choice. We met in a restaurant in London, and he *suggested* that I might like to invest some money with him. He told me outright that if I didn't, he was going to make the film public, selling the information to the highest bidder, and ruin my career. I begged him not to, and said that I couldn't afford it, but he didn't believe me. He said he knew how much I was being paid at the TV station and that if I didn't have the cash, I could borrow it. I had no choice but to say yes. I invested the hundred and fifty thousand pounds he asked for.'

'Where did you get the money from?' Birdie asked.

'I cashed in a term deposit I had at the bank and used that.' She slumped down in her chair; all the fight having gone out of her.

'Did you tell Dunkley?' Weston asked.

'I didn't tell a soul. It was too important to risk confiding in anyone.'

'Well, clearly, Dunkley did know. How?'

'I have no idea, unless he heard me on the phone to Witherspoon sometime and worked it out for himself. I was very upset at the time.'

'Did he drive you to your meeting with Witherspoon?'

'Yes, he did.'

'Are you sure you didn't confide in him after the meeting? You were upset, you'd known Dunkley for most of your life. He'd be an obvious choice to tell.'

'No, I definitely didn't.'

'Why do you think he waited until April to deal with Witherspoon when the blackmail actually took place in January?' Birdie asked.

That very same question had been on Seb's lips.

'Witherspoon tried to get more money out of me a couple of weeks before his death. But I said no. I didn't have any access to any.'

'Did he threaten you again?'

'No, he seemed to accept that I couldn't help.'

This wasn't ringing true. Why would Donald back down so easily, after initially being so aggressive?

'Can you give me the exact date of the phone conversation,' Birdie asked.

'I remember speaking to him on Friday 26 March at four in the afternoon. I was on my way back to Market Harborough for the weekend.'

'And the time before that?'

'January when we sorted out my *investment*. It was all done electronically.'

'Please could you show me the call log on your phone so I can verify this.'

'I left my phone at work, when your officers came. I forgot to pick it up.'

'Yet you remember the date you spoke to Witherspoon.'

'It was my wedding anniversary and I remember thinking it typical that the two men I hate most in the world were connected by that date.'

'Did Dunkley know about this second attempt to blackmail you?' Weston asked.

'How do I know? If he'd been listening to me on the phone, he might have done. You'll have to ask him.'

'So, the call came through when you were in the car. Did Dunkley drive you all the way to Market Harborough on that Friday?'

'He took me to the station and I caught the train as it's quicker at that time of day.'

'Is Dunkley still in love with you?'

'Again, you'll have to ask him.'

'How did you feel when you found out Donald Witherspoon was dead?' Birdie asked.

'I'd lost my money, and even though I'd told him there was no more, I still worried that he might disclose the film. That's the trouble with blackmail. It continues. It never stops. I was glad when he died.' She paused. 'I've changed my mind about not having my solicitor present. I'm not answering any more questions without her.'

It surprised Seb that she hadn't decided to ask for her solicitor sooner, considering the direction the interview had taken.

'We have finished with our questioning for now. You can go, but we'll be interviewing you again, at which time you're welcome to call in your solicitor to be with you,' Weston said.

Seb waited until Andrea Wood had been escorted from the interview room and then went into the corridor to meet Weston and Birdie.

'I think she was involved,' he said.

'I was thinking the opposite,' Weston said. 'What's your reasoning?'

'Do you really think that Donald would've given in so easily after she told him she didn't have the money? He was a desperate man. He'd extorted what he could out of his brother Edgar and his friend Tony Yates. He genuinely knew they couldn't pay him more. I can't see him not being more *persuasive* with Andrea.'

'That's for us to sort out. You're no longer part of the investigation,' Weston said.

'But—'

'We'll bring her back in for questioning after we've reinterviewed Dunkley. Your work here is done.'

FORTY-THREE

21 May

The phone was ringing on Birdie's desk when she walked into the office and she ran over and picked it up.

'DC Bird.'

'It's Tim,' the guy from forensics said. 'I've downloaded what's on the phone you gave me.'

'Great. Can you send over the call log straight away as we're about to interview the suspect. I need from before Christmas until the last entries, which should be the day he died.'

'Sending it now.'

She ended the call and within a minute her email pinged and she opened it up. She scrutinised the list of calls, of which there were hundreds, wishing that she had Seb's super memory. That gave her an idea. She pressed speed dial on her mobile for Seb.

'Clifford.'

'It's me. I'm in a hurry but hoped you could help. I need all the phone numbers we have for Andrea. I'm assuming they were in Donald's files.'

'No problem,' he said, and then proceeded to rattle off three numbers: mobile, studio, and home in Market Harborough. 'I take it you now have the records from Donald's phone.'

'I've got the call log for the last few months.' The phone on her desk rang again. 'Gotta go, the other phone's ringing. Thanks so much for your help. I'll fill you in on everything soon.' She ended the call and answered the other call. 'DC Bird.'

'Dunkley's solicitor has finally arrived, it seems she was caught up with another case and wasn't expecting to be called back. They're in interview room two,' the sergeant on the front desk said.

'Thanks, we'll be down in a minute.'

She printed off the call log, stuck it in a folder, and went to collect Sergeant Weston. She tapped on his open door. 'Dunkley's solicitor is here, she's with him in one of the interview rooms.'

He stood up, took his jacket from the back of his chair, shrugged it on and headed out of the office, with her following. 'Remember, our main objective is to find out whether Andrea Wood was involved, or whether she really was ignorant of what he'd done.'

When they entered the room Birdie immediately recognised the duty solicitor next to Dunkley, as she was often at the station. The expression on her face was one of complete disinterest.

After they sat down, Birdie started the recording equipment.

'Interview on 21 May, those present Detective Sergeant Weston, Detective Constable Bird and ...' Sarge nodded at the two opposite him. 'Please state your names.'

'Gillian Griffin, solicitor for the accused.'

'Aaron Dunkley.'

'Mr Dunkley, there are a few things we'd like to explore, following your previous interview,' Sarge said.

'You'll be wasting your time,' he muttered, 'I'm not saying anything else.' Dunkley folded his arms and looked away.

'We interviewed Andrea Wood earlier and she had a lot to say.'

Dunkley sat up straight in his chair and glared at them. 'Why? I've already told you it's nothing to do with her.'

'She told us all about the blackmail. Do you know what Witherspoon was blackmailing her over?' Sarge asked.

'I don't know and don't care.'

'How do you know she was being blackmailed?'

'I've already told you that I overheard a conversation she was having with Witherspoon. She'd already given him some money and he'd come back for more. That's all I needed to know. My job was to protect her and that's what I did.'

Birdie gave Sarge a little nudge, to indicate that she wanted to ask some questions, and he nodded.

'Let's go back to when you overheard the conversation between Andrea Wood and Donald Witherspoon,' She leant forward and pressed her hands on the folder in front of her on the table. 'What date was this exactly?'

'Um ...' He glanced upwards and to the side. 'It was on a Monday morning when I was driving Andrea to the studio.'

'Could you be more specific. What month?' she pushed.

'March.'

'Hmm, late March,' Birdie said, opening her folder and taking a look at the records in front of her. 'If it was a Monday it would be the 29th.'

'Yes, you're right. That's definitely it,' Dunkley said, sitting back in his chair, appearing relaxed.

'So you overheard a conversation on Monday, 29 March, and then decided that you were going to go and sort Donald Witherspoon out?'

'Yes.'

'What did *sorting him out* mean?'

'I phoned him up, pretending to be a client and asked to meet him. He suggested the Foxton Locks pub.'

'When you went did you intend to kill him?'

'I was just gonna warn him off but he was acting like a right prick showing me all these investments and making out he was something special and better than me. I told him I was going to invest a hundred grand and made out it was illegal money. He didn't care, all he had was pound signs in his eyes.' The solicitor tapped him on the arm and he turned to her. 'What?'

'There's no need for you to be saying all this. Wait until it gets to court.'

Birdie held her breath hoping he wouldn't listen.

'I don't care. I'm gonna to tell them what happened. I told Witherspoon that I'd parked in the top car park and asked for a lift up there, which he was quite happy to do. When we got up there, I told him I knew about the blackmail and it should stop or he'd be sorry. The bastard laughed in my face. I took out my gun and pointed it at him. He stopped laughing then. He was shitting himself. I made him write a suicide note to his wife, then I forced him out of the car and onto the wasteland. Then ...' he held out two fingers. 'Bang.'

Birdie flinched.

'Why did you move his car to the village?'

'So he wouldn't be found straight away.'

'And you say that Andrea knew nothing about this,' Birdie said.

In her peripheral vision she saw Sarge looking puzzled.

'Why do you keep going back to that? I keep telling you, I overheard a phone conversation on Monday, March, whatever date it was. And after that I decided to sort him out.'

'What you say is very interesting because I have Donald Witherspoon's phone records here.' She held out the pages. 'He didn't speak to Andrea, on Monday, as you said. He spoke to her on Sunday, the day before. You and Andrea should have got your stories straight. She said Friday, you said Monday, and it was actually Sunday. That's crucial because we know she wasn't in London that particular weekend. So you couldn't possibly have overheard the conversation.'

'That's it. I'm not saying anything else,' Dunkley said, his lips set in a flat line.'

'You don't need to. We have enough to convict the pair of you.'

FORTY-FOUR

21 May

'Well done, Birdie,' Sarge said slapping her on the back. 'Brilliant work. I'm proud of you.'

Warmth rushed up her cheeks. He rarely gave out praise, most of the time it was the opposite.

'It was teamwork. Donald's phone was found, and Tim in forensics rushed through getting the call log for me. All I had to do was check them against what Dunkley had said.'

'You got forensics to rush it through? Well, that's some feat in itself. I've no idea how you managed it.'

'Oh, well, you know what they say, Sarge. It's not what you know, but who you know.' she grinned.

'Right. Fun time over. It's time to question Andrea Wood. I had a text while we were in with Dunkley to let me know she's arrived with her solicitor and they're waiting in interview room four. I'm going to let you take the lead if you'd like to.'

'You bet I would. Thanks, Sarge. I really appreciate the chance.'

Birdie had been involved in loads of interviews in the past but she hadn't led in a murder investigation before.

'Don't let me down.'

She led the way into the interview room and after starting the recording equipment sat opposite Andrea. 'Interview on 21 May, those present Detective Constable Bird, Detective Sergeant Weston, and please state your names for the recording.' She looked across the table.

'Andrea Wood.'

'Kim Jones, solicitor for Ms Wood.'

'Thank you for coming back in to see us, Andrea,' Birdie said, deciding to take a less formal approach, because it often lead to a suspect being less on their guard and then they'd let things slip.

'Well, yet again, I didn't have much choice.' Andrea said.

'As you know, we've arrested Aaron Dunkley for the murder of Donald Witherspoon.'

'It's dreadful. I had no idea that he would do anything like that.'

'Yes, that's what he told us, too. He said he acted off his own bat. The trouble is, it doesn't quite add up and that's what I'd like to discuss with you.'

'I fail to see how I'll be able to assist,' Andrea said, a tremor in her voice.

'We believe you might have known what Dunkley had planned to do. In fact, you might have asked him to do it.'

'You've already asked me this and my answer hasn't changed. It was nothing to do with me.'

'I'm asking you again.'

Andrea's solicitor leant in and whispered something which Birdie couldn't hear.

'No comment.'

'That's your prerogative, but you might find that cooperating will help you in the long run. We'll put that to one side for the moment and return to the blackmail. You told us that Donald Witherspoon, having blackmailed you once, approached you again at the end of March, with a view to getting more money from you.'

'Yes, that's correct and I told him there was no more.'

She hadn't said that earlier.

'You also told us that Dunkley must have overheard you on the phone and took matters into his own hands.'

'That is also correct,' Andrea said, sounding much more relaxed.

'According to you, there was one conversation with Witherspoon in March and prior to that one early in the year when he blackmailed you for the first time.'

'Yes,' Andrea said, nodding.

'So the only way Dunkley would have known was from that one phone conversation in your car when he was driving you to the station for your journey back to Market Harborough, where you stayed for the whole weekend.'

'You're wasting my time, going over what we've already discussed.' Andrea scowled in her direction.

'I wanted to get your movements clear in my head because it's actually slightly confusing. You say you spoke to Witherspoon on the Friday, yet Dunkley says it was the Monday.'

'One of us must have got it wrong,' Andrea said.

Birdie pulled out the sheets of paper from the file and held them up. 'I have here the call log from Donald's phone. According to this, he didn't speak to you on the Friday, or the Monday. He spoke to you on the Sunday. The one day when we know categorically that Dunkley couldn't have heard because you were here and he was in London. So, how did he find out?' She paused and locked eyes with Andrea, but she wouldn't maintain the contact and looked away.

'What does it matter? He's admitted killing Witherspoon and said I didn't know a thing about it,' Andrea said.

'You know why it matters. What I think happened is that, knowing Dunkley would do anything for you, you asked him to sort out Witherspoon to stop the blackmail. You knew that if you paid him for the second time, there would probably be a third and fourth and if you refused he'd put the film in the public domain. You had no choice but to ask Dunkley to kill him'

'No. No. That's not what happened. I didn't ask Aaron to kill him. I just asked him to make it stop. I ...'

Gotcha

'And you didn't think for a moment that *make it stop* meant he would kill him?'

'No, I didn't. At the time I thought Aaron would warn him. Like he did with that Clifton chap ...' Her face visibly sagged.

'That leads me onto the next thing, *Clifford*.' Birdie said, accentuating his correct name. 'He was attacked by Dunkley and another male. From what you've said, I take it that you authorised it.'

The solicitor whispered to Andrea and then faced Birdie. 'I'm instructing my client to refrain from answering further questions.'

It didn't matter, Birdie had got what she needed.

'Andrea Wood, I'm arresting you for being an accessory to the murder of Donald Witherspoon, and an accessory in the grievous bodily harm to Sebastian Clifford. You do not have to say anything, but it may harm your defence if you do not mention when questioned something which you later rely on in court. Anything you do say may be given in evidence. Do you understand?' Andrea just stared at her. 'I repeat, do you understand?'

'Yes, I understand.'

'You will be escorted to the custody suite where you will be officially charged and dealt with,' Sarge said.

After the prisoner was taken away, Birdie and Sarge headed back upstairs.

'We've done it,' she said, unable to stop her smile which went from ear to ear.

'I was very impressed at the way you handled the interview and your whole input into the case.'

'Thanks, Sarge. But let's not forget Clifford. Without him we wouldn't have even known there was a murder to solve.'

'I suppose you're right,' he said gruffly. 'But I still don't like private investigators, if that's what he is now, interfering.'

She wasn't going to say anything as she didn't want to get in his bad books again.

'I've got some paperwork to do, and I'll see you bright and early tomorrow morning, Sarge,' she said as they reached the door to his office.

'Yeah, that'll be the day,' he replied, rolling his eyes.

FORTY-FIVE

22 May

'Let's go,' Birdie said to Seb as she came out of the station and saw him sitting on the bench outside. 'It's my treat.'

She still felt guilty about the way he'd been treated by Sarge yesterday. There was no need for her boss to have been so blunt. If it hadn't been for Seb, the case would've gone unsolved.

'Where are we going?'

'To the pub for something to eat. My stomach thinks my throat's been cut.'

'I wouldn't say no to something to eat either. Whose car?'

'It will have to be yours as I doubt you'd even get one leg in mine. It's not called a Mini for nothing. You can drop me back here later.'

She directed him to a pub on the outskirts of town.

'Is this one of your locals?' he asked, as they parked outside the old pub.

'Lots of pubs are my local,' she said, flashing him a smile. 'As you already know.'

They headed to the bar, and she picked up two menus, passing him one.

'I'm going for a Caesar salad,' he said.

'Don't be boring. The steaks here are to die for. Trust me.' He nodded his acceptance of her decision and she turned to the girl behind the bar who she knew. 'Meg, please could you get us two steak and chips. Medium rare for me, and ...' She glanced at Seb.

'Same for me.'

'Plus, half a cider and a pint of stout?'

'That's thirty-eight pounds,' Meg said.

Birdie reached into her handbag which was hanging over her shoulder and pulled out her purse. She rummaged through the cards which were all in a zipped section. 'Crap,' she muttered.

'Problem?' Seb asked.

'You're not going to believe this. I've only gone and left my card at home. *Again.* Could you—'

'Pay? Of course I will. I've subsidised your food every day so far since I've been here, so once more won't hurt.'

'Look, I'm really sorry. I truly meant—'

'I'm joking,' he said, holding up both hands. 'I don't mind.' He opened his wallet, took out a credit card, and paid.

They took their drinks to a table towards the back of the room, under the window.

'Seriously, I owe you one,' she said after they'd sat down. 'I really had intended to buy you a meal, to thank you for everything.'

She was back in Sarge's good books and there'd been no more mention of her having to sit behind the desk. In fact, he'd even consulted her on a spate of carjackings they were currently investigating.

'Call it my farewell meal.' He held up his glass and clinked it against hers.

'I'm sorry about the way Sarge behaved towards you after the Andrea Wood interview. It was uncalled for when you think of how much you put into this case, and that's even before considering the beating you took.'

He shrugged. 'Don't be. I get it. He didn't like me interfering as I'm no longer a serving officer.'

'I expect you having worked at the Met didn't help, either.'

'It doesn't matter, I wasn't offended. Has Andrea been interviewed again?'

'Yes. I was going to update you on everything. We interviewed Dunkley first, and he accidentally dropped Andrea in it by saying he'd overheard a conversation she had with Donald on the Monday.'

'She said it was the Friday,' Seb said.

'And it turned out to be on the Sunday when she was in Market Harborough. I had Donald's phone records and could check. Slam dunk to us. After Andrea was questioned again, she finally admitted that she'd asked Dunkley to deal with the blackmail. She thought he'd just give Donald a warning and not actually kill him. But she would say that. Although according to Dunkley he hadn't intended to murder Donald initially, just warn him off. But we'll never know.'

'Yet, when I was in the car with Andrea, she acted like she didn't want Dunkley to hear our discussion. She was a bloody good actress, that's all I can say. She must have already been covering her back knowing that we were getting close to what had actually happened. Did she admit to sending Dunkley to attack me?'

'Eventually, but she said Dunkley was to warn you and nothing more. We'll have to see what the jury has to say about it. Have you thought about what you're going to tell Sarah?'

'She needs to know what's happened as she'll find out when the case gets to court and all the details are released. I'll let her know that she was right about Donald and then take it from there.'

'When are you going to see her?'

'Tomorrow morning before I leave.'

Her heart sank, which was stupid as it wasn't like she didn't know he was going to be leaving.

'Are you going to miss Market Harborough?'

'Maybe. Under different circumstances, I'd have enjoyed it better.'

'What about work? You should really think of being a PI, you're so good at it.'

'I admit to enjoying the investigation, apart from being attacked, obviously. But PI? I don't think it's me. What about you, happy the case is over and you no longer have to act covertly?'

'You did me a good turn letting me help because now I'm sort of in the good books at work for helping solve a high-profile murder case. It means I'm no longer desk-bound, as Sarge has already allocated me some work.'

'But for how long will you remain out of trouble?' Seb said, tilting his head to one side.

'Meaning?'

He could read her like a book. Which was most discon-certing.

'You need to pull your socks up and make sure you get to work early and do what you're meant to be doing. There's no doubting that you're good, but you can't just rely on gut instinct when you're working in CID.'

She sighed. 'You're right, of course. I've decided to turn over a new leaf and buy a couple more alarm clocks. With long-lasting batteries.'

'How are you getting on with seeking your birth mother?'

She frowned as she remembered the email. 'Not good, I'm afraid. I heard back from the Adoption Contact Register and it seems my birth mother contacted them to let them know that she doesn't want any contact with me.' Tears filled her eyes, and she blinked them away.

'Does that mean you won't be pursuing it?'

'No, it means that I'll investigate myself without their help. I've no idea why she put in this request. But I need to know where she is. Even if we don't ever meet face to face.'

'Have you discussed it further with your parents?'

'They haven't mentioned it since I told them what I was going to do.'

'Are you going to tell them of your progress?'

'I don't think so. It's better if I keep it to myself as I don't want to cause them any more upset.'

If they asked her, then she'd let them know what she was doing. She wasn't going to lie to them. If they didn't ask, then she'd stay quiet.

'If you do want someone to talk to about it, you know where I am.'

'Thanks,' she said. 'I really mean it. You're the nicest older man I know.' She got up and gave him a hug.

'Ouch. You know, I am still bruised from the beating.'

'Don't be such a big wuss. Look at the size of you. A hug from someone like me isn't going to hurt.' She squeezed him tighter, and he responded by hugging her back. 'I'm going to miss you, you big lump. A lot.'

FORTY-SIX

23 May

Sebastian put out the rubbish and tidied up. Considering what had gone down in the place it was amazing that everything was in one piece. He'd packed his belongings last night and loaded them into the back of his car. Elsa's lead was hanging on a hook and when he picked it up she bounded over to him, her tail wagging in circles.

'Come on, girl, we've got one last stop.' He placed the key on the table, as instructed, and they left out of the front door which self-locked. Elsa hopped into the back of the car and lay down on the floor.

He drove them out to Rendall Hall and as Seb was opening the back door for Elsa to jump out, Sarah headed down the steps towards them.

'I heard a car on the drive and thought it was you. I've been on tenterhooks ever since you phoned. The finality in your voice set my mind in overdrive. Have you some news?'

'Yes, I do. Let's have a chat in the garden so I can give Elsa a run before we drive back to London.'

'You're leaving today? You didn't say.'

They walked around the house and into the garden. It was a lovely day, hardly a cloud in the sky. The flowers were in full bloom and everything smelt fresh after the rain they'd had the previous night.

'The most important thing you need to know is that the police have arrested someone for the murder of Donald.'

She faltered, grabbing hold of Seb's arm to steady herself. 'M-murder. I was right after all,' she whispered. 'Poor Donald. Even right at the end he was thinking of me and the boys by leaving clues so his murder would be discovered and his insurance policy not be invalidated. Thank you so much. If you hadn't looked into it, he'd have been classed as a suicide for ever.'

'You persuaded me. Initially I thought you were wrong but thank goodness you convinced me to investigate.'

'Do you know why?'

She might regret the *poor Donald* remark once she learnt of his actions.

'It seems that Donald was blackmailing several people into investing. He needed the money to keep himself afloat.'

'Blackmail,' she said, raising a hand to her mouth, a low moan escaping her lips.

'Yes, in total he got nearly six hundred thousand pounds.'

'Six hundred thousand,' she repeated. 'Yet the business still went down. Was it one of them who murdered him?'

'One of their employees, but it's unclear how much they actually knew.'

'Who?'

'I suppose it's going to come out anyway, but you must keep this to yourself. It was a woman called Andrea Wood. She's a presenter on breakfast television. Her driver, who'd known her since school, took it into his head to commit murder, after she'd asked him to warn Donald off. He was one of the men who attacked me, thinking I was getting too close to finding out the truth. Now it's classified as murder, you should be able to cash in your life insurance policy. You'll need to wait until the case goes to court though.'

'It feels like dirty money. If I do get it I'll keep just enough to help the boys through university and the rest I'll pay back to some of his clients. It probably won't help much but it's something.'

'I know of just the couple who would benefit greatly from your donation. I'll forward you their details,' Seb said, remembering Pearl and Bert Black, and the situation they were in.

'Thank you. I also have some news, and you're the first person I've told. I've decided to go travelling. The boys are at university and don't need me, so I'm free to do what I want. I'm fed up of rattling around in the house.'

'Who are you going with?'

'On my own. I've always wanted to go to South America, and that's my first port of call.'

'How long will you be away for?'

'I've no idea and not knowing feels great.' A warm smile swept across her face.

'What about this place?' He gestured to the house standing behind them.

'Well ...' She hesitated. 'I've had an idea. Hear me out before saying anything.'

He frowned. What was she going to suggest?

'I'd like you to move in. You can live here for free. All I want you to do is look after the place and pay the day-to-day bills.'

'You want me to move to Market Harborough?' he said, trying to process her suggestion.

'Why not? It's not like you've got anything else to do now you've left the police force, is it? You could become a private investigator and work from here, you're clearly good at it.'

'That's an option, but I need to think about it.'

Starting a new career from there wouldn't be easy, especially as a PI. He had no contacts, unlike in London. He shook his head. He didn't want to be a PI so why was he even considering it? Then again ...

He surveyed the glorious view surrounding them and breathed in the country air.

Would he really miss London?

'No rush. If you could let me know in the next few days.' She laughed and her face lit up. It was the happiest he'd seen her since he'd arrived.

'What would I do with my flat?' he said, more to himself than her.

'Rent it out.'

Did he want other people in there? He didn't have a mortgage as he'd brought the flat in Notting Hill outright with his small trust fund.

'Or I could leave it for when I need to stay in the city.'

'Does that mean you're saying yes already?'

Was he? The idea was becoming appealing.

'If I do say yes, and I haven't yet made up my mind, any time you wish to come back, do so. I don't need any warning. This is your house.'

'I don't envisage returning for a long time, especially if I know the house is going to be in good hands.'

'The boys can stay here during their uni holidays or at any other time and they too don't have to give me notice, they can just turn up. And I'll be here for them, if they need money, or advice and can't get hold of you.'

'So is that a yes, then?' Sarah asked, her eyes sparkling.

Was it? He'd never been rash in his life before. But what did he have to lose? He had no job. No girlfriend. He was a totally free agent.

'If that's what you want, then... Yes. I'll move in.'

A LETTER FROM THE AUTHOR

Dear reader,

Huge thanks for reading *Web of Lies*. I hope you were hooked on the Detective Sebastian Clifford series. If you want to join other readers in hearing all about my new releases and bonus content, you can sign up for my newsletter.

www.stormpublishing.co/sally-rigby

If you enjoyed this book and could spare a few moments to leave a review that would be hugely appreciated. Even a short review can make all the difference in encouraging a reader to discover my books for the first time. Thank you so much!

Thanks again for being part of this amazing journey with me and I hope you'll stay in touch—I have so many more stories and ideas to entertain you with!

Sally Rigby

www.sallyrigby.com

facebook.com/Sally-Rigby-131414630527848

instagram.com/sally.rigby.author

ACKNOWLEDGMENTS

Thank you to my writing friends, Amanda Ashby and Christina Phillips for always being there when I need help with plot and character issues. I'll be forever grateful for meeting you both so long ago.

Thanks, of course, go to Emma Mitchell for being such an amazing editor. Thanks also to Kate Noble and all of my Advanced Reader Team whose input I couldn't do without. I especially would like to mention Colin Spencer for his procedural input, and being at the end of an email whenever I have a question.

Thanks to Stuart Bache for coming up with such a brilliant cover concept for the series.

Finally, to my family, Garry, Alicia and Marcus, and my brother Andrew, thanks for your continued support.